I am not Raymond Wallace

Biography

Sam Kenyon is a writer, composer, performer and teacher. He studied English Literature at Emmanuel College, Cambridge, before training in Musical Theatre at the Royal Academy of Music.

After performing for twelve years, he developed a career as a composer and lyricist. At the Royal Shakespeare Company, he provided music and lyrics for *The Christmas Truce* (2014), *A Midsummer Night's Dream* (2016) and *Vice Versa* (2017). He wrote the book, music and lyrics for *Miss Littlewood*—a musical exploring the life of Joan Littlewood—which opened at the RSC in 2018, and which is published by Concord Theatricals. He is currently developing a musical about Gertrude Stein, Alice B. Toklas and Samuel Steward.

As a voice teacher, he works across styles and genres, with theatre, film and recording artists. He teaches at the Royal Academy of Music, as well as running a private teaching practice.

He lives in London with his partner, Mitch, and their daughter.

I am not Raymond Wallace is his first novel.

www.samkenyon.com

Praise for *I am not Raymond Wallace*

'Raymond Wallace goes to New York and like thousands before, discovers and re-invents himself. But this is 1963, a time when every gay man has to have "something of the spy about him". A sensual, moving story of masks and identities, across two continents and four decades. Sam Kenyon has the power to bring you up short with writing that captures all the contradiction of love and loneliness in a big city. I am not Raymond Wallace is a strikingly confident debut novel; not just good considering, but good absolutely.'
SAMUEL WEST

'Taking as his starting-point a real-life moment of queer history from 1960's New York, Sam Kenyon spins a marvellously stylish and often unexpected story, bringing things to a final boil in one of the most romantic backstreets of contemporary Paris. His denouement is as tough as it is touching—and this is quite some debut for a very first novel.'
NEIL BARTLETT

'A triumph. A primer for all ages.'
MURRAY MELVIN

'In this exquisite novel about the breaking of a human heart, a sad young man carries a torch for his first love. It's pre-Stonewall 1963. Men coming out come undone. Laws prevent giving consent to their own bodies. This daring love song of an anxious Prufrock wandering half-deserted streets embraces two generations of fathers, sons, and lovers yearning to find chosen family against all odds. A joyous literary triumph that moved me to tears. Shelve next to Michael Cunningham's Pulitzer winner, The Hours.'
JACK FRITSCHER
author of Mapplethorpe: Assault with a Deadly Camera

'I bloody loved it. A poignant and evocative reminder of how recently our love was impossible, of the lives that were lost in hiding, as well as the unsung heroes who paved the way for our freedoms today. It's also a beautifully told love story, deserving of a wide readership, not least because we all need more happily enough ever afters.'
STELLA DUFFY

Praise for *Sam Kenyon*

'*The masterstroke of the writer and composer Sam Kenyon is to tell this great theatrical figure's story in the muscularly informal and informative manner of such Littlewood shows as* Oh! What a Lovely War. *A magnificent evening.*'
DOMINIC MAXWELL, THE TIMES
on Miss Littlewood.

'*I felt the hairs stand on end at the back of my neck. An anarchic delight in the style of Miss Littlewood herself.*'
CATHERINE VONDLEBUR, WHATSONSTAGE.COM
on Miss Littlewood

'*The only problem with Sam Kenyon's delicately scored songs is that there aren't nearly enough of them.*'
ALFRED HICKLING, THE GUARDIAN
on The Borrowers

November 2022

Dear Laura —
with thanks
once more for
your help +
Support

I am not Raymond Wallace

Sam Kenyon

Sam x

Inkandescent

Published by Inkandescent, 2022

Text Copyright © 2022 Sam Kenyon
Cover Design © 2022 Joe Mateo
Author photograph of Sam Kenyon © 2022 Sam Allard
Sam Kenyon has asserted his right under the Copyright,
Designs and Patents Act 1988 to be identified as the author of this work.

This book is a work of fiction. With the exception of one borrowed name of a journalist
in this work, 'Doty' (see author's note at the back), all the names, characters and
incidents portrayed in it are the work of the author's imagination. Any resemblance to
actual persons, living or dead, events or localities is entirely coincidental.

A CIP record for this book is available from the British Library

Printed in the UK by Severn, Gloucester

ISBN 978-1-912620-22-7 (paperback)
ISBN 978-1-912620-23-4 (ebook)

1 3 5 7 9 10 8 6 4 2

www.inkandescent.co.uk

to Garry

for Mitch

Part One

Manhattan, 1963

& Other Regrets

Raymond Wallace

Manhattan, 1963

One

Raymond Wallace sits on his freshly-made bunk at the Railroad YMCA—eyes dry with jetlag; palms firm on the rough blanket—and glances at his wristwatch. As the minute hand hits eight o'clock, he adjusts his tie, stands up and—as a matter of habit—brushes his trousers down. His suit feels oddly loose on him, as though he has somehow shed weight during the transatlantic flight. Passing a mirror in the corridor he licks a finger and dabs it on a shaving cut from a sleep-deprived hand. He smooths his hair, thinking as he does so how he prefers the colour when it is like this, still darkly damp from the shower. He tries to avoid the eyes everyone back home says remind them of his father's, slips on his overcoat and heads out onto the street. The air is brisk, autumnal, and scented with yeast and iron: bakeries and brake dust. It is Monday October 14th, 1963, Raymond is twenty-one years old, and by the time he leaves Manhattan a mere three months later, on January 8th, 1964, he will have made the greatest mistake of his life.

As he crosses Lexington and looks left, his eye is drawn up and up and up to the zenith of what he recognises from his guide book as the Chrysler Building, its spire of concentric fans, shiny and elegant in the morning sunlight, accelerating and diminishing towards its peak. This fills his heart with twin senses of joy and ambition, senses which are assaulted almost immediately by the parps of determined traffic that send him dashing to the far kerb. His stomach still out of step with the time difference, Raymond stops at a diner on East 43rd Street, removing his coat as he enters. He is seated at a window table by a waitress who, handing him a menu stained with greasy fingerprints, immediately removes a pencil from her hair-wrap and licks the tip, studying his face as though for a portrait.

'Mmm-hmm?'

'Er…I would like some pancakes, please.'

Her lips curl into an appraising smile. She marks her pad without losing eye contact. 'Bacon?'

'Yes. And some eggs, please.'

'Scrambled, over easy, sunny side up?'

Raymond feels overwhelmed by the number of options. He turns the menu over as though the answer he seeks might lie on the reverse side. It is blank. 'I don't mind.'

'Over easy. Coffee?'

'Please.'

'Sugar?'

'No. Thank you.'

'Sweet enough. Cream?'

Raymond looks at her with unalloyed incredulity. 'In my coffee?'

'Accent like yours, Honey, you can pour it where you want.'

He eats ravenously, sipping at the coffee between bites, then—

checking his watch once more—wipes his mouth, pays his bill and is back on the street. As he begins the final approach to his destination—the offices of The New York Times at 229 West 43rd Street—his heart begins to beat faster; out of confidence, he tells himself.

Once through the revolving doors he is directed upstairs to the vast third-floor newsroom, the capaciousness of which has been facilitated by numerous regimented columns; the centre of which is dominated by a series of densely populated, curved desks, and the population of which has already rolled up its sleeves for the day's work. The curvilinear shape of the desks is echoed above the workers' heads by a circular structure from which hang lamps, themselves made of concentric circles, so that—it seems to Raymond—the very layout of the room stands in stark counterpoint to the intrinsic angularity of type-set columns, photographs and folded papers. The scent of male bodies, of soap, coffee, and the tart perfume of printer's ink; the sound of the woodpecker tapping of typewriters, the irritant scratch of nibs on notepads, the mutter of collaborative conversations and the roll and squeak of revolving chairs; the sight of lips moving silently as they rephrase sentences, and here and there the smoke signals of the day's first cigarettes.

A lady—red hair, pale green dress tied at the waist, her coat—a fur—slung over her shoulder—walks briskly past Raymond, brushing his shoulder heedlessly as she does so, then crosses the vast room at a pace and knocks on the glass of a hitherto unnoticed door, the interior of which is obscured by a lowered blind.

The door opens, but before Raymond can catch a glimpse of the figure inside, the lady has been ushered in and the door closed—and, for some reason, Raymond is convinced, *locked*—behind her.

He stands uncertainly, trying to catch someone's—anyone's—eye before realising that everyone is studiously avoiding him. He taps the nearest man on the shoulder.

'Excuse me, I'm sorry to bother you, but I'm here to see Mr Bukowski. Could you tell me which is his office, please? I'm Raymond. Raymond Wallace.'

'Bukowski? Office over there.' He wags a finger. 'But he's busy right now. You saw the lady?'

'I see. Do you know how long he will be?'

'Anybody's guess, pal, anybody's guess.'

'Ah. I'm here from England, and—'

'No kidding.' The man waves his hand vaguely over his desk which is empty except for a small pile of paper, printed with what seem to be adverts. 'Sounds to me like it's Dolores you need. Desk right outside Bukowski's door. Get yourself a coffee. She'll be in any minute.'

'Of course. I'm sorry to have bothered you.'

A column obscures Raymond's perspective so that it is only once he is halfway across the room that he sees the desk outside Bukowski's office.

A nasalised drawl comes from behind him. 'Can I help you, sir?'

Raymond turns and drops his eye level to a short bald man wearing thickly-rimmed glasses, waistcoat and matching trousers; his belly pulls his watch-chain taut.

'Oh. I'm waiting for Dolores. And Mr Bukowski. I'm Raymond. Wallace.'

'Nice accent, Wallace.' The man is panting as though he's jogged across the office. 'You are from England, I take it?'

'That's right. I'm here on a bursary. Three months.'

'Fancy. I'm Kleinmann. Photography.' He emphasises this last word as though divulging something of note.

'Wow. Pleased to meet you, Mr Kleinmann.'

'Call me Sam. My name's Samuel, but people call me Sam.'

'Alright, Sam. My name's Raymond. People call me— Raymond.'

And although he didn't mean to make a joke, Raymond is delighted when Sam laughs and slaps him on the shoulder.

'That's funny,' says Sam, 'you're a funny guy. Hey: I'll show you where you can get a coffee. You know,' he says conspiratorially as he leads the way past a series of office doors, 'Bukowski…well, he can take some getting used to, especially if you're new, like, he barely smiles, for example. But don't take any notice of that. And if you're in any doubt about anything—*anything at all*—then Dolores has the answers. She's his personal secretary? Look after Dolores, and she'll look after you.'

Sam leaves him shortly after this exchange, and Raymond stands, mug of coffee in hand, surveying the activity of the room. A few minutes later the slam of a door sends a shiver down Raymond's spine and he turns to see the woman in the green dress once more. Fur now across her shoulders, head sunk low, she darts defiant glances at the men she passes—each of whom studiously avoids her eyes—and strides towards the exit. A few minutes pass and then the man Raymond assumes is Bukowski steps out of his office and walks towards him. Late forties, his face inscrutable as a primed canvas, his thinning hair is parted to the left. As he approaches Raymond, he cocks his head and squints, eyeing him up like a pigeon.

'You here to see me?'

Something in Bukowski's manner makes Raymond feel as though he's in the presence of a Headmaster. 'Yes. I'm Raymond. Raymond Wallace.'

'Ah.' Bukowski sounds almost disappointed. 'I've been expecting you. You've got a coffee; I'll grab one for myself and then we can get down to it.'

Unlike the dull brown of the main newsroom, Bukowski's carpet is a dark green. A large, rather formal mahogany desk sits at an angle in one corner with a green-glass and brass lamp atop it that reminds Raymond of the lamps in the University Library at Cambridge. Next to the desk is a large filing cabinet that is so dark a green it appears almost black. In the corner opposite Bukowski's desk there is a second, smaller desk with a typewriter on top. In contrast to the bustle and activity of the main room, the office feels cool, like a sanctuary of sorts.

Two windows overlook the street. Raymond looks out to see the windowless brick walls of the building opposite.

'It's not what you'd call a view,' says Bukowski. 'Take a seat.'

Raymond sits in a small wooden chair against which a rather

elegant umbrella is leaning, and puts his hands on his knees.

'So: Professor Hurt, huh?'

'Yes. My Director of Studies.'

'Fancy.'

'Ha. He told me you had studied together.'

'Years ago.' Bukowski waves his hand as though the details are either sad, irrelevant, or both. 'But he tells me that you're quite the talent, which is why you're here, of course.'

'That's awfully nice of him.'

'Niceness is a luxury few people can afford, when it comes to bursaries. It's about talent, and it's about ambition. You ambitious, Wallace?'

Raymond nods, smiling broadly.

'Arthur mentioned an article about night climbers?'

Raymond flushes with pride. 'Yes. He—Professor Hurt—was particularly pleased with that one. I've got a copy if you'd like—'

'No. Tell me about it.'

'Well, pretty much by accident I came across a copy of a book, originally published in 1937, in a second-hand bookshop, called *The Night Climbers of Cambridge*: it's about undergraduates, mainly, who scale the walls and heights of the various college buildings in Cambridge—at night, of course. And I realised that last year was to be the twenty-fifth anniversary of the original publication date, and it's a rather notorious book, so I figured it was appropriate to mark this in some way.'

'You climb?'

'Oh. No. Fear of heights.' Raymond laughs shyly. 'It caught

my imagination for different reasons: the surprising amount of collusion with authority figures, for instance. You see, the real peril of climbing Kings' College Chapel is the getting caught; the actual climb—according to this book, at least—is the easy bit. Meet a policeman on your way back from an ascent, he'll happily swap climbing stories with you and you sleep a free man, whereas a bobby waiting for you at the bottom of a drainpipe? Rustication—expulsion—pure and simple. Dons are doing it, too, though of course they'd get the sack if they were found out. So it's a kind of secret, rebellious fraternity, and there is evidently a covert thrill that comes with that.' He pauses. 'But aside from all that, I think the thing that attracts me most of all is the perspective you must get. I can't think of many things that can be both literal and metaphorical, but climbing is one of them. The perspective you must get, being above it all. Alone, but not exactly lonely. Part of a highly-skilled, knowledgeable elite. And whilst I couldn't achieve the climbs themselves, I could appreciate them, metaphorically: so the simple fact of this book and its photographs gave me some escape—however momentary—some sense of a different set of possibilities outside what I described as *the gravitational pull of the establishment*.' Raymond realises he's glaring at the floor. 'So I wrote about that,' he adds, trying to sound casual and urbane, and looks up to find Bukowski is looking directly at him.

Bukowski's impassive face breaks so abruptly into a broad smile that it makes Raymond laugh. 'How old are you, Raymond?'

'I was twenty-one in June. I'm sorry; I can be terribly intense on subjects that captivate me.'

'An excellent quality in a writer, and utterly admirable in a young one. I can see why Hurt recommended you. What a pleasure, Raymond. I'd love to talk more, but I have much to be getting on with.'

'Of course, Mr Bukowski, and I'm sorry if my meanderings have taken up too much of your morning.'

'Bukowski. No Mr; just Bukowski. Listen: I'm going to introduce you to Dolores, my secretary, who will give you everything you need. I'll have a think and try to find you something which— what was the word you used?—*captivates* you, here, and I'll look forward to reading the results.'

As Raymond steps out of Bukowski's office that first time he feels vivid and valued in a way he hasn't felt for months. His return home after graduation; working the long, slow days in the sub post office: in his darker moments, these things had seemed so virulently and—though he can't put his finger on why— somehow *deliberately* anti-climactic that he'd felt practically cannibalised by his surroundings, whereas here he can be the person he knows he is at heart, and doesn't need—for the time being—to concern himself with anyone else's fears or ambitions for his life and times. Nobody here sees his father's eyes when they look into his.

'Well, good morning to you.'

He turns to find a woman—fifties, dark red hair drawn back into a neat pleat—reaching up to hang her coat on a hook behind

Bukowski's door. In the other hand she holds a compact. The mirror refracts erratically as she moves, sending spangles of light across the ceiling.

'Dolores?'

'All day long. You must be Raymond Wallace. We've been expecting you.' She brushes a shoulder clothed in a deep blue wool before shaking his hand.

'I'm very pleased to meet you,' he says. 'Everyone tells me you're the only person I need to know, here.'

'Oh, I don't know about that, Mr Wallace.'

'Raymond.'

'Raymond. Indeed. I'm, um,' she presses her lips together whilst checking in the mirror that her lipstick is even, 'sure we'll get along just fine.' She snaps the compact shut and slides it onto her desk. 'You're with us until the beginning of January: correct?'

Raymond nods.

'Good. Now then. I'm going to have a quick talk with Mr Bukowski, so you wait here; I'll be right back.'

As Dolores sidesteps her way past Raymond, knocks and disappears behind the door of Bukowski's office, she leaves behind her the scent of jasmine and roses, but also of something dryer, woodier; like nothing Raymond has ever smelt. He turns to her desk. Before him is a pale blue typewriter with cream-coloured keys behind which, hiding the machinery, a black screen bears a badge of cursive lettering spelling out the word *Olympia*. As his finger traces the lettering, he finds himself wondering how long Dolores will be, and whether—in fact—Bukowski mightn't already have changed his mind about Raymond's placement.

'Very good, Mr Bukowski,' says Dolores over her shoulder as she draws the door closed once more. She looks at Raymond's hand, still hovering over her keyboard. 'Everyone else uses an Underwood, here, but where I go, my Olympia goes. Call it a woman's prerogative. Now then, Raymond,' she says, smiling and looking kindly at him, 'I'll give you a tour, then I have a task for you this afternoon, and then tomorrow I'm to introduce you to a Mr Doty. Veteran. Celebrated. Spent time in Paris, now on the metropolitan staff here. He's got a new project which we'd like you to be involved in, though it's currently *top secret*,' she whispers, raising a sardonic eyebrow, 'so little people like me aren't supposed to know anything about it. But—well—he's an excellent journalist, Raymond. Excellent. Shall we?'

By lunchtime, Raymond's mind is whirring with scoops, scandals and op eds; with the hierarchy of reporters, copy editors and *backfielders*—such as Bukowski—whose role it is to assign and edit stories; with the extensive, correctional route to approval, and he has had his sense of scale shattered by the cavernous basement and its monstrous machines which—come printing time, he is told—make the entire building judder and quake in a quotidian reminder of the god they all serve.

By five o'clock he has witnessed the earthquake first-hand and—armed with a red pencil—completed the task of proofreading the previous day's paper. To his inestimable satisfaction he has found a series of errors in both spelling and grammar.

Dolores takes his marked-up pages from him and smiles. 'Nice work, Raymond. Home time. We're putting you up at the Railroad Y, right?'

'Yes.' He stifles a yawn, then grins like a child. 'I get to walk back the scenic route. The Chrysler's my favourite.'

'Best building in town.' Dolores smiles approvingly. 'You know, when I was a girl you could visit the very top for fifty cents.' She sighs. 'Still, at least they cleaned up the outside in time for your arrival.'

That night he sleeps heavily, his dreams full of hard-won footholds amongst shiny curved lines; of obscure, nocturnal adventures, and of not looking down.

Two

The following morning Raymond arrives at the offices to find a man waiting outside reading a book, a bookmark between his teeth. As Raymond approaches, the man takes the bookmark out of his mouth, slips it between the pages, closes his book and smiles. 'Wallace.'

'Yes. Mr Doty, I presume?'

'Correct.'

Raymond waits for Doty to proffer a first name, but he does not do so. Raymond laughs as though at a congenial joke, and offers his hand.

'I thought we could grab a coffee—you had breakfast, Wallace?'

'Yes, but I can happily have another coffee.'

'This suit. Love it. They said you looked unequivocally British. And they were right. Bukowski was uncharacteristically enthusiastic, which is like a medal, trust me.'

Doty wears a dark-grey single-breasted suit, a white shirt and a neatly-tied tie of the darkest blue. In his late fifties, he has a kindly, patrician face and wears a short stubby moustache the width of his nose. He ushers Raymond along the street until they arrive at a small café, its entrance concealed by scaffolding. The space is dominated by a polished wooden bar that curves from the entrance and glides along the length of the café; in the centre of the wall behind the bar there's a doorway obscured by a chain curtain, and attached to the floor all along the length of the bar are podium stools like wooden mushrooms. Doty perches on one, indicating for Raymond to join him. A head bobs up from behind the bar, shoulders rocking with the drying of crockery.

'Hey Charles,' says Doty, 'two coffees, please.'

'Coming right up,' says Charles, glancing and smiling briefly at Raymond before dropping his dishcloth on the countertop, turning and collecting two mugs from a shelf behind the bar.

Doty puts his book down on the counter between them in such a way that its title is obscured from view. 'Tell me, Wallace, what do you know about homosexuals?'

Raymond squints at Doty. 'Homosexuals,' he says after a pause, as though trying to remember what the word means.

'Inverts, deviants, degenerates: what do you know?'

Beneath the counter Raymond's right thumb finds a hangnail on his left hand. 'There was a chap at my college who was rusticated—sorry; expelled—for it,' he says. 'I had only ever thought of him as rather—I suppose the word is *flamboyant*—but then it transpired that there was rather more going on than that. A scandal. But I wasn't in his circle, so I wasn't privy to the gory details. Just that he—name of Stephen Bennett—disappeared to France. Paris, I think.'

'Paris is a fashionable choice for that type,' says Doty. 'The *overt* ones—the continent's lower moral standards allowing for greater freedom of expression. Characteristics?'

'Well, like I said: a kind of flamboyance. Confidence, really, that he was…who he was. Some found him to be defiant, which I can understand; I simply saw a man being himself to an extravagant degree.' His thumbnail finds some purchase on the piece of skin.

'You're not a homosexual, I take it.'

Raymond blinks slowly. 'I am a virgin, but that's not the same thing.'

Doty laughs like he's been punched, then pats Raymond on the arm. 'You're funny,' he says.

'Do you mind my asking what this is all about?'

'It's a tactical journalistic habit, non-disclosure. A terrific way of getting someone's truth out of them before they know it. An essential tool. I recommend it. Look: there's what many psychiatrists and medical experts are describing as an *epidemic* in this city, Wallace. And the thing is, I feel sorry for them. I mean, books like this,' Doty flicks the pages of the book before him, 'tell us the very latest in psychiatric and therapeutic understandings,' he taps his temple, 'and they're sick, you know? The result of inadequate parenting; absent or detached fathers, overbearing mothers; lack of a significant masculine figure in the household, et cetera, et cetera. And it can be cured. But if left untreated; when allowed to fester, untrammelled…' He trails off as Charles arrives with their coffees before disappearing behind the chain curtain. From the inside pocket of his jacket, Doty withdraws a chestnut-brown leather wallet, removes a few coins which he tosses onto the counter, then replaces his wallet. 'And in this city right now the saturation is such that a homosexual can basically live entirely amongst his own, so that he doesn't need to interact with normal society. I mean, on one hand, it's fascinating. It's like, well they say you can live a year in New York only speaking Spanish, you know? When you think of it like that—a foreign language—it's kind of sad, isn't it? Homeless, rudderless guys— like refugees—unable to lay down roots or get the benefits of the straight life.'

'So you're writing a piece on homosexuality in New York City.'

'On the growth of the *overt* homosexual. Front-page.' Doty smiles. 'Big deal, not just for a rising star like yourself, but me, too. What do you say?'

Raymond nods. 'Of course.' In a swift move, he yanks the hangnail off. A sting.

'Milton Bracker did a piece back in—oh, I want to say 1960?—but that was really more about the decline of the theatre district and suchlike. Only a half column specifically on queers, and it was almost comedic, you know? Talked about deviants in mascara who *walk with a swish*: that sort of thing. Between you and me,' he says, lowering his voice to a conspiratorial whisper, 'it kind of made me wonder whether Bracker himself wasn't one, you know? I mean: what kind of red-blooded journalist uses the word *swish*?' He sips his coffee and looks thoughtfully at Raymond. 'You know, Wallace, there's a thing they do, in the police. They're called "actors". They choose guys—let's say, a guy of around your age, your build, your looks—and they get him to visit places. Places…frequented by men of a certain persuasion.'

'Entrapment?'

'Ha! Jesus, no! Investigative journalism, Wallace. Immersive journalism. It's my specialty. Though you'll get much more traction than I would, for this particular investigation. Think of yourself as a decoy.'

'Who's the enemy?'

'Isn't that obvious? Though perhaps it's not "who", but "what". That is to say: a culture in which there are behaviours which run counter to societal norms is one thing, but when those behaviours are routinely criminal in nature, and when those behaviours result in vulnerability to other forms of criminal behaviour the picture shifts and the whole narrative needs adjustment. Good question, though. In the sense that one of the main tenets of psychiatric and therapeutic medicine is to understand the homosexual as a victim of his predilections, rather than a perpetrator.'

'Hate the sin; love the sinner,' says Raymond, slipping the side of his thumb into his mouth. A ferrous tang.

'Precisely. Victims of their own chronic obliquity.'

'Obliquity?'

Doty looks at Raymond's puzzled face with evident satisfaction. 'Indeed. Divergence from the norm, from moral rectitude… I guess that's why they call us guys *the straight ones*. Sexual inversion is, after all, a diversion from natural—*normal*—psychological and sexual development. Alcoholics are, similarly, victims of an addiction to self-destructive behaviours. And shame thrives in the dark, you know? One of the greatest transformational gifts you can give to a disease is to name it and give it room for open and frank discussion. Hence the front page.'

Raymond nods.

Doty covers his tie. 'What colour is my tie?'

Raymond smiles. 'Navy,' he says, without hesitation.

'My wallet?'

'Brown. Chestnut, I guess I'd call it.'

Doty smiles, evidently impressed. 'It might seem trite, but observational skills—and speed—are essential to a life in journalism. Listen,' he says, sliding down from his stool, 'I'll give you a bunch of reading to do, so that you can catch up—and if there's anything in addition you come across, bring it directly to me. Not Bukowski, and not Dolores; me. Got it?' He looks Raymond up and down. 'Now that is a quality suit.'

Raymond laughs. 'Thank you. For my twenty-first birthday present, my mother had three of my father's best ones tailored to fit me.'

'The man of the house.'

Raymond feels a knot clench his stomach.

'They're rather old-fashioned.' Doty reaches for his wallet once more and counts out four ten-dollar bills which he slides across the counter to Raymond. 'Ask Dolores for a recommendation. A clothing store. I imagine it'll be somewhere in the Village. A *boutique,*' he adds wryly, all the while holding Raymond's gaze. 'It's not a sartorial judgment, Wallace. It's the sort of place these guys work. *Fashion.* And a good-looking guy like yourself…I want you to spend some time there. Be an observant customer, then come tell me what you see. And along the way, get yourself something…' he waves his fingers as though filtering vocabulary. 'Trust me: with your accent and a *hip* outfit, the New York girls will fall at your feet.'

'This is a lot of money,' says Raymond, blushing.

'Expenses. Just bring me receipts,' Doty says, heading towards the exit. 'Meanwhile, let's reconvene November 1st and see how the land lies. Deadline November 26, so we have a while. Wallace? A pleasure.'

'Indeed,' says Raymond, slipping the bills into his inside pocket as Doty waves over his shoulder and is gone.

When Raymond returns to the office that morning Dolores looks at him over the top of a pair of spectacles the shape of which puts him in mind of a cat's eyes. 'Well?' she says, raising an eyebrow. 'How'd it go with Mr Doty?'

'Fine,' he says, looking unblinkingly at her, his lips twitching in mischief, 'if rather like being interviewed by my own mother for the role of her son.'

The peal of laughter that escapes Dolores' mouth takes everyone in the office—including her—by surprise. Waving nonchalantly to the heads turned in her direction, she smothers her laughter with a manicured hand, takes off her glasses and dabs at the corners of her eyes with the fourth finger of her free hand. Once she has her amusement under control, she shakes her head in contented disbelief. 'That is so much the perfect description of what it is to engage with that man, Raymond. Write it down now before either you forget it, or I steal it.'

That Saturday—Raymond's second in the city—he follows Dolores' instructions and takes the subway to Christopher Street. As he emerges from his subterranean journey he is at once astonished and relieved to find roads no longer in regimental grids, but fanning out at diagonals from the intersection. Consulting Dolores' hand-drawn map he makes his way West along Christopher Street itself until he finds his destination: a men's clothing store called, simply, *Threads*. In the window are three mannequins: one posed as though checking his watch, another with his arm around a third, who appears to be lighting a cigarette. Raymond thinks back on Doty's instructions. He notices his heart beating faster, once again. A bell rings as he pushes the door open, and a young man—perhaps just a little younger than Raymond himself—turns from his task of neatening a display of neckties and smiles.

'Good afternoon,' he says, stepping out from behind the low glass cabinet of the counter. 'My name is Joshua. Please let me know if I can be of any help.'

Raymond nods politely. In his tweed jacket and heavy woollen trousers, he feels as though he is dressed for another era. Joshua is slight and slim, and looks not unlike a mannequin himself, in a tailored shirt of the palest lilac and fitted black trousers. He looks Raymond up and down as though appraising him.

'I'd like to buy some clothes, please,' says Raymond. 'For myself. I've been told I look a little old-fashioned,' he adds, with a smile.

'How *rude*,' says Joshua, raising his hands towards Raymond's lapels. Raymond twitches and Joshua immediately drops his hands and takes a step back. 'Good fabric, good tailoring, good taste: these things are never out of fashion,' he says kindly, interlacing his slender fingers, 'but I can certainly recommend some items that might add a little...*freshness* to your wardrobe.' He leads Raymond towards a corner of the shop where shelves hold neatly-folded piles of cotton drill trousers in various shades, then scrutinises his build with a professional eye before selecting two pairs: one dark grey; the other, beige. 'These are of a lighter weight than your current pair, and a slightly slimmer cut, but they have some *give* in them which should prevent them from feeling at all *constraining*.' He smiles at this last word. 'And then for the top,' he adds, looking at Raymond's chest and shoulders before pulling open a drawer beneath the shelves, 'these have just arrived.' He withdraws two items—jumpers: one a dark, plummy red; the other a dull grey-blue—which he unfolds. 'They're called *sweater shirts*, and I have to say, they are a beautiful fit. Italian wool. They're lighter than a sweater, heavier than a shirt. Collared, buttoned and—like the pants—to be worn fitted, so they follow the contours of the body. They are both casual and smart.'

He pauses, looking at Raymond, who has almost forgotten his task of purchasing the clothing, so captivated is he by Joshua's demeanour and deportment. He wonders what it might be to move through the world as Joshua—with such elegant, understated confidence—and feels clumsy in comparison.

'Would you be interested in trying these on, sir?'

'Yes, of course. Please,' says Raymond, observing within

himself an encroaching sense of guilt as he considers betraying this man to Doty.

'The changing room is here.' Joshua draws back a curtain beside the shop counter to reveal a small cubicle with a chair inside. He carefully places the two pairs of trousers and the sweaters on the chair then nimbly withdraws, holding out an arm for Raymond to enter. 'I'll be right outside should you need any further help, or perhaps another size. But I think these should fit nicely,' he adds encouragingly. 'There's a full-length mirror out here, when you're ready for the *grand reveal*.'

Raymond glances at his reflection almost shamefully before ducking into the changing room. Joshua draws the curtain and Raymond is alone. He finds the relative quiet somewhat disconcerting, then hears the scratch of a record needle, a piano arpeggio, and a haunting voice sings about *sad young men*. Raymond unties and removes his shoes as the song continues, and hears Joshua humming along, every now and then joining in with the words. Raymond hangs his jacket on a hook, slips out of his braces and lets his trousers drop to the floor as he unbuttons his shirt. Scenes of drinking and drifting through bars come to his ears from the record player. Standing there in his vest and underpants he feels terribly shy, and is grateful for the curtain. He lifts the blue sweater shirt and slips it over his head. It fits snugly, cosily; he reaches for the beige trousers and pulls them on, too. They are indeed narrower in all areas, with a fit closer to a sports kit than anything else he has ever worn, and the fabric feels smooth and soft against his skin. He feels immediately transformed, and imagines that this is how an actor might feel when trying on a brilliant new costume. When he hears Joshua clearing his throat and asking whether he needs any help, Raymond takes a deep breath and draws back the curtain. As he does so he realises with a coy kind of giddiness that he longs for Joshua's approval.

The men of the song are now seeking *a certain smile*.

'Don't be shy,' says Joshua kindly, stepping back to admire Raymond's outfit. 'How do they feel?'

As Raymond steps out of the changing room, he is suddenly aware of Joshua's cologne—a dry, clean scent of bitter citrus—almost as though he has dabbed some more on whilst Raymond was getting changed. He turns to his reflection and is struck by the not unhandsome young man who now looks back at him. His hair has stuck up on one side, so he brushes it down, smoothing his parting once more. He looks for his father's eyes, but they are nowhere to be seen. From behind him, Joshua tugs at the bottom of the sweater, adjusting its position very slightly, and—almost without making contact with him—draws Raymond's shoulders back so that he stands tall; proud, even. Then, taking Raymond by the hips in a perfunctory manner, Joshua pivots him 90 degrees before dropping to his knees and tugging at the cuffs of the trousers. He looks up at Raymond and smiles. 'They just needed a tug,' he says, rocking back onto his heels before standing once more. Raymond nods and smiles back, his head a whirring combination of self-consciousness and delight at how he looks and feels. The trousers now hang neatly, following Joshua's adjustments, and as Raymond turns slightly, he sees how they show the outlines of his buttocks and thighs.

'You may find that the undershirt is now superfluous,' says Joshua, an extended forefinger pointing out the line made by Raymond's vest in the fabric of the sweater, 'not only in terms of warmth, but also in terms of its visibility,' he adds.

'Mmm,' murmurs Raymond.

Joshua brushes some lint off Raymond's backside; Raymond feels a pulse in his groin. He finds himself wondering what he might begin to want, should he stay longer in the shop.

'Would you care to try on the others?'

In choosing his response Raymond makes a silent pact with himself, the outcome of which will be determined by Joshua's reply to the question: 'are they are the same fit?'

'Identical,' says Joshua, confidently.

Raymond notes his own mild disappointment at this answer, but is resolute. 'No need, in that case; I'll take them all. Please.'

'Wonderful. And should you find anything not to your liking when you get home, you just come straight back to me, and I'll ensure you leave a satisfied customer.'

Raymond retreats into the changing room, draws the curtain and undresses once more. Once back in his own clothes, he returns to the counter where Joshua has packaged up his purchases in brown paper, and is making out the sales receipt.

'I have to say, I feel rather fusty, now.'

Joshua looks blankly at him. 'Fusty?'

'Fuddy-duddy. Old fashioned.'

'*Fuddy-duddy*: that's a great expression. Not at all. You look…
like a gentleman. May I have your name?'

'Wallace. Raymond Wallace.'

'Very good, Mr Wallace,' says Joshua, printing Raymond's
name on the receipt. 'With tax, that comes to twenty-six dollars
and seventy-five cents.' Raymond hands him three of Doty's
bills, and Joshua counts out the change. When he gets to the
dollars, he looks Raymond straight in the eye. 'Until they print us
a three-dollar bill,' he says, smiling expectantly as though sharing
a joke, 'we'll have to make do with individual ones.'

Nonplussed, Raymond smiles politely before pocketing the
change and slipping his parcel of clothing under his arm. 'Thank
you, Joshua,' he says.

Joshua tilts his head to one side and says, 'You're most
welcome, Mr Wallace,' then steps past to open the door for him.

It is only when Raymond is on the platform awaiting his
train that he identifies the overwhelming feeling he had during
his visit to the store as that of having been seduced; he swiftly
categorises this as an observation he will not be disclosing to
Doty. As he retraces his steps to the YMCA, in fact, he begins
the process of editing this entire experience so as to parcel up a
version fit for Doty that doesn't jeopardise its status within his
body and memory, and in doing so realises that the quality he had
most enviously and admiringly perceived in Joshua was, quite
simply, his apparent freedom.

That evening Raymond enters the showers to find another
man already there, and feels suddenly and immediately self-

conscious about his own naked body. He washes perfunctorily, stealing glances at the other man's impressive physique. Taller than Raymond, with dark hair fanning out from his breastbone almost up to his shoulders, his buttocks are meaty—muscular, like those of a race horse. He studiously avoids Raymond's gaze, and Raymond dries himself hurriedly before heading up to his room.

Later he is awakened by the sound of his door closing, bringing with it the twin smells of stale cigarettes and whisky. In allowing his eyelids to open ever so slightly, he identifies his new room-mate as the man from the showers. The air in the room suddenly feels charged with static. Raymond pulls the blanket up around his neck and closes his eyes tight.

Sometime later he hears an odd slapping sound and opens his eyes to find the man standing, leaning against the upper bunk, his head out of view, his naked body immediately before Raymond. The man's penis is fully erect and he is masturbating. Raymond's cheeks are ruddy with arousal. And humiliation.

'This what you want?' the man demands in a rasping whisper, his fist bobbing furiously. The head of his engorged penis looks grotesque—like something from a butcher's counter. 'I saw you. *Looking.*'

Raymond holds his breath, feeling the potential for violence in the air, then closes his eyes purposefully.

'Your loss,' slurs the man after a few long seconds, and he clambers into the upper bunk, the whole structure swaying violently as he does so.

After a minute or so of metronomic squeaks from the bed-springs above Raymond's head the man grunts his release, uttering the single word, *'faggot,'* as he does so before farting loudly and then—almost immediately, it seems to Raymond—beginning to snore.

When Raymond finally falls asleep he dreams once more of scaling the Chrysler spire, only this time, Doty is beneath him. Passing one of the triangular windows, Raymond sees a naked man dancing, his face out of sight, his genitals bobbing with his exertions, but then Doty asks him what he sees, and in cupping a hand to peer more closely, Raymond finds himself losing his purchase on the spire. As he begins to fall he is awakened by the sound of the door slamming. It is early morning. The man has gone. Raymond feels a tremendous relief coupled with a loneliness more profound than any he has ever experienced.

Three

Raymond returns to his desk on Monday morning to find a parcel wrapped in brown paper, a note scrawled across it:

R.W.,

For your Eyes Only.

Out of town this Friday; meeting postponed to 11/06.

Bring your notes!

Doty.

When Raymond opens the parcel he finds two additional textbooks: one by an Edmund Bergler entitled *Homosexuality: Disease or Way of Life?*; the other by Dr. Irving Bieber: *Homosexuality: a Psychoanalytic Study of Male Homosexuals.* Raymond swiftly tears the paper in two, wrapping each book in a sheet so that its title is concealed, and replaces them on his desk.

Those ten days are spent immersed in these books and the concepts and language therein. Raymond finds corroborations of Doty's commentary from the coffeeshop that first week, albeit in far greater, clinical detail: *close, binding, intimate mothers*; *violent, rejecting fathers*; *oral-masochism*—to give three pertinent 'causes' of homosexuality. To Raymond's surprise, both authors exhibit a sympathy for their subjects, coupled with a powerful conviction that—through the treatment of such causes—those subjects can be cured of their degeneracy. It is all so neat, so unflinchingly un-equivocal and so determined in its ambitions that Raymond finds himself considering Joshua, for example, and the man from the Y, and Stephen Bennett, for that matter, and wondering at the roots of their behaviours; at their parentage; at their solitude. The array of feelings he'd had in the clothing store and his hot blushes at his masturbating roommate he somehow manages to file away as though they are not pertinent. The overriding understanding he draws from all this reading is that salvation is expressly only for those who seek it; that the lucky homosexual is he who cannot be satisfied by the vicissitudes of his derivative, queer lifestyle, and who, desperate for respite, seeks professional advice, treat-ment and the hard-won enlightenment of *heterosexual adjust-ment*. Though he tries to read these accounts with journalistic objectivity, he finds they leave within him a residue that is both corrosive and corroborative, as though they are backing up argu-ments he has already heard.

Sometimes, in the evenings of these initial weeks, after he's had his supper, Raymond heads out into the corridored city. He might slip into a movie theatre and catch a picture; he might just walk, peering through the windows of shops and bars. Wherever he goes, however, he always feels like a spectator, and on those nights when he has wandered, he falls into bed with a melancholy kind of relief.

'The Heights Supper Club on Montague Street in Brooklyn had its license revoked last week,' says Doty when they finally meet again on the 6th November. He and Raymond are in the coffeeshop, once more. 'One of those places where a bell rings if the cops appear, and the boys know to let go their hold on one another and look butch. *Nothing to see here, Officer,*' he adds with a lisp, his hands splayed parodically.

As though trying to change the subject, Raymond hands Doty the receipt from *Threads*. He hasn't worn the clothes yet—though sometimes, alone in his room, he takes them out, holds them against his body, looks at himself in the mirror and wonders at who he might become if he *were* to wear them.

'Any hooks?'

Raymond shakes his head, remembering his prepared, redacted version of the encounter. 'Salesman, name of Joshua,' he says. 'Elegant, you might say, and perfectly respectful.'

Doty nods. 'Lingering eye?'

'Sorry?'

'Did he look at you with a lingering eye?'

'More than professional? I don't think so.'

'Found ways to touch you?'

'Lint,' says Raymond in a way that makes them both laugh.

'Did he—'

'Walk with a swish?' says Raymond, and Doty laughs again. 'It was a small shop so there wasn't much room to observe his gait.' Feeling as though Doty may be suspicious unless he proffers something more, he adds: 'He did make a joke, though—at least, I think it was a joke—about a three-dollar bill?'

Doty grins, raising an eyebrow, then—noting Raymond's blank expression, says: 'You're kidding: *Queer as a three-dollar bill?*'

Raymond shakes his head.

'Wow. You really *are* out of another country, Wallace. Another era, even. Tell me what you know about quinces.'

Raymond looks at him quizzically. 'Not a huge amount, I have to say.'

'They're a curious fruit. Inedible at the point of harvesting, they need to be tactically *blet*, which is to say that they need a period of time in complete darkness in order to ripen to sweetness. And if they touch one another during this time they will most likely rot. This is what I mean about the importance of bringing to light.'

Raymond is silent for a moment, then says, 'I'm afraid I don't understand. Your analogy would suggest that, once a homosexual comes out into the light after a time in obscure isolation, his flesh is ripe for the tasting.'

The glance Doty gives him in response is a wave of anger that foams into resentment before ebbing towards subdued admiration. 'You'll go far,' he says simply, and sips his coffee. 'Okay,' he then adds as though trying to regain the upper hand, 'our deadline remains November 26, so we have just shy of three weeks: plenty of time. Police Commissioner tells me they've got two joints in their sights at present: The Fawn on Washington Street and another down on Jane Street in Brooklyn. Licenses to be revoked just as soon as they gather sufficient evidence.' He stops abruptly, his face lit from within by inspiration in a manner Raymond finds faintly disquieting. 'You know, Wallace, given the success of your shopping trip, I'm now thinking that we can push the envelope on this…information gathering.'

Raymond looks at Doty as though at a chess opponent, awaiting his next move.

'Get you into a bar, I mean,' says Doty, placing his coffee cup on the counter as though in punctuation. 'What do you say?'

Raymond allows the corners of his mouth to curl into a smile of complicity. He now thinks of himself as two discrete figures: one, Doty's sidekick, covertly investigating the homosexual underworld, and a second who longs to enter that world as himself, to place himself amongst others who are—though he hesitates to even think this—*like him*. He swallows and nods.

'Good,' says Doty. 'Very good.' He pats Raymond on the shoulder in a paternal manner, leaving his hand there for a few seconds. 'Be careful, though,' he says. 'I wouldn't want you getting yourself into any trouble on my behalf.'

Raymond shrugs as though to indicate that such a thing would be all part of a day's work.

'Now then,' says Doty, 'may I take these notes with me? For the weekend?' he adds, lifting and tapping Raymond's papers into a neat stack.

'Of course, but they are for your eyes only,' says Raymond with a wry smile.

'You got that reference.'

'I was shaken by it, but not in the least bit stirred.'

'Didn't have you pegged as a Fleming fan.'

Raymond shrugs. 'I was blessed with a pair of unimaginative aunts,' he says, drily. 'The latest Bond appeared in my stocking each Christmas morning.'

'Ha.' Doty cocks his head to one side, looking him up and down. 'You know, Wallace? You could be a spy. Debonair, intrepid. British.'

Raymond laughs down his nose in feigned amusement.

Doty lifts a book-shaped paper bag and hands it to him. 'I'll swap your notes for this,' he says, standing up. 'See you next week, Wallace, and if you do go to a bar, I wanna hear all about it,' he adds, before slipping the papers under his arm and leaving Raymond alone once more.

A quarter of an hour later, as Raymond approaches the stairs to the third floor, he senses a presence above him. He glances up to see the woman from his first day, only this time her red hair is tied up and the fur is securely belted round her thin frame. She's shuddering and slightly out of breath as though from the effort of climbing. Her cheeks are flushed and a strand of her hair has fallen down and is stuck to her left cheek. She doesn't pull it away.

'Hello,' says Raymond gently, slowing down as he climbs the final stairs. 'I'm Raymond. Wallace. Are you okay?'

'I'm fine, Raymond. Thank you.'

As though Raymond has functioned as some sort of impetus, she pushes open the doors to the newsroom and enters, leaving the doors swinging behind her. Caught by some instinctive sense of discretion, Raymond stands in the stairwell for a second or two before heading back to his desk.

Kleinmann is sitting outside Bukowski's door, and looks at Raymond with an animated expression. He beckons him closer.

'*His wife!*' he whispers, raising his eyebrows in an almost comical, conspiratorial manner, and flicking his head towards Bukowski's closed door. '*They're not together anymore,*' he adds, excitedly, before spelling out his punchline: '*D.I.V.O.R.C.E.*'

'That's really none of my business,' Raymond says, turning away.

Then the office door swings open and the woman—evidently Mrs Bukowski—appears in the doorway. On seeing Raymond and Kleinmann, she turns to her husband with a brittle sneer and—her voice almost imperceptibly cracking with emotion—says: 'You have some visitors, Harvey. Two men: think you can handle that?' Then she leaves, head down, clutching her bag to her chest; and Raymond is certain—almost certain—that he sees her eyes fill as she walks away.

Kleinmann leans round the open doorway and begins to speak. 'Bukowski, I have those photographs you were look—'

Bukowski's voice booms out from within the office: '*NOT NOW, KLEINMANN: NOT NOW!*'

The shout echoes around the newsroom, the inhabitants of which freeze in the silence immediately following, before Kleinmann, combining indignation and sheepishness in equal quantities, leaves the room as quickly as possible.

Raymond pauses before leaning slowly towards Bukowski's door and—without looking inside—taking hold of the door handle and drawing the door to. He turns to find the entire office looking at him; some amused, some anxious: all curious. He shrugs and walks over to his place, sits at his desk and slips

Doty's latest book out of its paper bag.

Hours pass with Raymond reading away, making notes. Dolores comes over just after four o'clock, clutching a pile of papers to her chest. 'Er, Raymond?'

'Uh-huh?'

'Could I talk to you for a second?' Dolores is visibly uncomfortable.

Raymond stands up. 'Of course. Here?' He senses someone behind him raise their head but he doesn't look round.

'Follow me,' Dolores says, walking over to Bukowski's office. 'He's left for the weekend. Go in, I'll get coffee. Oh, and take these, please,' she adds, handing Raymond the papers.

Raymond enters Bukowski's office and hesitates before sitting down. The man isn't here to give his permission, which makes Raymond slightly uncomfortable, but he sits in the seat he sat in on his first day and looks around. It's only the second time he's been in here. He slides the papers onto the desk, on which he notices the backs of two photographs. He doesn't peek. He imagines that one is of Bukowski's wife, perhaps a wedding photograph; the other of children, possibly. He wonders whether Bukowski actually has any children; *it's none of my business*, he thinks. Seconds later Dolores enters with two cups of coffee, a cookie in each saucer. She kicks the door shut behind her and stands, leaning heavily against it, eyes closed, breathing heavily.

'Dolores, are you ok?'

She opens her eyes, taking him in, and says, 'Oh, Raymond.' Putting the coffees down, she shifts the papers on Bukowski's desk and perches herself on the edge. She hands one of the cups to Raymond, takes her cookie and breaks it in two before putting one of the halves into her mouth and chewing it slowly, all the while looking Raymond square in the eye. He holds her gaze for a second or two, then looks down at his coffee. There's a chocolate chip melting onto the side of the cup.

'There's something I need to talk to you about. Something kind of delicate.'

Raymond swallows. 'Dolores, if it's something I've done, I've—'

'No, Raymond, it's nothing to do with you. I mean, of course it concerns you, otherwise I wouldn't be talking to you about it, but it's not your fault. It's this article. The Doty article.'

Raymond darts a look at her. Dolores waves a hand in front of her dismissively. When she speaks, she does so in short bursts of rapid fire. 'I know, I know, Doty's told you not to say a word: that's just his way of garnering discretion and some weird sense of control. Does it with all the new guys, thinks it's charismatic. But it's Mr Bukowski who gets the final say, and to whom Doty answers, however grand he may be feeling after his sojourn in Paris. I need you—Mr Bukowski wants you—to…how to put it? To contextualise; to mitigate, to *cushion* the blows of Doty's instinctively conservative perspective. These titles he gives you: these are the guys who think the Kinsey Reports are some whacko zoologist's fantasies. And that the bible's a textbook? This latest one: Donald Webster Cory? He may well be a real, live homosexual, but he sure is a self-hater and he's only made the cut because he agrees with the others.' She pauses to take a bite of her cookie and a sip of her coffee. The tip of her tongue lingers at one corner of her mouth as she looks at Raymond as though making a decision. 'Mr Bukowski's wife is divorcing him. I can't say why. And Doty is not the most collegiate of colleagues. This article, Raymond…' She pauses once more, and for a second Raymond thinks her eyes seem full of pain. 'These articles affect people. They matter. And they matter not only to those who partake in Doty's point of view; they matter to those who don't, can't or won't, and those who—to take a bolder position—*shouldn't*. We have a duty to our readership to offer a selection of viewpoints.'

For a moment, they sit in silence. Raymond holds his coffee in front of him, somehow unable either to sip it, or to put it down. Then he remembers something. 'There was a report in the U.K. maybe five or six years ago—'57: that's right—the Wolfenden Report. Recommendations about removing penalties for *consenting adults in private*, amongst others. Might that be the sort of thing you mean?'

Dolores smiles and her shoulders drop. 'Yes, Raymond. Precisely.'

He sips and swallows. 'I mean, none of the recommendations were accepted by parliament, so the law in Britain remains the same.'

'None *was*.' Dolores gives a self-congratulatory smirk.

'*Touché.*'

Then her eyes widen in realisation and she snaps her fingers at him. 'Illinois,' she says.

'Sorry?'

'*They* passed a law. So there you go: Illinois.'

For a moment, there's a satisfied silence. When she speaks again, her voice is quieter than before. 'I mean, *consenting adults in private*: what is wrong with us? Where else—other than the Catholic church, of course,' she adds, wryly, 'do we expect to control every single aspect of someone's life? If you're straight you can beat your wife and no-one gives a damn, but if…' She tails off, takes another sip of her coffee, places the cup and saucer down on the desk beside her and rests her hands either side of her thighs. 'You don't socialise with anyone from the office, right?'

'Well, I, I mean, no. I hadn't thought of it like that, Dolores, but, no, I don't suppose I do.'

'That needs to be the case from now on. This divorce: it's messy. Not that all divorces aren't messy, but there's money involved. And some not very nice people. Well: one not very nice person. And Mr B's in the firing line. The reason you're in here today is because he trusts you.'

'Bukowski—'

'Trusts you: yes. He trusts you and wants you to…infiltrate— for want of a better word—this article in the most tactical and tactful way that you can. Can you handle this, Raymond?'

'Absolutely. I understand, Dolores. Thank you.'

'Thank *me*? No, no Raymond: thank *you*. Now,' she says, tapping his shoulder in a suddenly conspiratorial tone. 'Was Joshua helpful?'

Raymond nods guiltily as he recalls his conversation with Doty.

'What is it?' asks Dolores.

'It's just that Doty asked me what he was like—Joshua—and I told him.'

'Don't tell me: Doty's looking for descriptions of *overt homosexuals* to lend an air of credibility to his article.'

'I didn't mean to—'

Dolores points a manicured forefinger at him which she rotates as she speaks. 'You don't need to worry about anything,' she says. 'Doty's going to try to get you into all sorts of situations. Anything that concerns you from here on in, run it by me, first.'

'He talked of "actors". The police.'

Dolores laughs. 'Jesus. He's so *dramatic*. What is he, a plain-clothes journalist?'

'He wants me to go to a bar.'

Dolores' eyes snap wide open as she rises physically, like a protective swan. 'Now you listen to me, Raymond,' she says, her voice slightly hoarse. 'You go wherever you like. Get a drink in a bar. Whichever bar suits you best. But when you leave this office at five p.m. you're off duty, for god's sake. Don't let Doty manage your private life.'

Raymond breathes out in relief. Dolores looks at him as though she is about to divulge something when suddenly there's a commotion outside, a chorus of *NOT NOW, KLEINMANN!* and then Raymond and Dolores hear the frenzy of Kleinmann's voice.

'Excuse me, Raymond,' says Dolores, reaching efficiently for the door handle. She opens the door to reveal Kleinmann shouting in fury, each emphasis a yodel causing great delight amongst the packed office.

'I have had en*ough* of this *in*solence, this *dis*respect, this—'

'Mr Kleinmann?'

Kleinmann turns sharply, sees Dolores, glares at her. '*What?* I mean, *yes?* I mean I'm sorry, Dolores, I didn't realise there was anyone—'

'Mr Bukowski's not in the office, if that's what you're concerned about, Mr Kleinmann. Okay, everyone, show's over. Sam: take fifteen. Everyone else, get on with your work, cut the victimisation.' She turns back into Bukowski's office, pulls the door behind her, and—Raymond is almost positive—suppresses a smile. She purses her lips and looks at him. 'So, Raymond: we good?'

Raymond nods emphatically and turns to leave.

'By the way,' she says as his hand reaches the doorknob, 'Brooklyn's got some neat bars.' Raymond glances at her. 'Discreet. Should you happen to find yourself in the neighborhood, that is.'

He closes the door behind him then, glancing around the office, walks back to his desk a fraction taller. There is something about the complicity, the privilege of trust in what Dolores has told him that makes him feel as though he has been truly understood and valued for the very first time in his life, and Bukowski's request that he *infiltrate* Doty's article feels valorous:

a heroic quest.

That night he dreams of being offered slices of quince by a stranger. As much as he peers and squints, however, he cannot for the life of him find any definition in the man's features; the moon's light is too grimy for identification. The man lifts Raymond's hand and places a slice on his outstretched palm. Raymond is bringing it towards his mouth for his first taste when he is awakened by the discomfiting pressure of his hardened cock sandwiched between his belly and his mattress.

Four

That following Saturday afternoon Raymond has his hair cut at a barber's near Grand Central Station. He studies a large map of the city that hangs on the wall between mirrors as the barber gives him what he calls 'a college contour'—a smooth side parting, then finely clippered, fading almost into skin above the ears and the nape of his neck. Most excitingly for Raymond, the barber uses pomade to dress his new hair. It smells of coconut, and makes his hair look darker—as though, indeed, still damp.

Once back at the YMCA he showers, then puts on the beige drill pants and the blue sweater shirt. Opening the jar of pomade he'd bought at the barbers, he dresses his hair just as the barber had demonstrated, then checks his reflection as though preparing himself for an appointment he has yet to make. He finds himself smiling back at himself in shy admiration of his new appearance. He wants to share it. But not here. And not yet. He slips on his old English overcoat as a kind of coverall, buttoning it up to the neck, and as the lobby clock strikes seven o'clock Raymond steps out into the cold night of the city.

Picturing the map from the barber's, he turns left onto Lexington, takes in the glamourous, silhouetted beauty of the Chrysler spire, then shifts a block to Park Avenue from which he spies the grandeur of the Empire State Building. It puts him in mind of King Kong and Fay Wray—a woman in need of rescue—and then of Mrs Bukowski, emaciated by her grief. He shakes his head, reminding himself that he is now officially off-duty, and marches on. Half an hour disappears and he finds himself in Union Square. The glowing interior of a bar attracts him, and he cups his hands to look through the window. He sees a woman in a low-cut dress, hips swinging as she walks towards a table with a tray of drinks. One of the customers takes a bill from his wallet and hands it to her. She slips the folded bill into her cleavage with a wink. Raymond sees, but does not hear, the roar of laughter from the men at the table. One of them sees Raymond at the window and scowls at him as though Raymond has been caught spying, so he steps backwards, almost bumping into someone, before turning quickly and heading off again.

After Washington Square Park he passes Mercer Street, crosses Broadway, turns right onto Lafayette; left onto Prince; right onto Elizabeth, Baxter becomes Pearl which takes him to St James and the Avenue of the Finest, by which point he can smell the East River and can see the Brooklyn Bridge.

Once on the Bridge he pauses and looks up and down either side of the slatted walkway at the cars, the buses, the trucks pummelling the tarmac; he looks up to the pillars, the lights like fairy lights swooping between the posts; he thinks of suspension, of bridges and of water; of times in life when one is between things; and of how one only usually realises that once the parentheses are closed.

He looks left and sees the city at night: the shimmering, floating rooms of the many skyscrapers. To his right is a dark expanse, though he knows that somewhere in that darkness stands the Statue of Liberty. Whilst it is, indeed, a cold night, the shudder his body now makes might actually be that of anticipation.

He doesn't look back again as he continues his journey across the bridge. As the walkway comes to an end he meanders through the initial streets of Brooklyn, heading north to place himself on Water Street. He thinks of the club Doty mentioned, behind him on Montague, the one that had lost its license, and as he does so he feels that knot in his stomach once more. He goes on walking, weaving himself into the streets of Brooklyn. His watch tells him that it is now nearly nine o'clock, but he's not going back, not yet.

He crosses Gold Street, then finds himself on Hudson Avenue. When a man appears abruptly from the shadows Raymond holds his breath, feeling suddenly vulnerable, but the man just smiles at him as though in recognition before crossing the road and disappearing once more. As Raymond exhales, he feels somehow spurred on by this encounter and he walks the length of the avenue, eyes hunting doorways for clues. He feels instinctively that he is getting closer and closer to what he is seeking.

He reaches a set of gates: the dockyards. He thinks of the ships that come here from all over the world. From England. He imagines his mother descending a gangplank at the end of a trans-Atlantic voyage...

He turns away from this image and retraces his steps. After the junction with Evans Street he sees something he hadn't noticed earlier: a door with a ship's wheel as its window frame. Next to it is a boarded-up window, and next to that a second, unmarked door, above which a tiny bulb feebly illuminates a sign that reads *Little Navy*. And that's all there is—no other sign; nothing else. *Discreet, indeed,* he thinks. As though to gain perspective, he crosses the street and looks up at the building. It is built of brick, three storeys high, with a fire escape attached to the wall: an easy scale for a night-climber. As Raymond watches from across the road, a man in a dark overcoat appears and taps at the door. *Little Navy.* As the door opens and the man passes through, Raymond can see almost nothing other than a brief moment of light and outlines of some figures, but then the door swings back into position and it's dark once more—darker, in fact, than it had seemed before the brightness of the interior. It is a sudden desire to no longer be in that darkness that compels Raymond to march across the street and knock at the door. No answer. He knocks again. Still nothing. He is about to knock again, this time even harder, when he senses a presence behind him. He turns to see the man in the hat who had passed him earlier.

The man's eyes look deep into Raymond's. 'You going in?' he asks.

Raymond nods.

'What's keeping you?'

'They're not answering.'

'Ah,' says the man, before turning and tapping a sequence

on the door. The door opens and he turns to wink at Raymond before ducking swiftly inside.

Quickly now, losing no time, Raymond jumps inside the door before it closes and finds himself squashed against a tall, imposing figure: a large nocturnal creature with a beard, a round, bald head and eyes like stones. 'Sir?' he asks, in a deep and resonant bass.

'Mmm?' Raymond replies, feeling suddenly as though he may have made a stupid mistake.

'Did you want to go in?'

Raymond nods as though in slow motion.

'Do you know this bar?'

'Mmm,' Raymond lies. Though physically intimidated by the man, he perceives no immediate threat. The doorman, deducing correctly that Raymond can mean no possible harm, pushes a second—inner—door, with his left hand, and now the light from within shows the door to be covered in green baize—*like a snooker board*, Raymond thinks. He blinks as his eyes adjust to the relative brightness of the interior.

As he takes his first steps in the bar his legs suddenly feel tired from his long, cold pilgrimage, and though he doesn't look back he imagines the green door closing behind him slowly and not quite silently: with a little sigh.

Five

Raymond Wallace now stands in a strange bar in a strange city: no one knows where he is except himself. Or, at least, no one who knows *where* he is knows *who* he is, which amounts to the same thing. He is taking steps he's never taken before, and yet—when he looks back—this night will look precisely like what he's been moving towards for some time now. Bukowski; Dolores; Joshua; Doty; the books, the reading: all these point the way towards a certain epiphany, a certain honesty.

The bar is small and smoky. It is like all the bars in the world, and like no other bar in the world. Raymond is gradually allowing himself to be someone different, if only for tonight. He steps further inside, to the bar itself that runs along the entirety of one wall. He unbuttons his coat and sheds it like a carapace, revealing his new clothing with shy delight.

A barman appears. He is short, stout, and smiles a smile of simple munificence. Raymond orders a beer. When the barman slides it along the bar to him he looks at the bottle, beads of condensation appearing on the glass like sweat. He takes a sip. It's still a surprise to him how American and British beers are such different animals. This tastes like pop. Pop, and the promise of something intimate. Sliding a bill across the bar, he thinks of the barmaid in Union Square. The barman nods in simple gratitude, takes the bill and turns to ring it up at the till. Folding up his coat, Raymond places it on the seat beside him before sitting down, relieved to finally be off his feet.

A man steps up to the bar to his right. Raymond stiffens, but the man holds his hands up as though in submission and says, 'Hey, man: no problem.' He orders a beer and, after his first sip, bubbles froth his moustache. Raymond is just beginning to imagine what it might feel like to lick froth off a moustache when the man picks up his beer and wanders off, leaving Raymond alone once more. The barman slides his change back towards him.

Raymond realises that he hasn't actually looked around since he arrived. It is as though he is so certain that this was, indeed, his destination, that he doesn't need to pay attention. Or as though he is so nervous about what he might find that he cannot bear to look. Then music plays, a man's voice sings about a *Loverman*, of all things, and Raymond's eyes widen as he takes in the room. In one corner is a lone man dancing slowly, his vest—his *under-shirt*—riding up his torso. He is like Salome: shamelessly determined. His eyes are closed tightly, ecstatically. Raymond envies and admires his rhythm, his ease—and yes: that same freedom he'd seen in Joshua. He bleeds himself into the extraordinary and appalling concept of taking part. He fades himself out of one world and into this new one. After all, it is only for a moment. And although it is a world of strangers and unknown systems of thought, to Raymond it feels like coming home.

He suddenly longs to dance with a man. He closes his eyes

and imagines dance halls, partnered nights, some men leading; some following—some taking the woman's role, whatever that means, now—and the roles changing. Tuxedoed boys immaculately groomed leading each other around the floor, changing positions every eight bars. He opens his eyes again onto the brave new world into which he has entered, and feels the knot in his stomach begin to unravel, thread by thread. There are other men dancing now: one has his hand on another's hips. It is almost inconceivable to Raymond as to how that might feel, and he cannot shake off a concomitant repulsion. Nor, however, can he take his eyes off the point at which these two men converge. The man being held has his arms drawn back like wings, like an angel's wings. He leans away from his *partner*, and Raymond wonders what that word means now. He needs to learn a new vocabulary, or to learn new meanings for his existing one. This is a new order. There are codes he cannot possibly decipher, for he can barely process the information that his eyes are receiving.

The holding man has his hands on the angel's hips, as if delaying his flight. His thumbs grip the moment where the hips meet the abdomen. Now shrugging off that repulsion in its entirety, Raymond allows himself a new ambition: one day he will hold his hands thus, and will feel an angel at his fingertips. Raymond gazes as the holding man's thumbs slip through the angel's belt loops and, as they turn to the music and Raymond hears the singer singing of someone making love to him, *strange as it may seem*, he sees how the holding man's fingers wrap around the angel's waist to the crest of his buttocks. As if in slow motion

Raymond turns his head to the bar, realising as he does so that tears are simply streaming down his face, and he gestures for another beer. He shudders, now, with the relief of some ancient grief, and places his head on his hands. He hears a keening in his ears, like a loose wheel, and—under the spell of the strange music, and the images of these extraordinary men—it is minutes before he realises that the keening is actually his own cry, a whimper: it's him who's coming loose, though he cannot be quite sure as to whether he is falling apart, or falling open.

Right then, on the little finger of his right hand, Raymond feels the cold wetness of glass: refreshment, the beer he'd requested. He lifts his head, face snotty as a schoolboy's, and takes the bottle directly to his lips: a significant swig. He reaches for his wallet but the barman shakes his head, directing Raymond's attention instead to a man on his left. Raymond turns to thank him and, having turned, finds that he can no longer speak. For the man before him is the lone dancer—Salome—eyes so dark as to be black in this light; face as open as the moon's.

'It's on me,' he says. 'Drown your sorrows.' When the stranger blinks, his lashes close slowly as though not to take his eyes by surprise. His lips are a deep dark pink, his chin stubbled with black roots.

Raymond realises that he is staring. 'I'm so sorry. Terribly rude,' he says. 'Thank you.'

'There's nothing to thank me for. You look hot.' Raymond blushes. 'Warm,' says the man, as though qualifying himself. 'But yes: hot, too. Where are you from, anyway—Ireland?'

'England.'

'So, uh, God save the Queen!'

'Indeed. And all who sail in her.'

The man laughs. Raymond surprises himself at his ability to make a joke. Barely half an hour in this new world, and already tears and laughter. 'So, Mr Englishman, what's your name?'

'Raymond. Raymond Wallace.'

'A pleasure to meet you, Raymond. I'm Joey. Maniscalco.'

'A pleasure to meet you, too, Joey Maniscalco. You're the dancer. A great dancer, I mean.'

Joey shrugs modestly, but Raymond notes with satisfaction the smile his compliment has prompted. 'So, uh, what brings you here, Raymond? I mean, how did you find us?'

'I came out for a walk and I just sort of ... I just stumbled across it, really.'

'Where did you start from?'

'The Railroad YMCA.'

Joey's jaw drops open. 'The *Railroad Y*? Are you *kidding* me? You *walked*? No wonder you're crying.'

Raymond laughs. 'Yes. I needed to feel the ground beneath my feet. And to put some distance behind me. Once over the bridge, I was just wandering and then I saw this tiny light at the top of the door. A man walked in, and I followed him.'

'That's how most people find it, I guess. Serendipity, I think it's called.'

'Serendipity's not a word I use very often.'

'Me either, Raymond. But it seems the right word for tonight.

By the way: new pants?'

Raymond nods embarrassedly. 'Can you tell?'

'Well, I'm no detective, but…you left the tag on them. May I?'

Raymond nods. Joey gently shifts Raymond's elbow, darting a solicitous glance into Raymond's eyes as he does so, then reaches down to his waistband and lifts Raymond's sweater slightly to untie the tag. The brush of Joey's fingers across Raymond's skin takes his breath away.

'Done,' says Joey as though in triumph, placing the tag on the bar like a trophy. 'Listen, I didn't mean to, um—'

'I've never—'

'Well, actually I *did* mean to—and I hope that's okay. Sorry, I interrupted you. You've never—'

'I've never done anything like this before.'

Joey smiles, now—smiles, and Raymond is almost positive he even blushes. For the first time in the conversation Joey looks to his beer, conveniently empty. Raymond doesn't hesitate to make this his cue: 'Can I buy you a drink?'

'Sure, Ray. Can I call you 'Ray'?'

'You can call me whatever you like,' he says, feeling exquisitely daring.

'Well then, Ray. You can buy me whatever you like,' says Joey, breathily.

Now Raymond stops laughing—not because he isn't enjoying himself, and not because he doesn't know what's going on, but rather because he is enjoying himself very much and knows *precisely* what's going on. He takes another mouthful of beer, and is about to gesture to the barman when he hears Joey draw breath and say:

'You wanna come back to my place?'

And now Raymond cannot look at Joey—not because he doesn't want to, but because the decision to allow himself to want this—*Joey*—has so many implications that his brain feels ready to explode. This is a new language, a new algebra. Raymond knows that he can open this door onto a world of unbelievable beauty, yet he cannot seem to take responsibility for the opening of that door. He swallows his beer, hears Joey add 'I mean, only if you…' and realises that the doors are already wide open. He turns with a whole new set of tears in his eyes.

'Stranger, don't go all soft on me, now will ya?'

'Too late.'

Joey laughs kindly and nods in agreement. 'Too late,' he repeats and slips his left hand between Raymond's. With his right hand, Joey cups Raymond's left cheek, thumbing away his tears. Raymond leans his head into this tender touch like an indulgent cat. Joey removes his hand from Raymond's face, picks up the tag from Raymond's new trousers and presses his thumb onto the card, staining it with Raymond's tears. 'Watermark,' he says, making Raymond laugh, and then, as though spurred on by this, adds: 'Shall we?'

And now all Raymond Wallace can do is hang his head and follow. They open the inner door, nod to the doorman who smiles at them before drawing open the outer door. It opens onto the winter and it opens onto the night, and the happy couple shivers, more with anticipation than cold.

Six

On Johnson Street between Prince and Gold, Joey reaches for his keys, opens a door and leads Raymond up the stairway. Twin smells: an unfamiliar brand of disinfectant, and years of dust. The stairs are scratched and splintered, moulded by the passing of time, shoes, wardrobes, coffins.

Joey's front door is deep green—once gloss, now deglazed to a dull satin. He places the key in the lock, opens the door and holds it slightly ajar. Raymond is paralysed by this invitation; his heart beats so loudly he thinks it must be audible to Joey, who whispers, 'My papà is asleep in the other room; take off your shoes.'

Raymond stares at him in undisguised incredulity.

'This isn't a problem, is it?' Joey adds matter-of-factly. 'I mean, it's not a problem for me. And it's no problem for him, either.'

Since all of this is inconceivable to Raymond he decides, simply, to follow instructions: he unlaces his shoes, pulls them off and carries them in his hands like kittens. Joey closes the door and leads Raymond into a smallish room on the left. Striking a match, he lights a candle which he places on a table by the side of the bed. Raymond looks around, his heart still beating wildly. There is a small double bed, neatly made, its blanket tucked under against the frame, and a wardrobe in a shadowy corner. He wonders how many times Joey has done this. He feels suddenly nauseous. 'Where's the loo?'

'The what?'

'The lavatory.'

'The bathroom? Next door. You okay?'

Raymond bolts next door. There's a small nightlight already on. He leans over the enamelled toilet bowl. Seconds pass and his nausea recedes. He stands, rinses his hands, takes a good long look in the mirror, and whispers to his reflection:

'What on earth do you think you're doing?'

He splashes cold water on his face; the sudden chill serves to numb this doubt. He dries his face, checks his reflection, then returns to the bedroom. Joey has taken off his jumper— his *sweater*—and his jeans, and is sitting on the bed in a white T-shirt and boxer shorts. Even now, even having made it thus far, Raymond hesitates to make the first move in case he's misunderstood the situation. He walks over to the window and breathes onto the glass. It is somehow important to him that his breath still condenses; that this night obeys the laws of physics. His breath clouds the pane. He wipes the condensation with the sleeve of his jumper and looks out at the streetlights. He sees in them so many days of longing, of wondering: beacons of anticipation. In the morning they'll go out, as if realising the significance of this night. And tomorrow night he'll watch for them again. But tonight, he can't imagine how they'll look then, or with what eyes he might see them tomorrow. After tonight, Raymond cannot conceive of how he will read anything, ever again.

Joey is behind him. He touches Raymond's right shoulder. Raymond stops breathing. The windowpane becomes clear. A gentle pressure turns him round. Joey's eyes glint in the glow of the street lamps. He inclines his face towards Raymond's but Raymond does not move. Joey retreats, leaving a space between them. Raymond leans forward, then—half an inch before their lips meet—hesitates once more. This time, though, emboldened by Raymond's movements, Joey's face pursues him. Raymond wants to say, again, *I've never done this before*, but it's too late for all that, because the back of his head is touching the windowpane and Joey's lips are on his, and it's lucky there's a window sill to catch him because, as they kiss, Raymond's tired legs finally fail him, buckling under new sensations. Joey catches him, laughs, kisses him again, and Raymond feels the unctuous pressure of Joey's tongue parting his lips as Joey's hands drop to his hips, his thumbs at that crucial juncture, and Raymond realises now that this makes him the angel: Joey makes Raymond into an angel, and Raymond parts his lips to allow Joey inside. It's fast and it's beautiful and it's no longer clear who's doing what, who's leading whom. What's clear is that this night above all is when it all takes place. When Raymond becomes part of Joey, and when Joey becomes part of Raymond. This is, at last, the beginning. Which also makes it the end, in a whole other world. Because, after all, this is what takes place before everything else—though at the time, of course, there is only the moment: *this moment*.

Lifting his hands from Raymond's waist and putting his arms

around him, Joey pulls him tight against his chest. Raymond breathes in a deep breath, then lets out a tremendous shuddering sigh. Joey rocks him, holding his angel tight—hoping to make him stay, perhaps—then steps back. Raymond smiles sheepishly and looks deep into Joey's eyes, his pupils wide like eclipses; his cheeks flushed.

'Come on, stranger: let me take you to bed.'

Joey lifts Raymond's hands in his, and—walking backwards—draws him to the edge of the bed. Joey sits and, as he does so, Raymond makes out the tented evidence of his arousal beneath his shorts, and feels suddenly out of his depth once more.

'What is it?' Joey frowns.

'I don't know that I can do this. I'm sorry.'

Joey smiles resignedly, as though he has been half-expecting this. 'Don't be sorry, Ray,' he says. 'It's okay.' He pats the bed beside him. 'But sit a while, won't you?'

Raymond's head suddenly swarms with phrases from Doty's books, and he hesitates—his breath high in his chest—but then Dolores' words come to mind like a life raft and he consents to sit mere inches from Joey's bare thigh.

Joey swallows, then shrugs. 'We don't have to *do* anything,' he says in a way that almost makes Raymond smile. 'I mean: don't get me wrong, I'd *like* to, but ...' He leans forwards, elbows on knees, one hand worrying the other. 'I'm lucky: I get that. Here, I mean. But hey: aren't you here, too? So why not stay the night?' He smiles sincerely, holding his hands out as though in innocence. 'I won't touch you. I promise.' Then his eyes dart across

Raymond's torso and he adds: 'unless, that is, you want me to. You are seriously cute.' Raymond's face is suddenly wide open like a child's and now it's Joey who looks as though he might weep. 'Jesus, Ray: what did they do to you?'

Whilst Raymond can't point a finger towards a single person or event, still he feels a truth in Joey's acknowledgment that something *has been done* to him, and feels damaged. Then with a rush of clarity, he understands what Dolores means when she says that *these articles matter*—because now he can see that, if it is absolutely possible to be Joey, it is equally absolutely possible *not to be Raymond*; that circumstance has led him to be the way he is, feel the way he feels. This thought initiates fresh ambitions: the possibility of unravelling that knot within him, and of cleansing himself of corrosive residues. Tentatively, concern furrowing his forehead as though he is requesting something that will—not unreasonably—be refused, he asks, 'do you think you might hold me?'

Joey exhales through his nose in relief and says, 'Sure, Ray. I'll hold ya,' in the manner of a solemn promise. He shifts back onto the covered bed, beckoning for Raymond to join him. Raymond does so cautiously, before permitting himself into the safe embrace. Snuggling into Joey's armpit, resting his head on Joey's shoulder, he watches as Joey's eyelids flicker, then close. As Joey's breathing evens out into gentle snores, Raymond even allows himself a smile. The lights of cars migrate across the ceiling. He counts them like sheep, and they dwindle in frequency until it's just the two of them lying there together, lit by the lambent streetlights. Raymond bravely places a hand on Joey's belly, feels the somnolent rise and fall, and as he begins to drift off into the pleasurable safety of a dreamless sleep he understands—at last— what it is to *be alive*.

The memory of what Raymond sees when he next opens his eyes will give him pause—even fifteen years later, when he comes to this moment in his story—and his fingers will hover tremulously over the keys of his typewriter for a second or two, as he considers how to do it justice.

For when he wakes—still in all his clothing—he finds Joey still sleeping, outstretched like a landscape beside him, now naked but for the sheet that shrouds his lower half. Raymond buzzes with desire. At first, he only grazes with his eyes: Joey nuzzling the air as though in search of something; the pulse in Joey's neck, fluttering. But then—in the half-light of this winter morning—Raymond lets his fingertips quiver through the inky foliage on Joey's chest, over the tender nibs of his nipples; down the rising, falling abdomen towards the shadows of the sheet. If Raymond had turned his head right then, he might have seen Joey's eyes flick open, a smile curling his lips. However, Raymond is intent on his fingers as they lift the sheet to reveal Joey's cock unfurling like a fern, a dewy bead at its tip. Raymond draws a salty thread to his tongue and Joey's dick rears. Raymond tastes the perfume of urine as he takes the crown, taut as a mushroom, into his mouth. Joey's belly caves, his cock arches and Raymond finds that—so long as he holds his breath—he can suck right to the root. Joey's fingertips on the back of Raymond's neck send a surprised tickle down his spine as—now guided by Joey's moans—he works more urgently, loosening, tightening his suck, a hand on Joey's rucking balls. Withdrawing for breath—eyes bright, nostrils flaring—he sees Joey's legs scissor apart to open himself more honestly and Raymond dives to ensure that Joey's dick jolts and pumps its sap down his throat. A sudden exquisite pressure fills Raymond's own groin and he unbuckles only just in time to spurt his relief across Joey's thigh: his heart beats as though in applause. He shucks off his clothes, shifts back up the bed, his softening dick signing a snail's signature across Joey's skin. Joey draws up the sheet to cover the pair of them and his fingers ruffle the hair of his new-minted champion: released, relieved and revealed by the wintry morning light.

A knock at the door. A man's voice: 'Coffee.'

Raymond freezes. *Joey's father.*

Joey stifles a laugh. 'Just leave it outside, Papà,' he whispers. 'I'll be out in a minute.'

There is a grunt of acknowledgment from outside the door, then the sound of footsteps retreating and another door closing.

Raymond buries his blushing face into Joey's chest and Joey hugs him tight, rocking him from side to side. He takes Raymond's hands in his, brings them to his lips and kisses them. This makes everything in Raymond's world make sense; this tenderness makes everything worthwhile and everything possible. Raymond feels as if his entire being has been transformed, rejuvenated. He feels the irony as, at the age of twenty-one, he says to himself: *I feel like a young man.* He draws their entangled hands towards his own mouth, reverses the hold and kisses Joey's fingers, the backs of Joey's hands. He looks up to find Joey's eyes gazing inquisitively into his own. 'You stayed,' says Joey.

'I did.' Raymond swallows, suddenly concerned. 'What happened, just now. What I did. Is it okay?'

'Oh boy,' says Joey, shaking his head, 'they don't make 'em like you anymore, Raymond. Maybe they never did. You're the first guy who's polite enough to ask permission—albeit retrospectively—to give me a blowjob. Where'd you come from?'

'A long way away. A whole other world.'

And it is a whole other world. Raymond doesn't come from the world where you meet a man in a bar and bring him home; where the man's father makes coffee and leaves it outside the door. He doesn't come from there and yet he has now found that world for himself. He laughs at this thought as Joey kisses him on the forehead and slips a leg between Raymond's thighs. As their burgeoning cocks press together in a fine embrace they hear a jangle of keys.

'I'm heading out now, Joey,' whispers his father from outside the door. Raymond notes a lilting accent. 'See you there.' The closing of the outside door; the click of the latch.

There is a silence in the room, now. And a humming tension that emerges from this privacy. For now, with the daylight as their witness, in the blossoming tenderness of their embrace Raymond feels as though the entire chemistry of his body is changing. Now, under Joey's touch, Raymond feels like a piano string being tuned: he travels through infinite resonances within each split second and is transformed by the slightest shift in pressure from Joey's fingertips. He thrills as Joey's tongue traces the dark aureole of each of his nipples in turn, exciting them to prominence, then licks a silvery track of saliva across his navel towards Raymond's obediently rising cock. Just before he envelops him in his mouth Joey looks up, mischief twitching on his lips, says 'You just be sure to tell me if you want me to stop,' and then all is blurred: the most exquisite oblivion Raymond has yet experienced.

Seven

When Joey leaves for work—at the *ristorante*—later that Sunday morning, Raymond makes his way back to the YMCA, returning via the footbridge and approaching the city with an entirely different perspective than the one he had held just the previous night. He thinks of the moment when he said goodbye to Joey just now, for the very first time, and the curious sorrow he had felt. He slips his hand into his pocket to check for the fold of paper that bears Joey's phone number, then wonders whether he will have the courage to call. Joey had given him a look as they'd said goodbye, a look that lay somewhere between concern and loss—or the anticipation of loss—as though Joey understood all too well that someone like Raymond might never call.

Pulling his old overcoat tightly around him against the wind, he feels the distance between his new clothes and those old suits. His mind loops back to the evening of his father's funeral when he and Joan had been brushing their teeth.

Her face a foaming grimace, her speech muddled by the toothbrush in her mouth, she had said, 'You know, Raymond, that you are the man of the house, now.' Then she had looked at him with a mixture of incredulity and disdain before turning to the yellowed sink and spitting explosively into it as though in revulsion at everything he'd been and done up until that day. The same revulsion she'd shown when he'd wet himself coming back from the scrubland on the day of their father's death.

As he descends once more into Manhattan he is simultaneously descending the slope behind their family home, dragged away from his friends by Joan. He'd wrested his hand free once they were at the bottom and looked back towards Danny and Stephen, who were recommencing their game of fighter pilots and parachutes.

Joan had turned on him, eyes full of tears, voice full of anger: 'There's been a terrible accident.'

'What accident?' he'd said.

Joan had looked at him with a horrid sort of triumph simply because she'd known and he hadn't, and said: 'Father's dead, Raymond,' and then to his utmost surprise, she had reached for him and pulled him into her chest. She was quite a bit taller than him, then, and one plait had tickled his face. That's when he had realised his legs were warm, and wet.

Joan had stepped back and looked at him. The shocking sting of her hand on his cheek. 'That's disgusting,' she'd said, turning on her heel. 'And disrespectful,' she'd added over her shoulder before marching back towards the house. Raymond had followed her back at a distance, keeping close to the wall, hovering momentarily beneath a tree, out of the sun, hiding the dark shame of his piss-stained shorts by clinging to the security of shadows.

Once off the bridge, Raymond makes his way towards Second Avenue which leads directly to the YMCA: a simple corridor home. Once on Second Avenue he turns to look back the way he has come. He can no longer see the bridge that led him to Joey. He pulls up his coat collar and marches on.

Around 14th Street there is the sudden wail of an approaching siren. He turns to see a police car drawing up to the kerb, right beside him. He stops, suddenly and utterly convinced that they have come for him. His heart thumps as he watches a policeman climb out of the car and walk into a nearby restaurant. A few seconds later, that same cop emerges carrying a paper bag. He turns, acknowledges Raymond momentarily, then gets back into the car which drives off, siren blaring again. Feeling absurd in his paranoia, Raymond sets off once more.

The night of the funeral, he had had the first in what would be an ongoing series of recurring dreams about his father. They—he and Father—were driving along a country road towards a clifftop in his father's car—the one in which he had been killed, though in the dream his father says that they are in Chitty Chitty Bang Bang and laughs delightedly—and although even in the dream Raymond knows that they are not in a flying car, he too laughs at his father's laughter until he understands that, in his delusion, his father is heading directly for the cliff edge, and although Raymond tries to grab the wheel, his father's grip is stronger, and as they leave the cliff edge and begin the inevitable drop to the ground below, Raymond prepares to do a commando roll, and it was then that he had awoken, ashamed, the familiar wet warmth on his thighs and buttocks. He had got up quickly, stripped off his urine-soaked pyjama bottoms, then pulled the sheets off his bed and put them in a pile. Taking a fresh pair of trousers from the drawer, he had gone into the bathroom, wiped himself down with a flannel, then put on the dry clothing. Then he had gone out into the hall where he had seen his mother's door ajar. Torn between waking her up and risking a confession or returning to the discomfort of the rubberised under-sheet, he had quietly pushed open her door. She had been lying on her back, her mouth open, fast asleep. Very slowly, he had climbed into bed beside her and slipped under the covers, hoping that she wouldn't wake up. Her hand had brushed his hair. He had frozen. 'Thank you,' she had said, and he had known that, if he kept quiet and still, then he would have at least a few hours before she would find out the truth.

Somewhere around East 20th Street, he notices a photo of James Dean propped up in the window of a delicatessen. Feeling a sudden hunger, he buys himself a sandwich and a soda, which he eats and drinks as he continues his journey home.

The January after he had turned fourteen, Stephen had come round in a state of great excitement. '*Giant* is coming to the Gaumont,' he'd declared, almost before he was through Raymond's bedroom door. 'James Dean's last film, ever! I'm going on Wednesday afternoon. Come with me.'

'We've got school,' Raymond had said, in a whisper.

'Only Chemistry and Maths.' Stephen had leapt on Raymond's bed.

Raymond had got up and checked the corridor. Joan's door, opposite, was ajar. Raymond closed his own door and, only then, turned back to Stephen. 'Okay,' he'd whispered, a thrill blossoming in his chest, and they'd shaken hands as a pact.

On the day of the film, they had snuck in the fire door at the back of the theatre, after the cigarette break of the projectionist. '*Insider knowledge*,' Stephen had whispered mysteriously, and they had hidden on the back row. They nudged each other as Elizabeth Taylor beckoned Rock Hudson to bed; sat rapt as James Dean found treasure beneath his filthy feet; clenched their fists as he and Rock Hudson fought, willing Dean to triumph.

That Stephen had not checked the length of the film only became clear once the credits were rolling and they looked incredulously at their watches.

Raymond had panicked. He'd hurried out, pushing through the other audience members.

'Wait,' Stephen had shouted and then, when he had caught up, added in a whisper: 'We need a plan.' But just as he had said that, the very idea of a plan had become entirely superfluous, for there, standing with her arms folded tightly around her thick winter coat, was Mrs Wallace herself. She had turned brusquely, knowing full well that the boys would follow, and walked swiftly to her car. She had opened the rear doors for them as though out of exaggerated politeness, then slammed both doors and climbed into the driver's seat.

They had sat there in silence for a few minutes, and then she had turned round, leaning one arm on the back of her seat, and glared at them. 'The thing about blots,' she'd said, putting Raymond in mind of the oil that had covered Dean from head to toe following his strike, 'is that the whiter the shirt, the darker the stain appears.' Then tears had welled in her eyes and she had looked solely at Raymond. 'I can only imagine,' she'd said, her tone embittered by self-pity, 'what it is that I have done that makes you consider this an acceptable mode of behaviour. If it hadn't been for your sister…' Then she had turned the engine on abruptly, revved it up, and begun driving furiously.

She hadn't spoken to him for the rest of that day, nor the following one. At school he received a Headmaster's detention and had all privileges suspended for the rest of the term. At home, he was barred from spending time with Stephen: Mother had evidently spotted something in the association that she'd felt needed uprooting. Though Raymond barely gave him a moment's thought after the picture house incident and certainly didn't miss him. That Easter, Stephen had been sent to a boarding school, anyway, and then his family had moved away, so Raymond and he wouldn't see each other again until they matriculated at Cambridge four years later.

As he swallows the last bite of his sandwich Raymond finds himself simultaneously on Third Avenue, with the Chrysler tower in the distance, and in the tunnel beneath Emmanuel Street that night in his second term when he'd come across Stephen lounging on the steps by North Court.

'Wallace, my saviour!' Stephen had said, almost as though he'd been waiting just for Raymond. 'It's drunk out tonight, isn't it?' Stephen had added, groaning with the effort of standing. 'May I escort you?'

'I'm fine actually, thanks, Stephen,' Raymond had said, trying to dodge past.

'Don't be a spoilsport, Wallace. We go back a long way.'

Despite Raymond's protestations, Stephen had deftly and firmly hooked their arms together, making the journey across the court lurchingly awkward. At Z staircase he had dived to push the door open, then stood inside and indicated for Raymond to follow, as though it were his—and not Raymond's—staircase they were entering. As they had walked up the half-flight of stairs, he had leaned exaggeratedly on Raymond as though for assistance, so that by the time they had reached the top step their cheeks were nearly touching. When Raymond had then tried to extricate himself from his grip, he had felt the sudden pressure of Stephen's lips on his, smelt his sour drunkenness in his nostrils and then been assaulted by the grotesque, liver-like presence of Stephen's tongue in his own mouth. Raymond had reflexively pushed him away, and Stephen had staggered down the stairs, laughing. 'You, Wallace, know exactly what you are and what you want. You've always known it. And so have I.'

Raymond had shaken his head and turned swiftly to open his door. But as he'd flicked the lock behind him, his hand had quivered almost uncontrollably. From the safety of the half-closed curtains of his windows, he had watched Stephen's hobbling retreat across the court with a penitent sort of relief—as though he'd avoided something awful, but only by a whisker.

The following day was when the scandal had broken. For it turned out that, on leaving Raymond that night, Stephen had taken solace in the arms of the organ scholar and the pair had been discovered *in flagrante delicto* by a cleaner in the morning. As Raymond turns onto East 47th Street he reflects that—at the time—Stephen's consequent rustication had felt like a fortuitous reprieve.

Raymond expels any further thoughts of Stephen Bennett from his head and, for the remainder of his journey, indulges in infinitely more pleasurable recollections, slipping his hand into his pocket from time to time to touch Joey's phone number like a talisman.

On a bookshelf in the lobby of the YMCA that afternoon, he comes across a copy of Thomas Mann's *Death in Venice*. He has a vague recollection of having read it before, but can't remember when. Taking it to his dormitory, he lies on his narrow bed and studies the claustrophobic tale of the fifty-year-old Von Aschenbach and his fatal obsession with the teenage Tadzio; of Von Aschenbach's descent from his lauded position as celebrated man of letters to a parodic, tragic figure; of his impulsive decision to have his greying hair dyed an uncanny black, his pallid cheeks rouged; of his cherishing the odd insouciant glance from the callow youth, and of Von Aschenbach's piteous succumbing to the encroaching pestilence with which the city of Venice is afflicted that fateful summer. For Raymond, this reads not as a story of lust and obsession, of age and youth, but rather of the realisation of loss; the desire to regain that which is gone.

When Mann uses the word 'degeneracy' to refer to his hero's life, Raymond is reminded of a speech from a vicar in his first term at Cambridge, in which he had said—ominously, Raymond had always felt—that *the past depends on the future*—as though any sense of a good reputation was, as of that moment—and perhaps always is—defined solely by how one comports oneself beyond it throughout the remaining portion of one's life. At the time it had generated in Raymond a pendulous sense of responsibility which he had experienced as a sort of curse. Now, lying on his bed at the YMCA that first night after the night before, Raymond realises that, if he should die at that very instant then at least he would do so without the pestilence of his future mistakes.

When Raymond returns to his room after his evening meal that night he takes off his clothes, removes a small mirror from the wall and uses it to examine his body. He is looking for evidence that something has changed; that something from his time with Joey has remained, there, on his skin; or perhaps he is checking for signs of contamination. He looks and looks but doesn't find anything at all, and as he climbs into bed, he begins to wonder whether any of it—of last night—was real. And then, in the vertiginous moment just before he drifts off to sleep, he understands that it isn't whether it was real or not that is his query; it's whether he had deserved any of it.

Eight

When Raymond approaches his desk the following morning Dolores is standing outside Bukowski's office. She's hovering—she can't seem to stand still. Raymond hesitates, then calls gently across the floor: 'Morning, Dolores.'

She freezes—and then, without looking at him, walks across the office to join him. 'Morning, Raymond,' she says. 'I hope you slept well?' Before he can draw breath to respond, she continues, 'because we've got a day mapped out for us today. Mr Doty's in there on a surprise visit to Mr Bukowski, taking him through his ideas, point by insistent point. *Mrs* Bukowski's due in here with her lawyers at two. Mr Kleinmann's acting like a prize jerk, for whatever reason. He wants a meeting today, something exasperatingly inconsequential, and I haven't managed to tell Mr B yet because… well… Doty has been here since seven thirty. So: you take this,' she says, shoving a pile of photos into Raymond's hands, 'to Sam and tell him that they need to be archived by… let's say four o'clock. They need to be attributed and dated first, you tell him. That should take him some time. Most of them are untraceable—they've been in a drawer gathering dust since God knows when—but Mr Kleinmann's so goddamn proud he won't let up. He'll be lucky to trace *one* before four. So that's him.' She taps the rest of her papers, hesitating before continuing. 'You and I are going to take breakfast together—would you like that?— we're going to take a breakfast meeting right now and I'll take you through the rest of it. After that, you won't know any of it, right? And we can all continue just like last week ...right?'

Raymond nods to Dolores even though he has to admit to himself that, after his night with Joey, nothing can be *like last week* ever again.

He drops the photographs off with an infuriated Kleinmann before heading downstairs once more where Dolores meets him, her hair now tied up in a sea-green scarf, her coat buckled tightly around her against the November chill. Despite the fact that Dolores cannot possibly know anything about his weekend, Raymond nonetheless feels exposed. But then again, he acknowledges to himself, the point is that there is now *something to be known*, and also that Dolores has that preternatural capacity some people possess of making others feel the need to confess.

He and Dolores make their way towards a diner she knows. She ushers Raymond towards a table at the rear of the room and they sit down. She's got a little lipstick on—a pale pink—but no other make-up. She's plucked her eyebrows, Raymond notices, and they're starting to grow back ever so slightly.

On the wall behind her head there's a framed photo of Laurence Olivier, with a dedication: *To Jo-Ann, sunny side up! Always, Larry*—and an *x*. A woman whom Raymond assumes must be Jo-Ann approaches their table, somewhat suspiciously.

'Yes?'

'Two coffees, two bagels—you want a bagel, Raymond?'

'Sure. I'll have a bagel.'

'Oh my god! You're English? Say it again!'

Raymond blushes.

'And two coffees, please. We're in a hurry. Thanks,' says Dolores.

Raymond's eyes follow Jo-Ann as she bustles towards the counter and checks her hair in the mirror beyond. He thinks enviously of the customers at Joey's restaurant who get to observe that precious body with its secret scents and flavours; the herbal thicket of Joey's armpit; the funk of his come…then realises that he is staring at the reflection of Jo-Ann who, having adjusted an errant pin, now refocuses her gaze and clocks him looking.

'…which places Mr Bukowski in a very difficult position, as you can imagine. Raymond? Are you listening?'

Raymond's head snaps back towards Dolores. 'Uh, sure, Dolores—I'm sorry. Actually, no, I wasn't listening. Please begin again. I was in another world. Go ahead.'

'Mrs Bukowski found out.'

'Er, found out what?'

Dolores looks at him, meaningfully. 'About *him*.'

'Right.' Raymond hesitates. 'I'm sorry, Dolores, have I missed something? Is there something about Bukowski that I should know?'

'I figured you'd worked out by now, why Mr Bukowski—Harvey—can't deal with the article himself. It's about *him*.' Raymond frowns. 'Oh, I don't mean *personally*. But he's, you, know, *involved*. He knows some of the people, the places. The idea was originally mooted back in August but he dismissed it, said he didn't want to *offend the morals of our readers*. Then, early September Doty says he has a fresh lead from Murphy—Police Commissioner—so the whole thing rears its head once more. And at the same time, Laura—Mrs B—found out about Harvey. And told her *boyfriend*.' She toys with an unlit cigarette. 'Uh-huh, Raymond,' she says, clicking her lighter into flame and lighting her cigarette. She blows smoke upwards—like a smoke screen, Raymond thinks. 'The real trouble, though, comes when you consider Harvey's delicate position.' She pauses and looks Raymond directly in the eye. He holds her gaze for a second, then blinks and look down.

'Two coffees, two bagels. And your check.' Jo-Ann hovers beside the table, smiling at Raymond. He takes a coffee spoon, stirs one of the cups and draws it towards him, looking at the whirlpool he's precipitated.

Dolores reaches into her bag and takes out a dollar bill that she places on top of the check and pushes towards the waitress. 'Keep the change. Thank you,' she adds, impatiently.

Jo-Ann takes the money, makes a mock-curtsy and heads back to the counter.

'Dolores?'

'Yes, Raymond?' She spoons a spoonful of sugar into her cup and stirs, anti-clockwise.

'Who is Bukowski's boyfriend?'

Dolores stops stirring, draws breath and looks up at him. She twists her head inquiringly to her left, all the while holding his gaze.

'I meant to say,' continues Raymond, 'who is *Mrs* Bukowski's boyfriend.'

Dolores draws her head back to centre, relaxes her brow and smiles a kind smile. 'I'm so glad we understand each other, Raymond. I'm only telling you all this because I know I—*we*—can trust you.'

In the coffee bar before work over the following days she confides in Raymond.

'It was a seismic row that kicked it all off,' Dolores says that Tuesday morning. 'Laura stormed out only to return—hours later—*flammable* with vodka, to deliver a line Harvey just knew she'd not come up with herself: *You must be a fucking fag not to want to sleep with me.*' Dolores bites her lip. 'Harvey just…well, the penny dropped. Laura ran off to her mother's, and when she came back, Harvey thought she seemed different—better, somehow—and that maybe they could make things work. It was only a matter of time before the next row, however, and this time, instead of hitting the bottle, she called *Bert*,' Dolores says as though unimpressed by the very name, 'Bert is the *intrigue*, if we can call him that. Guy she'd met in a bar. A real small hitter: one of those real estate action men with dicks the size of noodles.'

'Sounds like what you might call, *corned beefcake*,' says Raymond as Dolores lights her cigarette.

'You,' she says, coughing with laughter and dabbing at her eyes, 'are the ticket, the absolute ticket! The surprising thing—to me, at least—is that Harvey feels zero bitterness towards her—on the contrary, in fact, he talks about feeling *guilty*—for god's sake!—for his wife's circumstances, so when Bert came to him with his subtle extortion plan—a little extra pocket money every week for him and Laura in exchange for,' Dolores adds wryly, '*respecting the choices of consenting adults in private*, he capitulated without negotiation.'

'You must have seen her, in the stairwell,' says Dolores that Wednesday morning. 'I get the feeling that the affair—such as it was—has run its course. It strikes me that she'd sooner weep in the offices than seek solace in the arms of Bert. Heartbreaking, really, when you consider the pair of them. She was quite the debutante, you know, and Harvey…brilliant, by all accounts,' she adds, ruefully. 'Now he's…well—' she indicates herself and Raymond, at the table. 'He's not really on this planet right now, so I've been managing the deadlines, the correspondence. And into this heady cocktail came a shot of Raymond Wallace himself,' she adds with a kind smile. 'Aloof yet affable, able to navigate awkward personalities, we spotted you the second you arrived in the offices,' she says, and Raymond flushes inwardly with a deep sense of belonging.

That Friday morning Raymond arrives at the café to find Dolores deep in conversation with another woman. Neither of them notices him approach, and it's only when he's at their table that he sees their hands are clasped together. Dolores' head snaps up, but she maintains her hold on the woman's hands.

'Raymond. This is my friend, Mary.'

Mary's hair is a smooth, rounded Afro; her lips are painted a dark purple. She smiles at Raymond, then bites at her lip. When she speaks her voice is breathy and deep. 'So you are Raymond Wallace.'

Raymond smiles and nods.

'I have heard so much about you,' says Mary. 'Not only,' she adds with a grin, adjusting her grip on Dolores' hands, 'from Dolores here, but also from young Joshua,' she adds, holding Raymond's gaze. 'And he's quite right: you are handsome.'

Raymond cannot help from blushing. 'I, er…' he falters.

Mary's face drops. 'I didn't mean to embarrass you, Raymond. I apologise. I simply meant that your reputation as a fine gentleman precedes you.'

Her sudden sincerity is almost comic, yet Raymond profoundly appreciates it. Releasing Mary's hands, Dolores shifts along her bench, patting it to indicate that Raymond should sit next to her. 'Mary has to go in a second,' she says.

'I know when I'm not wanted,' says Mary, mock-sternly, picking up her handbag. 'But before I forget, Joshua asked me to pass this on.' She opens her handbag and withdraws a slim pamphlet which she slides across the table. Raymond reads the title: *Mattachine Review*. As Mary reaches once more into her handbag, Dolores quickly places her hand on Mary's wrist. 'It's on me,' she says, insistently.

'You know I'll get you back.' Mary smiles and clips her handbag closed. She stands, kisses her fingertips—waving them first at Dolores, then at Raymond—and departs, leaving a voluptuous scent in her wake.

Raymond shuffles round to face Dolores.

'So that's Mary,' she says, smiling as though something significant has been acknowledged. 'And this,' she says, pushing the pamphlet across to Raymond, 'might just be our secret weapon. 'I hear there's an article about Illinois—perhaps you might read it, even get in contact with someone from the Mattachine Society who *might* be able to give us something more…*nuanced* than what I understand to be the general nub of Doty's current draft.' Raymond nods. 'Harvey's away for the day, so his office is free. The Society has a San Francisco telephone number right here,' she says, tapping her nail on the title page. Raymond nods, folds the Review, and slips it into his inside pocket. 'Actually, Raymond, I should really get back to the office. Some things to tie up before the weekend. Can we catch up later? Before you leave for the day?'

'Of course.'

Dolores leaves and Raymond orders himself a coffee. His hand moves reflexively to the pamphlet but then he thinks better of reading it in public. He drinks his coffee too quickly so that it burns his throat slightly, leaves some coins on the table then heads over to the offices.

He spends the day in Bukowski's office. One of the photos, it turns out, is indeed of Laura and Harvey's wedding day; the second shows a picture of a young Harvey and another young man, mortarboards on their heads, smiles on their faces. Raymond immediately recognises the second man as

Professor Hurt.

He picks up the phone to call the Mattachine number a couple of times, but always hangs up before he is connected. At around four thirty there's a knock on the door and Dolores enters carrying an envelope.

'Any luck, Raymond?'

'No answer,' he says quickly, patting the telephone in its cradle. 'I'll try again before I leave; or first thing next week. There's an article in here, though,' he says, abruptly lifting the pamphlet, 'that's really interesting. About blackmail and how the current laws in England actually play into the blackmailers' hands. Ironic, really. Unless, of course, we consider that blackmail can be seen to serve the purpose of those laws. Also, it says that the discretionary *skills*—for want of a better word—to survive as a homosexual in Britain right now are similar to those required to survive as a spy.'

There is a pause, and then Raymond and Dolores both laugh.

'Are you a *spy*, Raymond?'

'If I told you, Dolores,' he says, suddenly deeply serious, 'I'd have to kill you, and I really don't want to do that.'

They both roar with laughter once more.

'Oh Raymond,' says Dolores, sighing a deep and satisfied sigh, 'you are a tonic. But listen up, Mr Espionage: I do not want you to work at all, this weekend. This article will come and go, as will your time in this special city. I insist, therefore, that you do something memorable this weekend. Something that you will be able to look back upon with tremendous pleasure. Something you can't do in Britain, however Great it may claim to be. The details I will leave to your imagination, and of course I don't expect to be deserving of the finer points, but *live* a little, Raymond, would you? Loosen up. If you want to, that is,' she adds, kindly, before glancing down at the envelope. 'This arrived, and I assumed it must be for you.'

She hands him the envelope. It is addressed simply *To Raymond (from the U.K.), at the New York Times Offices.*

'It's been here for a couple of days, but took a while before it made it to me,' says Dolores. 'And now to you.'

Raymond turns the envelope in his hands but doesn't open it.

'I'll leave you in peace with your *correspondence*,' says Dolores, smiling.

When she closes the door behind her Raymond sits down at Bukowski's desk and opens the envelope. Inside is a plain postcard with a simple message in neat handwriting:

Dear Ray,
Friday at 2000: L. N.?
Yours hopefully,
J.

He finds himself blushing, smiling; he swiftly reads the card twice more, grateful for the sanctuary of Bukowski's office as he does so, then—his hands shaking—replaces the card in its envelope before burying it amongst the pages of the *Mattachine Review*.

When Raymond leaves the offices that night he reflects on his mendacity regarding the phone call. He hadn't, he was certain, needed to lie; he had chosen to, and he wonders whether he wasn't practising on Dolores a move he might need somewhere else in his life. He cannot as yet determine whether it was cowardice that made him hang up on each attempt, or whether there wasn't something about the task itself that simply felt too big for him; as though he is—however laudable the end might be—being used, somehow, as a foil to challenge Doty because in the fullness of time, Raymond will quite simply no longer be around. And then, because he doesn't want to think about leaving, and because Dolores insisted, after all, that he stop working over the weekend to *do something memorable*, Raymond draws a curtain over the New York Times and begins his weekend in earnest. Showered and changed once more, he puts on the other sweater shirt and pair of trousers he'd bought, then pomades his hair. As he checks himself in the mirror, he realises that, whatever his sad reflections last Sunday night, tonight he just feels a delicious hopefulness.

Nine

This time he doesn't walk; he takes a cab, which speeds him thrillingly through the lit-up metropolis and over the bridge into Brooklyn. Because he has some time to spare, however, he directs the driver not towards *Little Navy* itself, but rather to the corner of Johnson and Gold. Before anything else happens tonight he wants to be sure that the place actually exists. And there it all is—the block; the front door: he's remembered it well, though he cannot recall the number. Heedless of the honking traffic, he backs away onto the other side of Johnson. He counts up the windows of the block, trying to remember the perspective from which he had viewed the street, but all he sees are framed reflections of the night sky—a cloud passing over the moon—and he can't work out which apartment is theirs.

He imagines Joey approaching him on the street, now, looking up with him to point out his window before taking his arm and leading him once again up the stairwell into the bedroom where so much had taken place. He imagines their lovemaking once more, and turns himself on with the shocking thought of doing it again.

As the rain begins to fall heavier now, Raymond's heart is beating strong and fast, for the knot that began unravelling last weekend is loosening once again. He now knows it as a knot of upbringing, of inheritance and of implicit—and explicit—repudiations. A knot that can only, as far as Raymond is concerned, be undone in the presence of another, similar man—Joey, to be precise.

Checking his watch he walks swiftly now, almost running the length of Gold. He turns right onto Water and slows his pace as he reaches the junction with Hudson Avenue. Looking carefully at the few people there are around he crosses the road and turns right. It's not as he remembered it; it seems smaller now, even more discreet than last week. *You could easily miss it if you didn't know what you were looking for*, he thinks. In fact, he wonders that he ever noticed it at all. He crosses the street and then, looking left and right, right and left like a thief he steals quickly towards the door and knocks the code Joey had knocked on his chest the previous weekend: *two short, one long, two short*. As the door opens, Raymond smiles at the doorman before pushing open the baize-covered door and at last he's back in this world. His eyes as legible as a child's, he searches the faces of the men for Joey's. Some return his glance with a nod or a smile before turning back to their drinks, their conversations, their dances. He feels as though he's itemised every single face in the bar, but there is no Joey. Raymond curses his own arrogance at neither calling, nor responding to Joey's note. He begins to feel a terrible, craven stupidity when his arm is grabbed and his head turned by a hand and he sees Joey's face rushing in for a kiss.

The reality of this kiss is far better than anything his imagination could have come up with. They stand there in the centre of that bar, surrounded by men who've kissed a hundred men, who've seen it all, done it all, and if Raymond had been able to tear his attention away from Joey he'd have seen that something about the clarity of this embrace makes every one of those men stop, look, and feel nostalgia, ambition, envy.

'Hi, beautiful man,' says Joey.

Raymond laughs a happy laugh. 'Hello again. Where were you hiding?'

'I was just in the John. You got my note, then.'

'Ha-ha. Only just. This afternoon.'

'I wasn't sure you'd come.'

'Hmm,' murmurs Raymond, suddenly serious. 'I was surprised. Delighted, but surprised. I have absolutely no recollection of telling you where I work.'

'Well you did. I sent one to the Railroad Y as well.'

'Really?'

'You didn't get it?'

Raymond shakes his head.

'I'm glad I doubled up.' Joey looks suddenly concerned. 'Nobody opened it, did they?'

Raymond shakes his head. 'No, no,' he says, reassuring himself as much as Joey. 'I'm glad you wrote.'

'Well, you didn't call,' says Joey.

Raymond purses his lips and nods, conceding a point. 'Very, very glad you wrote. I…I walked past your apartment building just now. For old times' sake,' he adds, making them both laugh.

'But I couldn't remember your address.'

'One hundred and sixty-five. Apartment 7, 165 Johnson Street, Brooklyn, NY.'

Joey's voice is so stern it makes Raymond laugh again. Then he repeats, obediently: 'One hundred and sixty-five Johnson Street, apartment seven: I'll remember it.'

'You better. I move between here, the apartment and the restaurant,' Joey says. 'In a triangular routine, you might say.'

As Joey buys him a drink, Raymond looks around and understands that all these men embody the contemporary imperative to commandeer the language of their society on multiple, complex levels; that somewhere in the mind of each man here there is a dossier on a shelf detailing the necessary behavioural adjustments for stepping outside the door; that every single man in this bar, in short, has something of the spy about him. Then Raymond looks at the simple elegance of the back of Joey's head, the pattern of his hair, the downy nape of his neck, thinks of the kiss they've just shared, and of how the other men watched, and wonders what mightn't be achieved if the generosity of this audience in this bar were shared by the rest of the world. Then he feels a spark of resentment glow inside him that—as a grown man; as grown men—not a single one of them is accorded the simple, adult dignity of being able to give consent to his own body.

Joey turns back from the bar, handing him a beer. 'There you go.'

Raymond wrests himself from his reverie. 'Thanks.'

They sit on a bench near the door. Raymond is mesmerised by

the simple sight of Joey tilting his head back to drink; the stubble that spills from his chin to his neck.

'You know, in England we have pints of beer, not bottles.' Raymond sips.

'And it's warm, right?

'And it's warm: right.' He looks at the label of his bottle. 'It's not at all the same.'

'So I hear. I can't imagine *warm beer*. Sounds disgusting.'

'It can be pretty disgusting, actually. I've never understood it, myself. I much prefer this: it's like a soft drink.'

'There's nothing soft about American beer—you'd better watch who you say that to.'

'I'm sorry, I—'

'That was a joke, Ray.'

It is not surprising that Raymond spends most of his time blushing in this bar, and in the company of Joey. He feels so desperately naïve; that he can't even get jokes anymore. His mind is saturated with the intensity of the experience, and he feels as though his head will explode with the amount of information it has to process.

'I guess this must be pretty intense for you, right?' asks Joey.

'*Intense*: a great understatement.'

Joey places his hand on Raymond's knee. 'Do you like it?'

'God, yes. I like it. I don't know what to do with it, but I most definitely like it. You.'

'Don't you have places like this in England?'

Raymond guffaws in incredulity. 'I have absolutely no idea. I mean, I assume they—we—must have. But of course, I'd never go.'

'Why not?'

'Oh. Well, what if someone saw me there? I mean, I wouldn't know what to do. I wouldn't want to be seen there, in a place like that. Like this. In England, I mean.'

'But everyone here's the same, buddy. We're all in the same boat, as it were. Takes one to know one, right?'

Raymond smiles as the logic hits home. 'Of course it does, but—'

'Strictly speaking, we're all the same, here. With obvious differences. See that guy over there?' Joey tilts his bottle casually in the direction of a middle-aged man leaning on the corner of the bar by the jukebox. 'Midtown councillor; lawyer, too. You want theater tickets, he's your man. You're in trouble? He'll sort it out.'

'How?'

'By shifting papers, talking to people, making his presence felt. There's nothing that can't be done, here. That guy over there? Police chief.'

'Jesus.'

'Don't worry. There's nothing he's got on the rest of us that we ain't got on him. Queer as a three-dollar bill, as the saying goes.'

Raymond nods at this phrase, and wonders how many such coded phrases have passed him by, how many understandings he's missed. For some reason, he has an urge to tell Bukowski about this bar, the possibilities here; he feels like a child who's found an endless source of sweets. 'It's like a club,' he says.

'Not a club, Ray: this is life. This is the way life is, or the way life can be. Here, it's all possible; it can all be fixed. Sure, we've all got to watch our backs when we're outside, but this kind of place, it's vital. This is where we get our downtime. And here's where *we* get to live, even if it's just for a few hours every night, or when we can get away. Like I said, I'm lucky, I mean, with my father it's—'

Just then, the door opens and a man walks into the bar, his shoulders hunched over. *The end of the week.* He scans the length of the bar, and in the dim light, mellowed by the reflected refractions of the bottled malts sitting in front of the mirrors behind the bar, Raymond sees his boss's face, clear as day: Bukowski. In *Little Navy*. Raymond's mind whirs, and he thinks for some disconcerting reason of how easily he could now blackmail Bukowski himself; and then, just as abruptly, of how Bukowski could blackmail *him*, and then he shakes off these foolish thoughts, looks at Joey, and realises that he hasn't been listening to a word he has said.

'…and that has made all the difference—it's made my life so much more—I don't know—*comfortable*, I guess.'

Raymond takes Joey's hand off his knee, and puts it to his lips. 'Kiss me.'

'What? I mean, of course.'

'Kiss me, Joey.'

As Joey kisses him and Raymond feels his body responding to Joey's lips and the proximity of his body, something in his mind sits back, somehow, calculating the Bukowski situation. He can reveal himself to Bukowski or he can hide himself deeper in

Joey's embrace, lips, tongue…

Joey pulls back, his eyes shining with pleasure, and bites his lower lip in a way that seems so incredibly honest that it almost makes Raymond cry. Joey's voice is congested with desire. 'I want to see you naked again.'

They down their beers quickly, then get up, and while Raymond still hasn't made a decision as to whether or not to confront Bukowski, when it comes to it, he is relieved to see that his boss's back is turned as he and Joey make their way out of the bar, so he can, in all conscience, allow himself to be officially off-duty. *Serendipity*, he thinks to himself.

Just before Joey slips his key into the lock of his front door that night, he does something that Raymond will never forget: he reaches his hand between Raymond's legs, cups his crotch and, as Raymond closes his eyes in pleasure, Joey's other hand slips behind Raymond's head, drawing it down to plant a kiss on each of Raymond's eyelids. The simple confidence of these caresses strikes Raymond to his very core and he receives them as benedictions.

Sometime in the middle of that second night together Raymond awakes to find himself embraced by the curve of Joey's body—his abdomen against the small of Raymond's back; their legs intertwined—and feels the pressure of Joey's somno-lent erection between his own thighs. He reaches a hand back to stroke fur-covered buttocks. Joey murmurs grumpily, shifts slightly. Raymond turns his head so that Joey's stubbled chin rubs against his shoulder, then reaches down, languidly fondles the heavy sack of Joey's testicles and then—as a surge of energy courses through his lover's awakening body—feels a hand cup his own buttock, then a finger trace the rift between his legs, and a jolt of extraordinary erotic electricity runs through his body. He pushes himself backwards against Joey's cock.

'You want this?' asks Joey.

Raymond nods.

Joey reaches beyond him to a jar on the bedside table, unscrews the lid and takes a gob of unguent from it which he uses to slick on and around Raymond's anus, Joey's face the picture of concentration as he lets a finger slip gaspingly in, then out in exquisite increments, coaxing Raymond's body towards readiness. He replaces the jar, spits into his hand, slicks his erection, runs a finger hard along the underside to draw out a swell of his own syrup before easing the glistening crown momentarily in and then out of Raymond, in, and then out, teasing, seizing, eyes tight on Raymond's expression, fingers firm on Raymond's raised thigh.

There is a point when Raymond knows he is ready, feels an overwhelming need to be wholly penetrated, to receive his lover inside him in his entirety and when, steeling himself, one hand pressing down on the mattress, the other reaching for the small of Joey's back to gain some traction, he pulls him to him as he pushes back with a deep groan, riding the pain for the depth of gain, and feels himself opening up and Joey entering in and now their bodies are together and in his passion Raymond pulls Joey's hand towards his mouth, takes the base of his thumb between his teeth and bites down, hard. In response—teeth gritted and head thrown back in delight—Joey bucks his hips and thrusts himself yet deeper inside Raymond as though in delicious, benevolent revenge.

And in the heart of it and in the heat of it, Raymond experiences a moment of transcendental incredulity in which he cannot for the life of him understand why anyone could ever describe this as *sick, degenerate, perverted*, or anything remotely approaching *unnatural*, as he begins to understand the richesses of his own body's capacity and appetite for loving pleasure.

Ten

'How long are you staying?'

It's the following morning. Joey sits on the side of the bed, holding a mug of coffee between his hands. Raymond opens his eyes, and then—either in order not to break the spell of whatever it is that is growing between them, or in order to buy himself some time—he tells a little lie. A lie by omission, he persuades himself, but a lie nonetheless: 'I don't know.'

Joey nods perfunctorily, then sips his coffee. Raymond calculates that he has precisely seven weeks before he is due to depart. Seven weeks in which he might change the course of his life. He tries to imagine a world where he stays here, forever. He struggles to hold onto this image.

'Okay,' says Joey a few seconds later, in the manner of someone who has received precisely the answer they wanted.

'This placement I'm on,' says Raymond, as though adding credibility to his story, 'it's funded by a bursary from my college. I want to be a journalist.'

'Sounds like you already are,' says Joey. 'I mean, come on: The *New York Times*?'

Raymond laughs. 'Definitely a novice.'

Joey looks at him through narrowed eyes, and smiles. 'Not

if last night's anything to go by, you're not,' he says, putting his coffee down on the bedside table and pulling the sheet off Raymond's foetal body. 'But novice *journalist* or not, whilst you're here, we need to make the most of you, don't we? Papà's gone out for milk, and then I'd like to introduce you. Is that okay?' Raymond closes his eyes slowly, then opens them once more to find Joey's eyes looking kindly at him. 'He's cool,' he adds.

Raymond smiles, thinking once again of his mother who, he notes wryly to himself, is most definitely *not* cool. He remembers Dolores' injunction for him to *do something memorable, this weekend,* and nods. He even finds himself thinking that he'd quite like it if it *were* a big deal, he and Joey, together. 'Okay,' he says, taking Joey's hand. 'Last night,' he adds, 'was something. Really something. Thank you.'

Joey leans down and kisses him. '*You're* really something,' he says. 'And you're also really lazy. So get up. Get showered. You can borrow some clothes. I'll leave them out on the bed. Here's a towel,' he says, flinging one in Raymond's laughing face.

When Raymond emerges from the bedroom, his hair still damp from the shower, he is wearing Joey's T-shirt and jeans. He hears laughter coming from the other room, and although the door is already ajar, he knocks.

'Come in!' says Joey through his laughter.

Raymond pushes open the door. Sitting on a long couch beneath the window is a man in his forties who is smiling at him with Joey's eyes but a different mouth. He stands up and reaches his hand out towards Raymond. They shake hands. Something in the air reminds Raymond of Dolores, but he can't think why.

Joey speaks first. 'Papà, this is Raymond. Raymond, this is my Dad. What do you want to be called, Papà?'

The man brings his other hand to clasp Raymond's hand as he says something that takes both Raymond and Joey utterly by surprise:

'I think you'd better call me Papà, too.'

When Raymond crosses the bridge that Sunday afternoon, still wearing Joey's clothes, he feels as though his entire world-view has been revolutionised. He thinks of that first meeting with Papà, the simple clarity with which he had been welcomed by this man; of the laughter shared between the three of them as Raymond had regaled them with the story of Kleinmann's yodelling breakdown in the newsroom; of their fascination when he had told them of Mrs Bukowski, describing her as though she were a leading lady from a famous movie; of how impressed Papà had been that Raymond had graduated from Cambridge University; of how, when a certain song had come on the radio, Joey had suddenly started to sing, and with such simplicity and beauty that Raymond had almost laughed in delight, but when he had looked at Papà he had found that his eyes were bright with tears; of how, shortly after this, Papà had reached for a framed photograph, slipped it into Raymond's hands, and said, 'and now I'd like you to meet Sara,' and of how Raymond had felt the hairs on the back of his neck stand up and his own eyes moisten; of how, contemplating this photo of a young and beautiful woman—her eyes looking straight at him, a smile playing on her lips, her hair lifted slightly from her shoulders by a breeze—Raymond had been put in mind of Sophia Loren; of a second photograph Papà had then shown him in which Sara holds a young boy of perhaps three years old whom Raymond had identified with a rush of joy as Joey; of how this simple gesture of seeing his lover as a child had made Raymond feel at once more attracted to him, if that were possible; of how, removing the photos from his hands, Joey had slipped his own hand into Raymond's; of how Papà had smiled at this sign of reassuring affection, and of how—later that night, his body wrapped tightly around Joey's, with Joey deep inside him—Raymond had wept when he had come, and Joey had not asked why but had just held him, kissing his tear-stained cheeks.

That Sunday night, back at the YMCA, Raymond dreams of Stephen Bennett. They are out on the scrubland, playing with their kites, only now they are grown men. Stephen is fully-dressed, but Raymond realises to his horror that he is completely naked. Stephen laughs disdainfully. Then a kite falls, Raymond drops to the ground and rolls himself down the hill in an attempt to escape, though he knows in his heart that, once he reaches the bottom of the hill, Joan will arrive to announce—as though for the first time—the death of their father.

It is only when Raymond is en route to the offices the following morning that he realises two specific things: firstly, that older memories had not preyed on him as he had returned this time; secondly, that on the nights he spends with Joey he does not dream—or does not remember his dreams. And then Raymond realises that for as long as he can recall, he has lived—even in sleep—under tension, as though braced for attack, and yet there, in that apartment, in that bedroom, on that mattress, in that embrace, that same tension is cowed like a tamed beast.

That week, taking Dolores' suggestion, he wears the clothing he had bought on Christopher Street and feels a delicious if self-conscious pleasure at the compliments he receives. He only sees Bukowski once that week, on the Tuesday afternoon, and Bukowski looks at him in an odd way that makes Raymond wonder whether he might not have spotted him and Joey in *Little Navy*, after all.

On the Wednesday morning Raymond arrives at his desk to find, to his astonishment, a mocked-up cover of the Times with the stark headline: '*Growth of Overt Homosexuality in City Provokes Wide Concern.*' He grabs it and is folding it swiftly in half when he hears Doty's laugh.

'Gotcha, good and proper!'

Raymond turns, blending his fury into a sardonic smile. 'I thought,' he says, walking up to Doty in order to be able to keep the conversation at a low volume, 'that this was confidential.'

Doty shakes his head. 'I consider that no longer necessary, given that this will go to press next week. Take a look, tell me your thoughts. There's time to add something. If it's any good, that is.'

'Blackmail,' says Raymond, suddenly. 'I read a piece in a pamphlet I came across—the *Mattachine Review*?' Doty looks nonplussed; Raymond feels somehow vindicated. 'It's worth a paragraph, at least; it's pretty prevalent, as I understand it.' He thinks of Bukowski, now behind his closed office door, and hopes that he cannot hear their conversation.

Doty looks thoughtful for a second, then nods. 'Okay: a paragraph. Anything else?'

'Well, I was reading Thomas Mann's *Death in Venice* recently—'

'Old guy lusting over a youth? Very Greek.'

'Well, there is a passage where Von Aschenbach reflects on his literary ancestors and wonders how they might perceive his current, "degenerate" circumstances. It seems to me to be about a kind of generational expectation, a familial or societal pressure.'

'I'll stop you there, Wallace. Much as I appreciate a well-read colleague, this is not a dissertation; this is journalism.'

Raymond smiles tolerantly. 'I just thought that we could hypothesise as to what such pressure might mean for a would-be homosexual who retreats from that...*possibility*...under the weight of expectations from other family members.'

'I don't think that's useful for our purposes.'

'What are our purposes?'

'Keep up, Wallace. Healing. By bringing to light. Offering the possibility of salvation. It may seem grand, but a front-page story has the potential to have that effect. Listen: don't expect every idea to make the final cut. I can see your blackmail paragraph incorporating this idea but in a much punchier way.'

'I have one more suggestion,' says Raymond with a sudden resolve. 'I called the publishers of the *Mattachine Review*—based in San Francisco—'

'No shit,' interrupts Doty.

'—and I'm about to schedule a conversation with a member of the Mattachine Society later this week. I'll give you a transcript. It's a homophile organisation.'

Doty claps his hands together. 'Bingo, Wallace: exactly the kind of foil we need. I'm impressed,' he says, then looks Raymond up and down, a long index finger delineating Raymond's outfit. 'Swanky,' he says approvingly. 'I'm too long in the tooth for tight pants, but they look good on you. A little *faggy*,' he says, laughing darkly and patting Raymond on the shoulder, 'but then you Brits have always been able to pull that off in a way that we Yanks never could. Get me that transcript by close of business tomorrow—I'm taking Friday off, so can you—and I'll check it out over the weekend. By the way, did you make it to a bar yet?'

Raymond shakes his head. 'Not that sort of bar, anyway,' he says with what he hopes is a manly wink.

Doty slaps him on the shoulder. 'Understood,' he says before turning on his heel and leaving Raymond alone with his article.

Ostensibly prompted by contemporary closures of 'homosexual haunts' and the problem posed to society at large by the apparently increasing number of homosexuals swarming to the metropolis, as Doty had promised, the draft article details those various theories as to the causes of homosexuality as well as the outcomes of possible treatments of homosexuality with which Raymond is, by now, eminently familiar. As he reads a reference to codes used by the so-called *inverts* in order to distinguish one another, he smiles to himself about three-dollar bills. The article goes on to describe periodicals catering to the homosexual community as '*a kind of distorted mirror image of the straight publishing world.*' It also covers the parental anxieties concerning the 'seduction of minors' and the question of whether or not a single homosexual act would be sufficient to determine a minor's lifelong sexual preference, ie whether such an act could preclude the possibility of what Doty calls 'heterosexual adjustment'.

Under a paragraph entitled 'Impossible Dream', Raymond reads that '*most homosexuals are condemned to a life of promiscuity—the cruising of bars seeking casual partners.*' Raymond thinks of what he and Joey have done; of what he and Joey are doing, and he wonders whether this is all they have together. He finds himself disturbed at what feels like a burden of evidence against the manner and location of their meeting, even of their very union itself. Nonetheless, and emboldened by his reading, Raymond makes good his lie to Dolores later that day and calls the San Francisco phone number once more, this time staying on the line. He arranges a conversation—anonymity assured—with the society's president, no less, for the following afternoon. When he gets through the next day, his notepad and pen at the ready, he hears a stern, serious voice at the other end.

'Mattachine Review, hello.'

'Hello, my name is Raymond Wallace, and I am an intern at The New York Times. I'm working alongside a Mr Robert Doty.'

'Hello, Mr Wallace.'

'Hello. Mr Doty is writing an article on what he's describing as a *growth in overt homosexuality in New York*, and—'

'It's a hate piece?'

'Oh. No. Well, not if I can avoid it.' Raymond finds himself stammering. 'I'm providing—hopefully with your help—other perspectives; real life. Lives. Mr Doty tends towards the work of certain so-called *experts*—psychologists. Bergler, Bieber ...'

The man laughs drily. 'Sounds like your Mr Doty *tends* towards conversion therapy.'

'Well, there is that,' says Raymond. 'I hear that one bunch is awfully proud of a twenty-seven per cent success rate on that front.'

'They're not concerned about their seventy-three per cent failure rate, then?'

'I'm so glad we understand each other,' says Raymond, smiling. 'It's a front-page piece, so I hope you'll appreciate my desire to provide a balanced perspective,' he says, and then—once more grateful for Dolores' eloquent humanity—he adds, 'these articles matter.'

'They do, indeed.'

'In that spirit, would you mind answering a couple of questions?'

'Fire away.'

'I'm interested to know when you first knew that you were a homosexual.'

'Oh, I can be very specific,' says the man. 'I was thirteen and a half, and my mother had bought a book on British artists. In it there appeared a work by Henry Scott Tuke, entitled *Ruby, Gold and Malachite*. Do you know it?'

'No, I'm afraid I don't.'

'I recommend it,' says the man with a laugh. 'It's of six young men, bathing, three entirely nude; the others partially clothed. One of them is on a rock, tentatively lowering himself into the water as though fearful of the cold, whilst another stands, his butt facing the viewer, looking at his buddy, and then another sits on the boat hiding his modesty with a well-positioned hand. It was only a grainy black and white reproduction, but from the moment I saw it I knew exactly who and what I was, and who and what I wanted to do. You know,' he adds as though remembering something suddenly relevant, 'Randolfe Wicker—look him up, if you haven't already—did this survey recently, in which he asked a bunch of us whether we would change if we could. You know what I said?'

'I'm all ears,' says Raymond, his pen poised over his notepad.

'I said, *I'm forty-four years old. I've been a homosexual for thirty of those years. I have none—none—of the social and emotional history of the straight world. Of normal dating. I would be lost in the world of heterosexuals and heterosexuality. At sea in a boat with neither a sail nor a rudder.*'

Raymond scribbles furiously. 'I have one more question,' he says. 'Would you consider there to be any benefits to…your life-style?'

There is a silence on the other end that lasts long enough for Raymond to wonder whether the connection has been lost. Then the man sighs. 'It isn't insurmountable, the hatred that comes toward us,' he says, 'but it is tiring. And distressing. But let me tell you—Raymond, is it?'

'Yes.'

'Raymond, I know myself. And I look around at my peers, my straight peers, and I see their unexamined confidence in their own positions in society; I see their desperate competition to retain those positions, and I have to tell you, whatever is being postulated by the so-called experts Mr Doty is quoting in this article of his, that I have seen more breakdowns from straights than from queers. No doubt about it. Life kicks the shit out of everyone by the time they get to my age. But it's the ones who are still clinging to illusory fantasies of their own significance who fall the hardest. So, no: I wouldn't wish to be anything or anyone other than who I am.'

'I am deeply, deeply grateful for your time, Mr—' says Raymond, reflexively.

'Nice try,' says the man, laughing.

'I didn't mean to—'

'No one ever does,' says the man. 'Goodbye.'

It is only on Thursday afternoon when Raymond has typed up the transcript of this conversation, handed it to Doty, and is on his way back to the YMCA to shower and change that he wishes he had asked the man one more question: why, if he were so simply and evidently confident in his own existence and so secure in the courage of his own convictions, did he insist so assiduously on anonymity? And then another question begins to form in Raymond's mind—albeit in an unrefined, shadowy form—prompted by those thirty years the man mentioned: If he *hadn't* been a homosexual for as long as thirty years, might the man have felt somehow *less* lost in the world of heterosexuals; and if so, what increment did he feel marked the point of no return? As Raymond's mind begins to formulate this he feels a kind of bereavement, or perhaps more accurately—though he won't formulate it in these terms at this point in his life—a sense of auto-betrayal, as though his very thought processes are undermining him. But once in the showers of the YMCA that evening as he washes his body, preparing himself to be loved once more, he imagines, running down the drain, not only the dirt of the day and of the city, but also the blackness of newsprint, as though he has been marked—imprinted, even—by Doty's article, and is now doing his level best to cleanse himself of its corrosive residue.

Eleven

'We're going out,' says Joey, sitting on the side of the bed.

'Where to?' asks Raymond through a yawn.

'The *ristorante*,' says Joey, looking every inch as though he's just thrown down a gauntlet. 'It's Papà's idea. He wants to introduce you. To Gianna.'

'Aren't you both working?'

'No. Friday's our day off. One of them.'

'Right. Well, then,' says Raymond, immediately trepidatious at the prospect of this new frontier. 'I'd better get up, hadn't I?'

Joey looks at him languidly and slowly draws the sheet back on Raymond's nudity. 'If you don't get up this instant, I'm gonna need to get back into bed with you. And Papà's waiting.'

Joey takes hold of Raymond's genitals and squeezes gently, then takes the scent to his waiting nostrils, all the while holding Raymond's gaze. Joey nods approvingly. Raymond laughs, hops out of bed—his swollen penis bobbing absurdly—and gets dressed in a flash, once more wearing Joey's T-shirt and jeans, pulling his sweater over the top. 'Ready!' he says, seconds later, adjusting his crotch.

'Papà?' calls Joey. 'Rip Van Winkle's up. We're good to go.'

Out on the streets now, they walk in a row—like a team,

Raymond thinks—and he finds himself struck by the physical freedom of these men; the way in which they casually stroke his shoulder to emphasise a point they are making, or guide his body through traffic with a brief touch to the base of his spine. He feels treasured, welcomed.

After ten minutes or so they stop opposite a restaurant with two large windows separated by a central doorway. Above the door is a neon sign of cursive lettering that reads *Gianna's*. Zig-zagging fire escapes lead Raymond's eyes up to the roof, where a rail runs across its width.

'It's quite a place,' says Raymond.

Joey smiles modestly. 'It's not ours, you understand, but it is our family's.'

Papà pushes the door open and a bell rings. He gestures for Raymond to enter. Inside there are maybe fourteen tables of two different sizes—some for two; others for four—in differing configurations. At the far end is a long, pale wooden counter behind which is a shelf filled with empty wine bottles, congealed candle wax down their sides. To the left of the counter is a door which opens swiftly at the sound of the bell.

'You came!' says a short, dark-haired woman in her early fifties, her hair held back from her face by a scarf tied at the base of her skull. She appraises Raymond with her eyes, smiling all the while. 'So this is your English friend,' she says teasingly to Joey; then to Raymond, she adds, conspiratorially, 'I have heard nothing about you. Not a single thing.' Her accent is a mixture of agile Italian and acerbic Brooklyn. She winks, takes Raymond by the elbow and leads him to a seat over by the counter, where he is joined by Papà and Joey. 'I am Gianna, Sara's cousin, in case you didn't know,' she says, one hand on her chest, the other holding Raymond's hand firmly before letting go to indicate the entirety of the restaurant in a grand gesture, 'and this—142 Smith Street—is *Gianna's. Benvenuto*; welcome.'

Raymond looks shyly at Papà and Joey who are smiling back at him.

'*Raymond si è laureato a Cambridge,*' says Papà proudly, '*e ora sta lavorando al* New York Times.'

'So you said, Giuseppe, so you said. *Va bene,*' says Gianna, pursing her lips and turning her head to one side as though all the better to scrutinise the object of their conversation, 'but are there real *ristoranti Italiani* in this *Cambridge*, huh? Or even in England? Have you ever tasted true Italian cooking?'

Raymond draws a deep breath and shakes his head resignedly. 'I very much doubt it,' he says.

'Well, that will not be true by the end of the day,' says Gianna with a wink. 'And you,' she says, taking Joey by the chin and looking him straight in the eye, 'have something in your eyes… are you in love, Giuseppe? Is she anyone I know?'

Joey screws up his face, pushes her away playfully and laughs. Raymond watches him intently. 'I tell you what I am,' says Joey, patting his stomach. 'I'm hungry.'

Gianna nods sagely, one finger tapping the side of her nose. 'Well, later I will have some *minestrone alla Sara,*' she says knowingly, 'as well as risotto…*alla Sara, evidentemente*; sorry

Raymond,' she adds, turning to him, her hand stroking his shoulder, 'you must forgive my lapses into Italian when these guys are around. You will have heard of Sara. You may even have seen a photo of her. What you have not yet had,' her eyes misting with mischief, 'is the taste of Sara's particular brand of genius. We call her *La Contrabandiera*, which means—well, perhaps you might guess, Raymond, with your degree from Cambridge University?'

Raymond grins at Gianna's playful challenge. 'I read English, but anyway…contraband?'

'Sure,' says Gianna, 'but it describes a person: *contrabandiere*. Come on, now,' she adds, clicking her fingers as though in impatience.

'Smuggler,' says Raymond.

'*Benissimo*,' says Gianna, patting his head tenderly. 'Bright boy. Yes. When Sara arrived in this restaurant after her ten long days at sea, she sat down—'

'Gianna,' interrupts Joey. 'Can we do the full history once there is some food in front of us, *per favore*?'

Gianna stands as tall as she can and pretends to slap his face.

'Rude boy,' she says, laughing. 'But yes: I will bring something for your hungry young stomachs. Giovanni?' she adds, turning to Papà before walking around the counter towards the doorway beyond it. Papà follows her into the kitchen.

When they are alone, Joey takes Raymond's hand and squeezes it momentarily.

'She can be pretty bold,' he says.

'She's wonderful,' says Raymond, releasing his hand self-consciously.

'That thing she asked me—about love?'

Raymond picks up a fork and turns it between his fingers. 'Mmm?'

'She doesn't say it all the time.'

'Right,' says Raymond, glancing up to see Joey's dark eyes looking straight into his own.

Joey places his fingertips on his chest, then opens them expansively in a shrug-like move that is at once self-confident and self-deprecatory. 'I'm a simple guy,' he says. 'And I can't lie. Neither can my eyes.'

'Right,' says Raymond, wishing now that he hadn't withdrawn his hand from Joey's.

'But I'm also realistic. And whatever is going on in here,' he says, tapping his chest beneath which his heart beats, 'is A: delightful; B: without expectation, and C: my responsibility.'

Raymond shakes his head in disbelief, then nods in understanding. 'I find you incredible,' he says under his breath.

'Try not to,' says Joey seriously before turning his head abruptly towards the counter.

Raymond looks up to find Gianna, followed by Papà, both carrying trays. As she approaches, he sees plates with slices of some sort of pie; Papà's tray is laden with coffee cups.

'*Torta Pasqualina*,' says Gianna, placing a plate in front of Raymond. 'You British may be comfortable eating a huge meal at any time of the day or night, but we Italians like to stick to a routine, you know? Since we come here, to this land of *brunch*, we have adapted. Somewhat,' she adds with a smile. 'And I know you guys like eggs for breakfast. Try.' She hands him a fork, scrutinising his expression as he takes a mouthful of the pie.

'It's delicious,' he says, chewing thoughtfully. 'Spinach?'

'Close,' she says. 'Borage. Ricotta. And a boiled egg, for good measure.'

'It's just what I needed,' says Raymond. 'Thank you.'

'You are so welcome,' says Gianna. 'Now then, Joey, am I *good to go*, as they say?'

'Gianna,' says Joey through a mouthful of pie, 'take the floor.'

'Well,' says Gianna breathily, sitting herself down beside Raymond, one elbow leaning nonchalantly on the table. 'It is 1939. A notable year. Spring. Giovanni and Sara arrive after ten long days at sea, she heavily pregnant with this one,' she says, ruffling Joey's hair, 'and she comes in *still* looking like a fashion plate. She sits down, over there,' she says, her eyes scanning Papà's and Joey's in an evidently well-rehearsed speech as she lifts the hem of her skirt and turns it over, 'and she asks me for a pair of scissors. I bring them to her, and she starts cutting the threads. Like a crazy woman. I said to her, *sei matta?* Are you mad? but she ignores me and carries on cutting at these threads. Cut, cut, cut. Well,' says Gianna, clapping her hands together. 'Then, can you guess what she brings me, fresh from her hemline?'

Raymond shakes his head.

'Saffron. Well, not saffron exactly, but the corms. The bulbs. For me,' she says, her fingers tapping her clavicle, 'this was the equivalent of gold. I mean: what a genius! And the meal I have planned for you today, of course, will incorporate some of the saffron strands from Sara's corms. From the rooftop,' she says, pointing skywards.

'That's quite the story,' says Raymond, laughing.

Papà smiles wistfully. '*Veramente*, indeed. She was so worried they would be confiscated when we arrived, or that they might rot if kept in their box, that she sewed them into her skirts that first night on the ship.' He shakes his head. 'What a woman.'

'And what is more,' says Gianna, waving her finger at the three men as though dictating that the conversation will not take a morbid turn, 'she applied her spirit of *invenzione*—Raymond?'

'Invention, Gianna.'

'*Bene*—to her cooking. One morning very early Sara went out for a walk and she comes back with what?'

Raymond looks at her, nonplussed.

'A shawl. Full. Of nettles. Her poor hands!' says Gianna, shrugging and worrying her palms with her fingers. 'I said to her again, *sei matta, Sara?* But she just smiled and said, *aspetta di averlo assaggiato:* wait until you've tried it. So I wait, and I wait, and finally she comes to me with a bowl of soup, and I'm thinking, *so this is a minestrone, no?* But then I see that this little genius of the kitchen has added her—*come se dice*—foraged food to it. And, well, I taste it, and it is'—she kisses her fingertips in delight—'*Buonissimo*. The most delicious minestrone you will ever taste. And free! And you will taste this, Raymond, today!'

Gianna speaks with the gravity and promise of a ringmaster

galvanising the crowd before a show. Raymond puts the final forkful of pie into his mouth and takes a sip of coffee. It is rich, and strong, and delicious.

'Proper coffee,' says Gianna, reading his expression. 'That's all you're having, you understand, for now? Otherwise, you will spoil your appetites,' she adds strictly, piling their empty plates onto her tray.

The morning passes in story upon story, mostly of Sara, but also of Joey as a young boy, the scrapes he would get himself into—and how often he would get himself out of them, by singing.

'I swear to god,' says Gianna at one point, crossing herself and looking skywards, 'I truly believe that this boy—I should not call you a boy, anymore, I know, Giuseppe, but I cannot help it—could sing his way out of the grave! You won't have heard him, of course…'

Raymond raises his eyebrows. 'Actually, I have. Last week.'

'Is that so?' Gianna's voice, so firm and vibrant before, becomes a sudden whisper. She looks up to the ceiling, sniffing deeply as though overcoming some great emotion, then looks at Joey who is nodding. 'Is that so,' she repeats, this time to Joey, as though a huge weight has been lifted. 'That is good news,' she adds with a delighted laugh before turning back to Raymond. 'Now then, Raymond, either I talk too much or you don't talk enough. You must tell me all your secrets, especially if they will improve my cooking. You have managed to divulge not one single piece of information about your family. Tell me something.'

'What do you want to know?' asks Raymond, feeling suddenly exposed.

'Your mother's name.'

'Margaret.'

'An excellent name,' says Gianna. 'Now: your father's occupation.'

'He was a draughtsman.' The past participle seems to echo around the restaurant. Raymond smiles before adding, 'He died. In a car accident. I was very little.'

'I'm sorry,' says Gianna.

'My sister married a sub-postmaster,' says Raymond, as though this decision was somehow connected to their father's death. 'He's called Gerald. He has an absolutely massive moustache. And terrible teeth. They have two children: Barnaby who is seven, and Gillian who is five. To date, neither has shown any evidence of a sense of humour, but I live in hope.' He is hugely relieved when the other three roar with laughter. Gianna puts her hand on his shoulder and squeezes, gently.

Other staff enter as the morning draws to an end and—as customers arrive in dribs and drabs, gradually filling up the waiting tables—Gianna bustles around, expertly delegating tasks to other waiters; swiftly re-joining their table whenever she has to leave them. When they eat, they do so in a reverent silence, the three Italians looking furtively towards Raymond as he takes his first bites, as though he is either an expert, or they care deeply about his opinion. Raymond is thrilled by the flavours—the herbal tang of the nettles; the hay-like sweetness of the saffron threaded through the creamy risotto—but far more so by the welcome he is given by Gianna. He pronounces the food completely delicious, prompting a cheer from the other three which fills him with a childlike delight and makes the rest of the restaurant turn to look at them. At one point after their first courses have been cleared, Gianna goes to the counter and switches on the radio just in time for the strains of a bluesy, sonorous saxophone to fill the room, then walks swiftly back to the table, crosses her arms firmly beneath her bosom, and looks expectantly at Papà. At first he shakes his head, smiling, but then, to Raymond's astonishment, stands, takes Gianna in his arms and—as Doris Day begins to sing '*Hooray for Hollywood*'—they dance elegantly through the restaurant, prompting laughter and applause from the other punters. Joey hums along, initially resisting Gianna's imprecations to him to sing out loud, then caves in and stands to sing. Almost as soon as he does so, however, the music stops.

'*We interrupt this program to bring you a special bulletin from ABC radio.*'

'Oh come on!' groans Gianna. 'Play the music!'

The announcer continues: '*Here is a special bulletin from Dallas, Texas: Three shots were fired at President Kennedy's motorcade today in downtown Dallas, Texas.*'

There is a collective gasp from the restaurant. Gianna's hands grip Papà's arms.

'*This is ABC Radio. To repeat: in Dallas, Texas, three shots were fired at President Kennedy's motorcade today. Stay tuned to your ABC station for further details. Now, we return you to your regular program.'*

There are a series of beeps on the radio. Raymond looks, horrified, at Joey, who holds his stare.

'Ladies and gentlemen, to add to this bulletin from Dallas, Texas, there is a possibility that the president —' The announcer pauses momentarily. *'—Mr John F. Kennedy, has been seriously wounded. Now we ask your attention to stand by on this bulletin.'* There is another pause. *'Here is some more information that is just coming in, this is from the Associated Press. It says, President Kennedy was shot today just as his motorcade left downtown Dallas. Mrs Kennedy jumped up and grabbed Mr Kennedy. She cried, "Oh no!" The motorcade then sped on.'*

From outside the restaurant a voice shouts, *'The President's been shot!'* and some customers stand reflexively as though this might help, somehow. Joey, still standing, looks to his father as the announcer continues:

'And from the United Press: President Kennedy and Governor John Connally of Texas were cut down by an assassin's bullet, as they toured downtown Dallas…'

An hour or so later the radio announces the death of President Kennedy, at which point Gianna stands up and switches it off. The restaurant slowly empties of its dazed clientele leaving the four of them sitting around their table by the counter.

'He was the first Catholic to enter the White House,' says Gianna.

Papà flinches and changes the subject. 'Hey Ray, shouldn't you be at the offices?'

Raymond shrugs. 'Oh, I don't think so. I'm not on the front line in that sense. The piece I'm working on…' he begins, and then immediately regrets it. 'The department, the guy I'm working with, he's not, it's not news,' he says, in a way that makes the other three laugh, despite everything.

'What is it, then?' asks Joey.

Raymond feels a chasm open up inside himself as he considers how to describe the article. 'It's about psychology, really, and um, some police reports, and how the city is changing in all sorts of ways. To be honest,' he says, suddenly relieved at the possibility of finding an exit strategy from this conversation, 'I don't really know whether I am allowed to talk about it.'

'Oh well then you mustn't,' says Papà. 'Must he, Joey?'

Joey shakes his head. 'No,' he says, but still Raymond feels like a traitor, somehow. Or perhaps he feels simply that he has betrayed himself.

Joey stands. 'You want some help, Gianna?'

Gianna waves her hands sadly. 'Thanks, Giuseppe, but we've got it covered. You go home. Some day off, huh?'

Joey nods and Papà and Raymond stand to leave.

'You come back soon, you hear?' says Gianna, cupping Raymond's face in her tired hands.

'I promise,' says Raymond. 'And thank you.'

'You have a kind nature and a good appetite: an excellent combination. Go well.'

She shoos them out of the restaurant. The three men walk aimlessly for a few minutes but then Papà takes them both by the arm. 'Come with me,' he says, crossing the road with them and heading purposefully down Bergen Street towards the river.

'Where are we going?' asks Joey.

'You'll see,' says Papà, who has now released their arms and is walking a few steps ahead of them, setting the pace.

They pass the beautiful, imposing brownstone houses of Congress Street and then—as they draw closer to the river—those houses drop away to be replaced by low-rise red brick warehouses and the odd, isolated apartment building. As they pass the Redhook Firehouse—the engine house locked, its windows boarded shut—a man appears from round the corner, staggeringly drunk. 'It's a conspiracy!' he shouts, waving a brown paper-wrapped bottle at them as though in evidence. 'The communists are coming. Run!' He dashes towards them; they hold tight to the side of the building as he runs past, wailing. Papà strides on. Gradually—flanked by two channels of long four-storey-high brick warehouses, winches at the windows—the end of the road comes into view, and Raymond can smell the river. Suddenly, Papà turns right, checking once on Joey and Raymond's progress before ploughing on once more.

'Where are we going, Papà?' asks Joey again, but Papà just beckons them over his shoulder.

At the end of the road there is a low-rise warehouse on the left, scrubland ahead of them, then water. Papà stands on the scrubland and takes a deep breath. He looks at Raymond, then points out across the body of water.

'The Statue of Liberty,' says Raymond.

Papà shakes his head. 'Ellis Island, where we came in. When Sara…after Sara, I would come here. On my days off. Just to know, you know? That this was still here. Where we came in. Where our lives began.'

Papà puts his hand gently on Joey's shoulder then suddenly grabs him in an urgent hug, sobbing into his chest. Joey strokes his father's head tenderly. Raymond stands, watching them, wishing somehow that he were a part of them, and then, to his astonishment, Papà reaches out a hand for him and draws him into their embrace, an embrace the like of which Raymond has never experienced. He stands there, hugging and being hugged, and then to his puzzlement he begins to weep, too. And while it is entirely possible that Raymond is crying for the dead president he never met, or for Joey's mother who he also never met—or, indeed, for his own father who he cannot truly remember—he realises as he stands clinging to these men that he feels more included and more loved by this new family than at any other point in his life; that now that he knows this love, he can never *not* have known such love, and he decides that it is most likely, in fact, that he is actually weeping for the old Raymond, the Raymond who lived a lonelier life of less love.

After a few minutes Papà draws back his head and smiles. Shorter than the other two, he gently pulls each of their heads down and plants a kiss on each forehead. 'Thank you. For indulging me and my pilgrimage. When Gianna speaks of Sara…'

'It's as though she's in the room,' says Joey.

Papà nods, then laughs heartily. 'That's the wonder. And the horror. Now: let's go home. That is, unless you two have somewhere else to be?' he adds, an impish glint in his eyes.

Joey and Raymond laugh, shaking their heads, and the trio walks slowly back to the apartment.

That night after supper Papà brings down a bottle of bourbon and three glasses from the shelf above the range. 'We don't have any ice. Joey? Would you? Janice downstairs usually has some.'

Joey groans in mock-moodiness, slips on his shoes and disappears out the front door.

'How do you drink it, Ray?' asks Papà when they are alone together. 'Neat? On the rocks?'

'Oh, neat is fine, I suppose, but I'm happy to wait for ice, too.'

As though in anticipation of Raymond's answer, Papà hands him a brimming shot glass. 'This one doesn't count,' he says. 'We'll pretend this one never happened.' He raises his own glass. 'To new friends and old countries, Raymond.'

'*To new friends and old countries*: that's a great toast, Papà.'

'Shut up. Drink!' And Papà laughs a loud laugh before flinging his head back and downing the Bourbon in one. He draws the back of his hand over his mouth before shaking his head in a powerful shudder. 'Quick, before Joey gets back.'

Raymond puts the glass to his lips, takes a deep breath and sucks the alcohol into his mouth, almost coughing at the burning sensation on the back of his throat. He shivers with the woody heat of the vapour and raises his empty glass. 'New friends and old countries,' he says again, and then, as though fortified by the alcohol, 'Papà, can I ask you a question?'

'Be my guest,' says Papà, sitting down on the sofa and arching his back against the cushions.

Raymond sits in the chair opposite. 'You are a Catholic, I presume?'

Papà smiles tolerantly and taps his fingernails against his glass. 'There is a distinction to be made; a distinction *I* make, at least,' he says carefully, as though wishing to avoid causing offence, 'between believing and agreeing.'

Raymond feels suddenly impelled to push the conversation. 'Then I don't understand.'

'What?'

'Joey and I…and then you, here. I just…I don't understand. Why it's okay? If it's okay.'

Papà leans forward, his elbows on his knees, his hands together in a move that reminds Raymond uncannily of Joey. 'It's none of my business, Raymond. I don't understand it, if that's what you mean,' he says, looking at the floor as though reading a map. 'But loss focuses the attention on what remains and on what matters. What remains is Joey. And what matters is that Joey is…Joey. Not what I might want him to be; not what the world might think he should be, but who he is in himself. And if that is…' Papà pauses, confused, as though he cannot work out what word to choose. Then he looks seriously at Raymond for a second before his face bursts into a smile. 'If that is you, here, now, then who am I to ask for something else?'

There is a silence after this. Papà looks as though he is going to add something, but then chooses not to. Raymond strokes the blanket hanging over the arm of his chair, and then—as though identifying something he'd suspected for a while—brings it to his nose and sniffs. 'What is this?' he asks.

Papà grins. 'Sara's blanket. It's good, right?'

'I know it, though. Dolores—a woman in the office—wears it.'

'*Mitsouko*. Guerlain. Sara wore it. I don't have the faintest idea how, but that blanket has held her scent these three years. Traces, at least. The first time I could afford to get her something nice, you know, I got her a bottle of that perfume. She wore it every single day.' He shakes his head as though at an amusing memory. 'When we'd go out—she had this string of pearls that her mother had given her when we left Italy—she would put on her perfume and then just stand there, waiting, before putting on the pearls. Like some ritual.'

Raymond remembers watching his own mother dressing for an evening out. 'It's the alcohol in the scent,' he says as though by rote, his mother's voice echoing in his ears. 'It causes them to lose their lustre. She—Sara—was waiting for it to evaporate.'

Papà nods, looking suddenly freshly bereft, and then Joey returns with a bowl of ice.

Much later, in the quiet sanctity of the bedroom, Joey lies on his back, his hands casually interlaced behind his head. Raymond sits astride, bracing himself with his left palm on Joey's breast-bone as he sinks onto the thick reassurance of Joey's cock, allowing it to open and own his body. He looks down beyond the turgid confidence of his own erection to the conjunction of their bodies and feels as brazen as a centaur. Pushing down harder;

squeezing ever more tightly, Raymond slicks his middle finger with spit, reaches behind and—as his palm brushes teasingly against Joey's testes—allows that finger to trace the furred ridge down to Joey's anus, circling and probing before flicking the tip inside. As Joey gasps—his left hand grasping Raymond's thigh; his right thumb thrumming Raymond's left nipple—his body bucks and arches, tightening around his lover's digit and they accelerate towards a leap until—their orgasms galloping together—with each pulse of Joey's root Raymond's own cock swells and spurts and it's like Joey's come is Raymond's; like Joey comes *through* Raymond, and as Raymond feels in his finger the dying bursts of Joey's release and in his body the breathy echoes of his own, he feels as though—through coming together—they may, at last, have arrived.

When Joey falls asleep soon afterwards, Raymond feels sorry to be left awake with his own company, and though he manages to persuade himself to acknowledge Papà's acceptance of him, still he doubts, and he doubts, and he doubts and so, as he begins finally to drift towards Joey in sleep that night, and on the subsequent nights, he clings to him as to a harbour.

Back at the offices on Monday it is as though he has returned both to and from a different time zone. Dolores beckons him over. She is holding an envelope.

'Doty's furious,' she says, under her breath.

'With me?' asks Raymond.

'Jesus, no. With everyone else here. This article. It's been delayed. Of course it has. There is *other news*. Mid-December.

And Doty's already booked his Christmas break. He leaves on the 13th; we now go to press on the 17th.'

'But if he's—we've—finished it already, what's the problem?' asks Raymond.

'Oh,' says Dolores, as though about to reveal something she had considered utterly obvious. 'He's frightened. That Mr Bukowski will change it. And there's not a damn thing Doty can do about that, except maybe blame Lee Harvey Oswald, or Jack Ruby, or even—God rest his soul—President Kennedy,' she says, looking down at her nails and pausing momentarily before looking directly at him. 'I should tell you that it's not in Doty's gift to give you a day off. If it wasn't for Joe eavesdropping over there,' she indicates a young man a few desks away from Raymond's, 'I might have gotten worried. It's not your fault, Raymond,' she adds, lowering her volume almost to a whisper, 'but I did leave you some messages. At the Y. Over the weekend. I thought it might be an interesting time for you to be here.' Dolores puts her hand on his shoulder. Raymond feels a panic rising in his chest. 'I mean, wherever you were,' she says, giving his shoulder an almost imperceptible squeeze at this point, 'I just hope you were amongst friends.'

Raymond knows that he is blushing and can do nothing about it.

Dolores takes off her glasses, squints at him then purses her lips and shrugs. 'You know you don't have to hide anything from me,' she says matter-of-factly before sighing heavily and adding, as though in cryptic explanation of this fact, 'It's a broken world.'

Raymond swallows hard. 'Is there anything I can do?'

Dolores laughs. 'To fix it? Actually: yes,' she says. 'You can make a plan as to what precise edits you'll be able to make when December 14th comes around. You know: the stylish kind that even Doty can't argue with. And it's possible Bukowski will need you this week to check updates on the assassination. Oh, by the way,' she says, handing him an envelope. 'This arrived for you on Friday.'

As Dolores walks away Raymond sits at his desk and looks at his mother's handwriting on the envelope. He opens it, withdraws and reads the letter, then puts it back in the envelope. He picks up the *Mattachine Review*, turns to a random page, but cannot focus and tosses it aside. Then he takes out the letter and re-reads it. Stuffing it into its envelope with finality this time, he slides it far across his desk. He thinks of Papà, reading the floorboards like a map, and scans his desk as though trying to orientate himself.

As agreed with Joey and Papà over the weekend, after he leaves the offices that Monday night—November 25th, 1963, the day on which John F. Kennedy's body was laid to rest—Raymond heads to the Railroad Y, collects his belongings from his locker, hails a cab and moves into Apartment 7, 165 Johnson Street, Brooklyn, NY.

Twelve

The following weeks—those leading up to Christmas 1963—will prove to be the happiest of Raymond's life. He fits into the world of the Maniscalco men like a piece into a jigsaw, and they discuss Christmas together with childlike excitement.

Meanwhile, contrary to Dolores' ambitions, by the time the December 17th deadline for Doty's article approaches, Doty has already had both the headline and ninety per cent of his article approved at the highest level. All the same, when Doty leaves that Friday night in the middle of December he does so with a stern word to Raymond. 'You're the custodian of this,' he says, putting his hat on his head as though in punctuation. 'Don't disappoint me.'

Raymond smiles reassuringly and shakes Doty's hand. 'Have a good Christmas,' he says.

'Unlikely,' says Doty. 'The wife's family. But thank you. You too.'

That Sunday, Raymond, Joey and Papà take a trip to Central Park where they watch the skaters, and Raymond wonders what it might be to glide arm in arm with Joey. At one point, Joey puts his arm casually around Raymond's shoulders.

'Smile,' says Papà, his camera poised.

Joey and Raymond grin guileless grins as the shutter clicks and captures them, forever.

On Monday afternoon Raymond knocks on Bukowski's door.

'Come in,' says Bukowski.

'Hi,' says Raymond, and closes the door behind him.

Bukowski sits squarely at his desk, his pen poised over a typewritten page. 'The Doty article,' he says, looking at the pages Raymond is holding.

'Yes,' says Raymond, handing over the script. 'Update from yesterday: another bar lost its license—The Fawn, on Washington Street. I adjusted the opening paragraphs to reflect this.'

Bukowski reads these and nods. 'Ok. Anything else?'

Raymond tilts his head in disappointed acceptance. 'The final few paragraphs contain the key additions I made,' he says, watching nervously as Bukowski jumps to that section. 'It's not much,' he says, 'but I think for those who do read the article in its entirety, it at least leaves us in the hands of the ... *subjects* themselves.'

Bukowski reads silently. He flicks back to the opening, rolls his shoulders, then rereads Raymond's adjusted sections. 'Do we need this "*strange, ambivalent attitude of the homosexuals themselves*"?'

'It's one of my least favourite lines, and there's some pretty stiff competition for that particular prize,' says Raymond, surprised at his own candour, 'but it's one of Doty's from an earlier edit, and I think it politic to deploy it here. If nothing else, it reveals the partisan nature of the writer.' Raymond pauses. 'Actually, I also added the paragraph a third of the way down column three,' he says.

'Show me,' says Bukowski, scanning the page.

'Here,' says Raymond, pointing at the passage, 'under *Blackmail feared*,' he says and then immediately wishes he hadn't said it out loud.

Bukowski bites his lower lip. 'Illinois, huh?' he says. 'Okay. And what about this other guy at the end, the guy from…*Mattachine*, is it?'

'Insisted on anonymity. But I think his words are no less powerful for that. And it's really as a trade-off for that line of Doty's that I wanted to finish with his,' Raymond adds, his heart-rate increasing slightly as he worries that he is over-justifying himself.

'Lost in the world of heterosexuals,' reads Bukowski, 'not much ambivalence about that. That the final line?' he adds, turning the page but finding no additional material. He looks impassively at Raymond, who swallows, then nods. A shy smile plays on Bukowski's lips.

'Professor Hurt was right about you. Said you had a keen eye for the power of rhetorical flourishes.'

Raymond smiles tentatively. There is a knock at the door.

'Who is it?'

'Dolores.'

'Come in.'

Dolores enters and closes the door behind her.

'I'm happy for this to go to press,' says Bukowski, winking at Raymond before standing and handing Dolores the article.

Raymond blows out his held breath. Dolores looks at him

proudly and smiles. 'Nice work.'

'You haven't read it yet,' says Raymond.

'Okay, golden boy. I'll be sure to peruse it on the way to the typesetters.' She hands some papers to Bukowski. 'I'm gonna need your signatures on these by the end of the day. Raymond? Lunch.'

Over lunch, Dolores details Raymond's next project: the correspondence they anticipate following the publication of Doty's article. 'Our readership has a habit of jumping on this sort of thing,' she says. 'That's why Doty's such a popular writer. And why this gets the front page. And that's your job—selecting the letters to be printed. You know all too well the poison in that piece. And putting you on it will give the illusion of continuity and balance.'

Raymond smiles. 'Understood.'

'Good,' says Dolores. 'Now listen, honey: you look rejuvenated these past weeks. Anyone I should know about?' Raymond sees a sudden image of Joey's face kissing him goodbye that morning. He looks at Dolores, daring himself to tell her, but just shakes his head. She waves a hand towards him. 'Well, if you should find yourself at a loose end,' she says casually, 'Joshua's single.'

Raymond darts a shocked look at her to find her staring right back at him. Dolores takes a cigarette from her case and offers Raymond one, which he accepts. Lighting his first, she brings the lighter to hers, draws lightly, then blows out a wisp of fragrant smoke. 'Takes one to know one,' she says, flicking the lighter shut, the fingers of one upturned hand tentatively touching her chin, her pinkie scratching slowly at her lower lip.

Raymond looks down to see his cigarette shaking. Dolores takes his hand in hers as though to calm him. He pulls his hands gently away and takes a drag. 'The silly thing, Dolores,' he says through an exhaled plume as he stubs out his cigarette, 'is that I don't actually smoke.'

Dolores bites her lip, shakes her head and laughs. 'You get me every time with your dry humor, Raymond Wallace. Every. Single. Time. And I admire your discretion. In fact, I rely on it. One day before you leave, however, I plan to catch you with your guard down.' She takes another drag on her cigarette and Raymond wishes he hadn't put his out—if only so that he would have something to do with his hands. 'Talking of which, when do you leave us, Raymond?'

'Well I'm due to leave on the 8th.'

'That sounds as though you have other plans.'

Raymond notices his hands are shaking. He looks up into Dolores' eyes. 'I haven't worked it out, yet.'

'I see. Now listen,' she says, as though having thought something through, 'I've no idea what your plans are for Christmas, but if you would like to, you'd be very welcome to come to mine. There won't be many of us—me, Mary, and a few other friends. And you. If you'd like to, that is.'

Raymond smiles, deeply touched, not least because Dolores' invitation somehow adds even greater value to the gift he already holds: the secure knowledge that he, Joey and Papà will be spending Christmas together.

'That is awfully kind of you, Dolores, and I would have loved to have come, but I do have plans, already.'

Dolores takes another drag of her cigarette, bites her lip, then breathes out slowly. 'Glad to hear it.'

'Friends of the family,' he adds: a superfluous lie.

'Good,' says Dolores, pursing her lips as though used to metabolising other people's half-truths. Then she smiles kindly and asks, 'and do you need to buy presents for these family friends?'

'Yes,' says Raymond, also smiling now. 'In fact, I was wondering if I might ask your advice.'

Dolores stubs out her cigarette and clasps her hands in front of her as though their conversation has taken a simply fascinating turn. 'I'll need to know something about them in order to be able to help properly,' she says while Raymond nods and blinks away sudden, surprising tears.

Sometimes, during these weeks, faced with the prospect of such a different festive season, Raymond finds himself thinking of all his Christmases past: of all the steam from all the pans of mushy vegetables and all the paper hats glued to sweating foreheads; of how his mother always seems to be managing disappointment at any present she opens as though one of them might just be the gift she was after—but not this year, not this year; of all the cloyingly sweet sherry and all the stale mince pies and all the endless questions, and he despairs at how—even at this distance—these memories exert such a weird magnetic pull on him with their predictable, disappointing routines. Then he shakes them off, secure in the knowledge that, whatever this year may hold, he will only have to enter the Overcooked Old World for the duration of a long-distance phone call. At other times, he imagines a series of woollen threads leading from the respective births of Papà, Joey and himself—one drawing Papà from Lombardy in 1919; one drawing Joey from Brooklyn in 1939; a third drawing Raymond from Gloucestershire in 1942—and all these threads being woven into a tapestry of the three of them. In such moments he wonders whether he might not tell his mother about Joey, and Papà, and their life together, and what that might feel like. And he tells himself that he still has time; that his die has not yet been cast, that he can still be ambitious about all his future Christmases.

Thirteen

On Christmas day Raymond wakes early to find Joey already awake, propped up on one arm, watching him. He reaches a hand to smooth Raymond's hair.

'Merry Christmas, Mister Wallace.'

Their ankles intertwined, the sheet barely covering their naked bodies, Raymond feels a vibrant desire, pulls Joey on top of him and kisses him until Joey catches his fervour, reaches for the jar on the bedside table and anoints Raymond's dick. Then, his lower lip between his teeth, his back arched, Joey sinks exquisitely down to join them together, and they ride their way to festive glory. Afterwards Raymond lets his hands fall to Joey's thighs and smiles as his thumbs stroke the junction of hips and waist: he has found his very own angel.

That afternoon, just as they are finishing their lunch—*tortelloni in brodo*, followed by a delicious roast capon—the phone rings in the hallway. Joey goes to answer it, then returns swiftly. 'It's for you, Ray.'

Bracing himself, Raymond walks quickly into the hallway and picks up the receiver. 'Hello?'

'Hello?' says Gerald's voice, 'is there anybody there?'

'Gerald.'

'Raymond. Happy Christmas, old boy. How are tricks?'

'Happy Christmas to you, Gerald,' says Raymond. 'Really rather good, actually, thanks. Is Mother there?'

'Sipping a sherry whilst we charge around with the brats. Margaret?'

There's a shriek from one of the kids followed by a burst of raucous laughter.

'Raymond?' his mother says, rather loudly.

'Mother. Happy Christmas.'

'At last,' she says, as though Raymond is somehow late. 'Happy Christmas to you too, dear,' she says. 'Where is it, exactly, that we are calling?'

Raymond looks momentarily back to the half-open door through which he can see Joey and Papà in conversation. 'A friend's apartment. Joey. And his father.'

'I see.'

There's a silence that Raymond feels he ought to fill. 'Chap from the paper. Terribly nice.'

'Are you sure that's not too much of an imposition on them? Having a stranger for Christmas?'

'We're not strangers, Mother. And they invited me.'

Joan's voice suddenly bursts onto the line. 'Happy Christmas, Raymond!' she yells. 'Found yourself a girl yet? I bet they all go absolutely *dizzy* for your accent, don't they?'

Raymond laughs a forced laugh. 'Happy Christmas, Joan. Give the children a hug from their favourite uncle.'

'What did you get?' she asks, and Raymond is momentarily

transported back to their childhood.

'We haven't done presents, yet. We're doing them after lunch.'

'How very novel!'

Then it's his mother once more. 'You must remember to thank them from me, this Joey, and Mr—?'

'Maniscalco.'

'Golly. Are they—'

'Anyway, how is everything?'

'Oh,' she says as though affronted at being interrupted. 'Absolutely as it should be I suppose. Overexcited children with too many presents and everyone riding terribly high on the Christmas spirit. All jolly festive,' she adds without a hint of festivity in her voice.

Raymond feels a sudden resolve. 'Mother,' he says steadily. 'I've been thinking, and—'

'Oh, you don't want to do something silly like that, Raymond,' she says, half-jovially.

'I've been thinking of staying on a while longer.'

'Well I've got some news, actually. That is, that I'm definitely coming. To collect you. I arrive on the 4th. Little Christmas present to myself. Thought we'd have a few days there together before I bring you home on the 8th. It was a trip your father and I had dreamed of making. But that would have been on a boat, of course. Anyway, you can tell me all about your ideas then, if you like.' Raymond is silent. 'You've gone awfully quiet. Is the line dead?'

'No, Mother. I'm here,' he says, as though through fog.

'Good. Now this Joey,' she says, making Raymond wish that he hadn't told her his name. 'What does he do?'

'Works in a restaurant.'

'I thought you said he was from the office.'

'Oh, sorry; I meant his father.' He scrambles for a plausible answer. 'Archives.' Another silence. 'Mother, I can't—'

'I did say in my letter,' she says, interrupting him in a tone that pierces him even from this distance, '—I assume you did receive my letter, Raymond?'

'Yes—'

'It's just that you didn't respond. I realise it was only a suggestion at that stage, but once I'd had the idea of making the journey—and, as I say, in the absence of a response—well, it seemed somehow *fitting*. As an end to your time away. I hoped you'd be pleased. I certainly didn't mean to disappoint you.'

'It isn't that.'

'Besides, Gerald went to an awful lot of bother to sort out our tickets.'

'Mother—'

'Then that's settled. I'm excited,' she says, no excitement in her voice, then: 'It's funny, but you'll never guess who I bumped into at Midnight Mass. The Bennetts. Of all people. Stephen is still cowering on the continent. Quite right, too, I suppose. Still: can you imagine? I know how hard it is to have a son abroad, albeit for a few months, so their circumstances are, frankly, heartbreaking.'

Raymond hears Joan calling in the background: *This is costing us a fortune, Mother! Why on earth are you prattling on about the Bennetts, for goodness' sake?'*

'I am so sorry, Joan,' says his mother sardonically. 'I'm sorry Raymond; apparently I should be sticking to some sort of script. My mistake. Is it all terribly sad over there?'

'What do you mean?' asks Raymond, nervously.

'Oh. I would have thought that things would have been at least *somewhat* muted. As a mark of respect. For Mr Kennedy. And Mrs Kennedy, of course.'

'Ah. No. Not terribly.'

'People have a habit of forgetting all too soon.'

'*A fortune!*' says Joan once more, and then the children's voices scream in imitation of their mother.

'I should let you go,' says Raymond, utterly desperate for the conversation to be over.

Once the receiver is safely back in its cradle, he stands still for a few seconds. After the noise of the phone call, the relative peace of the hallway feels almost eerie. He steps into the bathroom and closes the door. There is a coward in the mirror. He splashes his face with cold water and a sob emanates from his chest. He curses himself for ignoring the letter. Could he have held her off? He doubts it. Replaying their phone conversation in his head he views his failure to challenge her as endemic, and his future as though from a nauseating height. Drying his face, he heads into the bedroom where he sits down heavily on the bed. To his dismay, the knot that he has managed to keep undone these past few weeks is now tighter than ever, and he wonders, will he ever be free of its bind?

A figure emerges from the corner; Raymond yelps.

'It's only me, Ray. It's only me,' says Joey, walking towards him.

'Why were you hiding?'

'I wasn't *hiding*,' says Joey, laughing, 'I was getting your present. From the wardrobe.' He sits down next to Raymond on the bed. 'Why were *you* hiding?'

Raymond drops his head into his hands and presses the heels of his palms into his eye sockets. After a few seconds he lifts his head and looks at his hands. 'I was looking for courage. I thought I might have left it in here.'

'You'll find it when you need it,' says Joey, putting one hand on Raymond's shoulder, the other on his stomach in a move that is so intuitive it makes Raymond laugh. 'Does that tickle?'

'No. It's perfect. I have a knot there,' says Raymond, as though confessing. 'And you help me untie it.'

They hear the sound of a cork popping in the other room. Joey grins.

'Well, at risk of making a terrible pun, there are some ribbons on some presents which also need untying. So, if we might take a break from the untying of *this* knot,' he says, patting Raymond's belly, 'Papà is evidently waiting to make a start.'

Raymond reaches under the bed for two parcels—one quite large; the other, a small rectangle—and, carrying them with great care, follows Joey back into the other room to find Papà pouring three glasses of what looks to Raymond like champagne. Raymond puts his parcels down carefully on the floor.

'*Spumante*,' says Papà, handing him and Joey a glass each, then raising his own. '*Allora*, what was that toast we made, Raymond?'

'To old friends and new countries,' says Raymond, beaming.

They toast and drink, then sit around the table once more.

Papà pushes a present towards them. 'Open this one first,' he says impatiently.

'Who is it for?' asks Joey.

'I guess it's for the pair of you, really, or even the apartment itself,' says Papà, his fingers dancing across the tabletop.

Joey and Raymond pull at either end of the ribbon and unwrap a beautiful silver frame holding the portrait of the two of them from Central Park. Raymond smiles a broad smile. 'This is a marvellous present,' he says.

'Mahvellous,' says Joey in delighted imitation.

'Thank you thank you thank you,' says Raymond, and Papà draws him into a warm hug.

'I remember the feeling,' says Papà, 'when we first arrived. We didn't have to deal with phone calls back then, but we did receive some pretty awful letters. I never really understood: they chased us away, then resented us for not begging to return.'

'Why did they chase you away?' asks Raymond.

'Okay you two: that's enough misery,' says Joey, taking them each firmly by the shoulder. 'Presents!' he says as he hands Raymond a small gift-wrapped box.

Raymond opens it to find a silver watch with a shiny black leather strap. He lifts it carefully out of the box and puts it on. 'It's absolutely beautiful,' he says.

Joey grins. 'Take it off again,' he says excitedly.

Raymond undoes the strap and Joey takes it from his hands and turns it over. On the rear side is another watch face.

'You can flip it,' says Joey, demonstrating. 'Two different times. It's for someone who may need to find themselves in two different places at the same time.'

Raymond feels as though a delicious joke has been played on him. 'It's perfect,' he says, slipping the watch over his wrist once more. 'Now then,' he adds, reaching for the smaller parcel. 'This is for you, Joey.'

Joey opens it. Inside is a long gold chain at the end of which hangs a large, single pearl. Joey slips it over his head, nodding. 'I love it,' he says.

Raymond looks at Papà and they share a smile.

'This is specifically for you, Raymond,' says Papà, handing him a parcel. When Raymond unwraps it he finds a stack of five pocket notebooks, each held closed by an elastic band.

'For your writing,' says Papà. 'Hemingway swore by them, apparently. Little shop in the Village that sells French imports.'

'Wonderful,' says Raymond. 'Thank you. This,' he carefully lifts the larger parcel onto the table, 'is for you, Papà. Well, perhaps this is actually for the apartment itself.'

Papà tears at the paper to reveal a cardboard box with the word *Columbia* printed on it. He opens it and looks inside. 'Oh,' he says, his eyes glistening, 'a record player!'

In that moment, in addition to the genuine enthusiasm he sees in Papà's eyes, Raymond spies something else, something plangent, and he realises that what he had interpreted for all these years as some sort of petulant pickiness in his mother was in fact nothing of the sort; it was simply that each present she opened represented yet another that she could never share with her husband.

Raymond pulls a final, thin parcel out of the bag and hands it to Joey. 'You'll be needing one of these.'

As Papà sets up the player Joey unwraps the parcel and gazes at the red and white cover. 'Papà, take a look at this,' he says, turning it round.

'*Judy Garland, Carnegie Hall*,' reads Papà.

'My sources tell me that it's an absolutely phenomenal album. Four Grammy awards,' says Raymond.

'You won't know this, but she was Sara's favourite singer,' says Papà. 'She always said that Judy had a gypsy's soul,' he adds, then frowns suddenly, as though he's said too much.

'Let's put it on,' says Joey, drawing one of the records out, placing it carefully on the turntable and, as the overture emerges from the speaker, they look at one other as though they are witnessing their very own Christmas miracle.

When Gianna drops by with a dessert for them later on, she insists on hearing Joey sing.

He sings '*You made me love you (I didn't want to do it)*,' his voice sonorous and expressive, giving Raymond the delicious impression that Joey is singing at once to him, and about him.

'You should do something with that,' he says, when Joey finishes.

'Shouldn't he, though?' says Gianna.

Joey laughs.

'I'm serious,' Raymond says.

'He's right,' says Papà.

Joey looks at them with a kind of bored tolerance and shakes his head. Gianna gives Raymond a look that is as much like a nudge as a look can be.

'Okay,' says Raymond, taking his cue. 'Let me put it this way: if you don't allow at least a few people to hear your voice, at least every once in a while, the world will be very much the poorer for it.'

Papà leans back, laughing down his nose as if there's no challenging Raymond's logic; Gianna claps her hands together and stares at Joey who—after locking eyes with Raymond for a moment—nods to her, as though conceding a point.

As she leaves that night, she turns to Raymond. 'It's cold out. Tell me you're not making that long journey back to your YMCA tonight,' she says, patting his cheek affectionately.

'He's staying over,' says Papà quickly.

Gianna beams, kissing Raymond on each cheek. '*Va bene*,' she says. 'That's good to hear. *Buon Natale, ragazzi!*'

That night as they lie in bed, Joey lies on his back beside Raymond, the gold chain glistening; the pearl sitting proud of his solar plexus.

'Gianna doesn't know,' says Raymond, finally.

Joey purses his lips as though he has been caught out, somehow, then shakes his head. 'Gianna's wonderful. But I think you can imagine that she's not exactly celebrated for her discretion.'

'Ah,' says Raymond.

Joey takes hold of his pendant and murmurs something.

'What?' asks Raymond, finding himself almost afraid of the answer.

Joey turns towards Raymond, nuzzles his neck, and whispers: 'Nothing.'

'Nothing?'

'Something and nothing.'

'Something?'

Joey lifts himself up onto his haunches, smiling conspiratorially, takes Raymond's right hand in his and places it, palm down, on the centre of his chest.

'Yours,' says Joey, and beneath the wiry warmth Raymond feels the clear, strident beat of his heart.

'Is it as simple as that?'

'It can be,' says Joey, then lies down, kisses Raymond's shoulder.

'Right.' Raymond's voice is weak. He cannot find the strength to take Joey's hand and place it on his own chest; he falls asleep wishing he could.

For the first time ever in Joey's arms, that night Raymond dreams—a dream of seas, of deep waters and of oysters. Grains of sand, their rough edges gradually peeling off the lining of oyster shells to become something new and precious: he hears the scratching and scraping as though it is highly amplified, or as if it comes from within his own head. He dreams of walking down a dimly-lit path, seaweed crunching beneath his bare feet. At the end of the path is a glow which blossoms into a closed oyster shell, a thin line of light emanating from its lip. Raymond picks up the shell, prises his thumbnails in between the shell's seal— the wafer-thin edges crumbling and flaking as he does so—and begins to gain some purchase on the smooth inner lips. Creakingly, the ancient hinge gives way, but when Raymond opens the oyster it is empty. He turns to find his mother, seated at her dressing table. In her reflection he sees there are a few dozen pearls hanging around her neck. Between her fingers she is holding the one she has stolen from the oyster in his hands.

'Thread this for me, would you?' she asks casually. 'Don't worry; I put my perfume on earlier.'

He lets his shell fall to the ground, then reaches obediently towards her. Dropping the pearl into his palm, she looks at him through the mirror and smiles. 'People have a habit of forgetting all too soon.' She lifts her hair away from the back of her neck and as he reaches for the clasp he awakes—his heart beating timorously like the wings of a caged bird—to find Joey asleep beside him, his back turned. Raymond's hand hesitates over his lover's body—as though both desirous and fearful of waking him—then reaches instead for one of his new notebooks. He writes down the dream in the hope that doing so will remove its haunting power, then just lies there, listening to Joey's calm breathing, and watching headlights meander across the ceiling.

Fourteen

Back in the offices on Monday 30th December, Raymond opens two letters concerning Doty's article. The first—dated December 18th from a certain Robert W. Wood of the First Congregational Church in Spring Valley—criticises Doty's journalistic integrity as well as identifying holes in his declared research. Delighted by its challenging tone, Raymond manages to edit it down to end the letter with the sentence: '*Perhaps at some future date [Doty] will do further research and discover there is much to be said in favour of the homosexual.*' Though the letter does refer to homosexuality as a 'psychosexual problem' it nonetheless quenches both Raymond and Dolores' thirst for printable criticism of Doty. The second letter, dated December 27th, from an Alfred A. Messer, M.D., postulates that '*many unsolved homicides in New York*' are committed by homosexuals as a result of misinterpretation of heterosexual males' behaviour, and follows this with an assertion that a man might participate in homosexual activity '*in order to degrade his partner and thus build up a feeling of "manliness" in himself,*' adding, parenthetically and to the delight of Dolores as Raymond reads it out loud to her in Bukowski's office, '*This was very frequent in the German S.S.*'

'These are ideal,' says Dolores. 'The first is sufficiently erudite as to justify its criticism; the latter writer is clearly a lunatic, and therefore a perfect complement to the first. Now then, Raymond,' she says, taking off her glasses and looking at him with some sadness in her eyes, 'the unfortunate thing about this is that it draws this project to a conclusion. You leave us next week.'

Raymond swallows nervously. 'Actually, I haven't decided, yet.'

Dolores looks delighted. 'Oh! Well, then. I can talk to Bukowski, see if there's anything he can do to persuade you. When do you need to decide by?'

'My mother arrives on Saturday for a few days. I'm hoping to tell her I won't be returning with her.'

'Hoping?'

Raymond nods.

'And what might get in the way of that?' asks Dolores.

'My mother,' says Raymond, drily.

'Hmm. Can I meet her?' she says, making it sound as though she's got a plan.

Raymond laughs. 'Er…I don't see why not. Though I should warn you: she's indefatigable.'

'That makes two of us, then, doesn't it?' Dolores catches sight of Raymond's watch and immediately takes his wrist in her hands. 'This is beautiful,' she says, her thumb coveting the face.

Raymond blushes. 'A present,' he murmurs shyly.

'Mmm. From someone who cares, I'd wager. How did my recommendations go down?'

'Like a dream,' he says, smiling at the memory of Papa's face when he'd opened the record player; Joey's when he'd withdrawn the pearl. 'Thank you.'

'So when exactly can I meet Mrs Wallace?'

'Well, she arrives on Saturday morning, so perhaps, if you're free, Saturday evening? For a drink?'

'Sounds delightful.'

That Friday evening once Raymond has tidied his desk he turns towards Bukowski's office. As he does so the door opens and Mrs Bukowski appears. She looks at him with a curious expression—contrition, perhaps—before nodding and disappearing across the newsroom and out of the double doors. Raymond knocks on the glass of Bukowski's door.

'Come in? Ah, Wallace. Close the door. Take a seat.' He looks up at Raymond over the top of his glasses, then removes them and places one end of the frame between his teeth. Raymond sits in the seat where he had sat on that very first day, though now that feels like a memory from a distant era.

'I wanted to thank you,' says Raymond.

Bukowski smiles. 'My pleasure,' he says. 'You've been a real asset to us. I'll be sure to provide you with a glowing reference.'

Raymond smiles somewhat sadly. 'Thank you,' he says, closing his eyes for a moment.

'Everything alright, son? You look a little…'

Raymond opens his eyes and looks directly into Bukowski's. He sees some kind of reflection in him: a man old before his time. Or perhaps he just sees himself, old before his time. 'How do you bear it?' he asks abruptly, then puts his hand over his mouth. 'I'm terribly sorry, Mr Bukowski; I shouldn't have—'

But Bukowski waves his hands at him, shushing him soothingly. He folds up his glasses and places them neatly on a pile of papers before interlacing his fingers and resting them on his desk. When he speaks he does so carefully and deliberately, as though talking someone down from a ledge. 'If you are referring to what I think you are referring to, Raymond, then after much deliberation and soul-searching I have come to the following conclusion: under the current laws in our respective countries, living—and I use that word advisedly—with this predilection comes down to one of three things: courage, compartmentalisation, and conformity. If you have the courage to *"step into the light,"* as the song goes, then you will, by virtue of that courage, be able to face almost anything. If not, but you find you can manage a compartmentalisation of your life into drawers—like that filing cabinet over there—whereby you present one version of yourself in the office; one at the family gatherings, and another in…' he looks unblinkingly at Raymond, '…*Little Navy*, let's say, then you can make that work. For you.'

Barely breathing, Raymond looks away from Bukowski. He sees the filing cabinet. It bears a number of dents, as though it's been kicked a few times; paint is peeling off in places. It seems—at least to Raymond—to be somehow disappointed by its experience to date. He looks down at his hands and knows that the disappointment is his, and his alone. Then he thinks of the different Raymonds he is—with Joey; with Mother; with Doty—and feels overwhelmed, almost frighteningly so.

Bukowski clears his throat. 'And if you haven't the stomach for either of those, then conformity it is,' he says, as though reading Raymond's mind. 'Though, for what it's worth, I don't agree with Doty and his psychologists who think that we can be changed. Trust me; I speak from experience on this,' and he laughs sadly. 'I have seen men travel from conformity through compartmentalisation to courage and thereby a freedom, of sorts; I have not known anyone to navigate that route in the opposite direction. There are consequences of any and every decision, of course,' he adds with a shrug. 'I have known men who have chosen to die rather than live with any of these.' He looks sincerely into Raymond's eyes. 'I thought about it, myself, actually. Quite seriously.' He pauses for a moment, looking momentarily out of his window. 'No. I chose compartmentalisation. Which, by the way, sure has had its consequences. On others, as well as on me. This thing that Laura—my wife—has been doing, for example.'

'It's none of my business,' says Raymond, quickly.

'I'm afraid that's not entirely true, as you'll see,' says Bukowski, returning his gaze to Raymond. He opens a drawer and removes the envelope Raymond recognises immediately as that containing the note he had received from Joey. He freezes. Bukowski slides it across the desk towards him. 'Laura managed to acquire this from your desk at some point. Perhaps you left it lying around, or something. She confessed to me that she planned on using it, somehow. I have to say,' he says, surprising Raymond with a light laugh, 'I can't imagine what she hoped to prove by its contents; she certainly didn't have an answer when I confronted her. There's nothing intrinsically incriminating about it, but codes are there to be deciphered. And possibly as part of a portfolio of details, it might be perceived as compromising. I hope that, by returning this to you, you will be able to remain in control of your own circumstances. Think of it as a salutary lesson in care and discretion.'

As Raymond takes the envelope and buttons it securely into his inside pocket, he wonders what else he might have left lying around.

'Laura isn't a bad person, Wallace. She's trapped; or she *feels* trapped. No,' he then says as though determined to take responsibility, 'she *was* trapped. And she's really, *really* sad about that. And she's lashing out. But the money I give her...we've just been discussing it, actually...it's really nothing more than she would receive if we were to divorce, you know? It wasn't even her idea. And Bert—this guy she'd been hanging around with—he slunk off as soon as she suggested anything more...permanent. So Laura and I decided to try to make a nicer version of these... transactions...with less of the drama, and hopefully far less pain.'

Raymond nods once more. 'I'm glad to hear it,' he says.

'You know, Wallace,' says Bukowski, looking suddenly thoughtful, 'if you were to decide that you wanted more time here, I think we could make arrangements. Another bursary, at the very least, or even—thinking longer-term—a visa, perhaps, in the absence of any evidence of *moral turpitude*, of course,' he says as though trying to make a joke before adding, with sudden and genuine sincerity, 'like I say, Raymond: you're a real, live asset. No doubt about it.'

Raymond smiles sadly, shaking his head almost imperceptibly. 'That's…awfully nice of you.'

Bukowski nods regretfully. 'No, it isn't. It's awfully *accurate* of me. And, as for the rest of it, you just let me know when you've figured it all out. Hell, if you *do* figure it all out, for Christ's sake come and tell me, would you?' he adds, trying to lighten the mood with a smile.

'I should be going,' says Raymond, yet stands hesitantly. Then, as though he has made some sort of decision, he steps forward, reaches across the desk and shakes Bukowski's hand. 'Thank you again,' he says earnestly, 'for everything, but especially this conversation.'

'You be sure to give my very fondest regards to that professor of yours whenever you see him next,' says Bukowski, looking suddenly terribly young. He indicates their picture on his desk, saying, 'we would have been around your age then, I guess.'

Raymond bids Bukowski farewell and leaves the offices just as the subterranean machinery kicks into gear, making the building groan and shudder. As he steps through the revolving doors he thinks back to the day he first arrived and imagines filing the entirety of those three months into a cabinet drawer before sliding it shut.

The following evening Raymond Wallace sits on a freshly-plumped sofa at the Excelsior Hotel, his palms firm on the velvet cushion, and glances at his wristwatch. As the minute hand hits seven o'clock, he looks up to see Dolores enter through the revolving door. She is carrying a large shopping bag. Raymond gestures to her, adjusts his tie, stands up, and—as a matter of habit—brushes his trousers down.

'My mother is just freshening herself up,' he says as Dolores approaches. 'Take a seat. Would you like a drink?'

'Oh, I would adore a martini. With an olive. In fact,' she says, a twinkle in her eye, 'make it a dirty one.'

Raymond calls for a waiter and orders the same drink for himself. As they sit, Dolores fingers the lapel of his suit jacket.

'Very smart,' she says as though somehow a little disappointed, then: 'You look pale, Raymond.'

'I got you a present,' he says quickly, sliding a wrapped box across the table towards her.

'Snap,' she says, looking at him cautiously before handing him her shopping bag.

He watches her open her present first. As soon as Dolores sees the trademark gold and yellow box she lets out a little yelp, then looks at him and shakes her head. 'How did you know?'

'I smelt it somewhere else and recognised it as your perfume.'

'It's too expensive,' she says.

'No, it's not,' says Raymond, feeling suddenly emotional.

'Well, open yours, then,' says Dolores, spraying her wrist and sniffing delightedly.

Raymond pulls a large rectangular parcel from the bag and unwraps a frame. He turns it over to see a picture of Manhattan by night: two globed lights shine brightly on the left, then just off centre is the Chrysler building, office windows lit up in a patchwork. The spire itself is an obscure silhouette against a grey, cloudy sky, as though the photographer was walking away but turned back just to capture this final glimpse; the whole image, in fact, has the air of an afterthought. Raymond places the frame on the table.

'It's not illuminated,' says Dolores, as though apologising, 'but this is what we mere mortals see on an average night. It's by a photographer called Elliott Erwin. Mary used to run a gallery down in the Village—next door to *Threads*, in fact—and she had this in her lockup.'

Raymond finds himself suddenly unable to speak and Dolores takes his hands in hers. The waiter returns with their drinks and the bill on a tray. Raymond frees his hands and reaches into his inside pocket for his wallet only to find he has withdrawn his passport. He corrects his mistake—though not before clocking that Dolores has noticed it, too—and slips a bill onto the tray. As the waiter withdraws, Raymond sees his mother—in the dark green dress usually reserved for vicars and solicitors; the large amber brooch clinging to one shoulder—descending the staircase across the lobby. He waves to her before returning his gaze to Dolores, his heart beating wildly.

'How did he take it?' she asks quickly. He holds her gaze, unanswering, then blinks very slowly. 'Ah,' she says, as though in some pain. 'Will you—?' But he shakes his head almost imperceptibly.

'You must be Dolores.' Her voice seems almost rudely loud.

'All day long,' says Dolores reflexively, turning to Raymond's mother with a smile and taking her proffered hand.

'I hear you and Raymond have been working very closely together. I'm terribly glad we have this opportunity to meet.'

'Mrs Wallace—'

'You may call me Margaret.'

As the two women begin to get acquainted—and despite managing to appear genuinely interested in his mother's opinions—Dolores darts odd, concerned glances towards him, ministrations which he finds indiscreet and embarrassing. He looks away to the rich, mahogany panelling, the large mirrors with their cut-glass edges, the square columns that divide the lobby into sections and the pairs of curtains that flank them as though poised to sequester that portion of the room at a moment's notice. Lacking something to do with his hands, he adjusts the position of the framed photo on the table in front of him—but this only puts him in mind of the photo upstairs, zipped tightly into his bag: Joey and him in Central Park. That morning he'd taken it as a sort of talisman, though now it seems merely stolen contraband.

'Is that a bee?' asks Dolores, extending a hand towards his mother's brooch.

Mrs Wallace draws back. 'It's fossilised,' she says, almost proudly.

'It's beautiful,' Dolores says, almost sincerely, and reaches instead for her glass.

In 1978, Raymond will have that very brooch on his desk before him as he writes, and will examine its macabre glamour. He will imagine the moment when the slow, viscous sap first caught the bee's leg—or wing, perhaps—and the ensuing agony of asphyxiation. And he will understand how the bee died by increments.

But back then—in the hotel foyer—music comes from hidden speakers, lambent strings over a bluesy shuffle, and Billie Holiday sings of a cold night, and a deep longing.

Raymond is, of course, transported by this—back to that first night in *Little Navy* when another version of '*Loverman (Oh Where Can You Be?)*' had come on and he'd watched that bold stranger dance like an angel waiting to be captured before weaving into his life and changing everything forever— but only in the way that one can be momentarily captivated by distant memories: with absolutely no sense of agency. After all, a different person could have seen this music as a cue to stand up, make his excuses—weathering Mother's protestations; bathing in the glow of Dolores' cheerleading smile—retrieve his bag from upstairs and hop in a cab to interrupt Joey's evening shift.

Raymond Wallace, however, simply sits perfectly still, looks at Dolores and his mother making more or less convivial conversation and realises with a sort of detached, disenchanted curiosity that these two women are almost exactly the same age.

R.W., 1978

Part Two

Rue des Rosiers

Paris

February 8, 1983

Dear Raymond,

Life never ceases to amaze me. Its secrets, its tricks, its tragedies. I never imagined writing this letter, but now life has offered me an invitation that I cannot refuse.

A few days ago, I was up in the 18th arrondissement sorting out my citizenship papers. I had an hour between appointments, so went for a walk and came across a small bookshop on rue Simart called *Les Mots à la Bouche*. The words in the mouth? I don't know why I went in, but I did, and there I found a few shelves of what is known here as *Littératures Étrangères*—foreign titles, mainly English. The word *Manhattan* caught my eye on one of the spines, so I pulled it out. *Manhattan, 1963 & Other Regrets* by Raymond Wallace! I couldn't believe it. I paid for the book, attended my second appointment—I am a French citizen now—and brought your book back home. Joey and I now live in the Old Jewish quarter. It's called *Le Marais*, which translates as the swamp. It's nicer than it sounds.

I've just finished it. Well, the Manhattan 'regret' at least. Wow! Twenty years is an age in some ways, and a heartbeat in others. You knew us just a few years after Sara's death, when it was all still so raw. I find it amazing that, however short our time together, we never shared with you so many details. Perhaps we were just glad to be with someone who hadn't witnessed all that pain.

It's interesting, your choice of the word, 'regrets', because I always regretted not being more honest with you back then. I feel that even more now, having read your book. That conversation we had the night of Kennedy's assassination, for example: I didn't tell you everything I could have—in fact, I told you almost nothing—and I don't know whether it would have made any difference then, anyway, but I figure it's worth a shot now.

I know something of shame, Raymond. I know something of hiding my true identity. It is in my blood, after all.

My grandparents were born in Lithuania. They arrived in Lombardia towards the end of the nineteenth century. They were Romanies—gypsies, some people call us. (That explains the darkness of our eyes which you write about!) They were blacksmiths—farriers, actually—and part of the decision to settle involved taking the name of our occupation: Maniscalco. They hoped it would help disguise our nomadic history, I suppose, as well as giving us a useful role in the community. Everyone needed horseshoes, back then…

By the time I was born there was almost nothing of the Roma about us—the odd lullaby, the odd recipe, but nothing else of our language—except, of course, our skin colour: a few shades darker than that of our new neighbours.

Sara's family lived in a nearby village, and her father—a successful grocer—brought his horses to us to be shod. So we knew each other from childhood. But still, somehow, when we fell in love, we knew instinctively that we had to keep it secret. We danced with others at the festivals, even courted other people from time to time, but the most precious place in each of our hearts was kept for the other.

One evening in early September, 1938, I was working alone at the forge. The sun was just beginning to set. I heard footsteps and turned to find Sara approaching, in tears. I put down my tools. She told me that her mother had discovered a love letter of mine, and that she was sending her away—to a convent—the next morning. I felt helpless as a puppet. I implored her to stay with us (I knew my parents would agree). But she insisted that, should they do so, we would all become outcasts. And I knew she was right: whatever integration we might have achieved, there were always limits. Would always be limits, for people like us.

By now Sara's tears were dry, and her face clear and determined. She pointed to a stool and told me to sit down. I did as she said. (I always did!)

She removed her cardigan and put it on a bale of hay. Then she did the same with her dress until she was before me in just her petticoat. I sat as though pinned to that stool. I had left an iron in the fire, and it glowed white, I remember. She lifted my apron, pressing the dirty panel against my chest, unlaced my pants and reached for the evidence of my passion. I could barely breathe...As the fire puttered, we made love on that stool as if our very futures depended upon it. It would turn out, they did. As I felt myself getting close, I tried to lift her off but she just clung tighter, her hand covering my mouth, silencing my moans.

Afterwards, she dressed quickly, kissed me and made me swear my fidelity to her. I laughed. I could not have been more absolutely hers than if she had taken the iron out of the fire and branded me right there and then.

And then she was gone.

When morning came and the news of her departure filled the mouths of the local gossips, I hid my true feelings and wept only with the horses. I felt like an animal: used and discarded.

The next time I saw her was the end of January. She was being dragged through the snow towards the stables by her mother who was hissing at me, calling me *Zingaraccio porco* (Gypsy pig!) saying that no matter what I did I could never change who I was. She swore that as long as she lived I would never see Sara again. Sara's mouth was a thin line. Her hands were on her belly, covering the tiniest of bumps. Our eyes locked. She nodded. My mind buzzed as her mother dragged her away.

There was a woman—also Romany—name of Analetta, who lived in a cottage nearby. I had known her my whole life. In fact, Analetta taught me to read and write (and also made the most delicious poppy seed cake!). She was like an aunt to me. Two days after the revelation, she turned up with a letter from Sara. This whole thing, she wrote, was the result of a gamble she had taken that night in September, to seal our destiny. Sara's parents naturally planned for the baby to be given to an orphanage at birth, but if we married, she wrote, they would be powerless. I was overwhelmed by her reckless, crazy genius. And I also understood that she had sacrificed everything to be with me: her family, but also, her reputation. Of course, I agreed. Of course! Analetta took my reply to Sara in a pile of laundry, then ensured that my letter was burned as soon as Sara had read it.

However, as we were both below the age of majority, we needed parental consent. Analetta assured me there would be no impediment.

Two days later—like something from your Shakespeare—Sara and I were married at sundown by a priest two villages away. My parents were there as witnesses, with Analetta. Sara wore a grey veil to denote our sin, but beneath the dull fabric, her face was beaming. I was so nervous that I could barely say her name. Just as we said our vows, Sara's father, Giuseppe, ran in, and I feared our plan was doomed. But he just nodded to Analetta, kissed Sara, and picked up the pen.

We had to move quickly to minimise the scandal. Sara had a cousin—Gianna, of course—in a place called Brooklyn—perhaps you have heard of it…My parents gave us the box of saffron corms that Gianna told you about; Analetta gave us a pouch containing five gold coins as well as her secret recipe for poppyseed cake. There was, I am still surprised to say, some small expression of love that came Sara's way from her mother the day we left, and in that exchange she also gave Sara the string of pearls that Sara would protect from the perfume for the rest of her life. Bearing these gifts, along with the one she carried in her belly, Sara and I took the train to Genoa, where we boarded the ship that would take us to the New World and a clean slate.

As Sara and I embark, I will pause. It is touching and tiring to write about the past…also, Joey is due home any minute, and I haven't yet found the moment to tell him about your book…or this letter, for that matter …

Sam Kenyon

Joey,

I should have written this letter nineteen years ago, when you and Papà had left for the restaurant and I was alone in the apartment. But I feared then, that if I tried to articulate my reasons for leaving, I might find myself incapable of doing so. I left you quite simply because I was convinced that there was no other option available to me. In the phone conversation with my mother on Christmas Day she had announced that she was coming over the following week. In the bedroom shortly afterwards, you told me that courage would come when I needed it; I am afraid you overestimated me. For, in the days that followed, I found I could not imagine a version of life where I told her about us; I simply couldn't countenance inflicting that pain on her. Then this terrible thing happened: because I couldn't—or didn't—justify our love, I began to find it wanting. Since then I have come to understand that desires are not to be thought away and that love is not to be anatomised—or, more accurately, that an anatomisation of love is an autopsy. I don't know how to say this without sounding ridiculous, but I am, nonetheless, terribly, terribly sorry at how late I am.

Mother arrived that Saturday morning, and we left the following Wednesday. I went along with whatever she wanted to do, which seemed the simplest route—at least at first. I threw myself into tourism overdrive: The Statue of Liberty, Ellis Island, The Met, and skyscrapers galore, hoping, I should add, that you might magically appear—to rescue me? No such luck. Mother found my compliance suspicious. Said she didn't understand what was wrong with me,

187

and of course I couldn't explain.

Dolores had given me a photo of the Chrysler Building as a leaving gift. She knew I loved that building. At dinner on our last night, as a waiter removed our dessert plates, Mother announced that she couldn't understand the appeal; that that building above all buildings struck her as being "full of its own sense of self-importance," an assessment that felt more personal attack than architectural critique. I wanted to scream, but managed to just push my chair back, stand up and walk out. Out of the hotel, onto the street. It was freezing and I had no coat with me, but I couldn't go back in. I marched around the block, fuming. Perhaps—again—hoping you might just happen to be passing. After about half an hour I returned to the hotel to find the waiter from dinner standing outside, smoking. He smiled sympathetically and offered me a cigarette; we smoked in silence. As I dropped my spent cigarette to the floor I glanced furtively up. His eyes met mine and he nodded. I muttered my room number and entered the hotel. To my relief, Mother had the Do Not Disturb sign hanging from her door. A half hour later there was a knock at mine. The waiter had whisky on his breath. He closed the door behind himself and I backed into my room. Ten minutes later, after he'd buttoned himself up, he went, and I wept.

At breakfast the following morning—to my unconcealed astonishment—Mother apologised unreservedly. Said she hadn't realised how fond I had evidently become of this city; that she understood it might take me some time to settle back into life at home. I was so flummoxed I believe I was even on the verge of confessing you to her, but then the waiter—the same waiter—appeared, served me as though I were a complete stranger—which, in all sorts of ways, of course, I was. Whether out of superstition or cowardice, I took this as a sign I should hold my peace.

(That encounter was the first example of what would become a thwarted

sort of pattern throughout my life: I set out looking for you, but settle for the discomfort of strangers: disconsolate, fleeting unions with neither history nor future. I am a night-wanderer: under cover of darkness I search for someone who might explain me to myself; I reach out to other clandestine philanderers for some kind of solace, and perceive my failure to find solace as the failure to find you. I am only looking for one man, yet find tens, perhaps hundreds. So what began that night in the hotel as an indiscretion has become the point, the drug, the anti-quest: my opium.)

When I finally made it onto the plane I must admit to a feeling of seismic relief: new circumstances where nobody knew me the way you had known me; where nobody could catch me, or quote me. A clean slate, you might say. The seat next to us was occupied by a young primary-school teacher called Carolyn who had accompanied her aunt back to New York following a family funeral. Chatty, friendly; pretty, I suppose. I was rather a cold fish at first, by all accounts, but I warmed up during our journey together, with the help of a gin or two. Mother, however, was immediately taken with her and by the end of the flight had, in fact, arranged for Carolyn to visit us in Gloucester that half-term. I'm afraid I remember almost no details of that visit, other than that Carolyn was—I would come to understand—characteristically kind to me, and that I—now back once more in the drudge of the sub-post office—appreciated her undemanding attention. However, since the onus seemed to be on me, as the man, to pursue our relationship, such as it was, and since I just didn't have it in me to be that man, we lost touch shortly after that. Mother was furious.

Because leaving you had been so ghastly, I feared that beginning anything new with anyone else might necessitate re-examining, raking over that pain. So for years I kept you and your absence—precious and excruciating, familiar and hideous, reassuring and undermining—deep within me. And for a long time it worked—the prejudice I felt at the impossibility of our love, the guilt of leaving you, the self-flagellation at the nexus of these two…each time I questioned my reasons for leaving, for example, I chastised myself with the unquestionable absurdity of staying. And gradually, inexorably, the question became shorter and the answer came quicker until I was no longer aware of any particular exchange taking place. This whole circle was reduced to a minuscule spasm of psychological activity. It became part of me.

Around that time, I had a dream that would become recurrent: it is as if I am awake in our bed in the Johnson Street apartment just as I was that Christmas night, and I turn to see that you're lying beside me, your back turned. I see—exactly as I did—the curve of your spine, the down in the small of your back, your raised hip, the slope of your buttock—I see all this, and I want you. I reach out to touch you, but you just evaporate.

The very first time I dreamt this I awoke screaming. Soaked in sweat, revulsed by my own arousal, and almost drowning—if only*—in my own tears. I had traced, without touching, the curve of your torso, before reaching down to nestle my palm in the small of your back. But where our skin should have touched, my hand went right through. And the more frantically I tried to hold on to you, the faster you disintegrated.*

I reached out and you disappeared: a fair exchange, *you might say.*

When I next had the dream, months later, again I reached out—and again you disappeared. But the third—maybe the fourth—time, I didn't reach out; I just gazed. I read your every curve and dimple, caressing and commemorating you with my eyes. And since I no longer reached, you no longer disappeared. What a night I spent then, once I'd comprehended the dream's logic. I'd found the goose that laid the golden egg! I could spend entire night's sleep gazing at you, basking in the heat of your body, secure in the love of your turned back.

And while I still woke up weeping, it was as the weeping at the annunciation, at something divine: they were tears of relief that you could somehow remain in my heart; that you held strong in a place that I hadn't destroyed. The pain of solitude each morning after became my penance, my hangover, and in some strange way I took comfort in that. I transmuted my betrayal into a curiously beatific chastisement.

(Looking out my window, I see that it has started snowing. Last week, surprised by the warmer days, the bulbs began to poke up through the unfrosted earth. These are signs of shifting geographical meteorological patterns, the subtle moves on one side of the world that create explicit alterations on the other. What moves are you making on your side of the world, Joey? I suspect that deep down I've always denied the mutability of time; I've always tried to pretend that time can be held—that, for example, I could hold you in my heart and memory and yet leave you. A watch with two faces. I sometimes feel as though I have spent my entire life in a different time zone to the one in which I appeared.)

I got a job in London. Over the next decade I would become a rather well-respected journalist, renowned in certain circles for my arch commentary and— yes—the power of my rhetorical flourishes, as my old professor had once said. I had hoped that the metropolis might offer me either shelter or solace; company or clarity. But outside the office, away from my typewriter, I simply found myself living the life I had been trying to avoid. I had traded the beauty of you and me for a life of unlove and unpassion; for more failed unions and disappointed trajectories; for the untouchable, uncertain smiles of other sad, young men. I sat by myself in bars that just felt like anaemic parodies of Little Navy, and I feared I had become the Bukowski I had met that October.

Some years later, Carolyn left a message for me at the paper. When I called, she told me that she was in London for a few days, and wondered whether we mightn't meet up. Over dinner she confessed she'd just ended a rather dis-heartening relationship with a colleague, and needed cheering up. Somehow, we made each other laugh, and it didn't seem dishonest or disingenuous when we fell drunkenly into her hotel bed. And whilst it was no grand passion, it was perhaps precisely that that made it so attractive to me: whatever it was that Carolyn and I shared would never, in either my mind or body, threaten to usurp what you and I had shared.

Does it sound utterly ridiculous to say that I proposed? It certainly sounds ridiculous to me, now that I have put it down in this cravenly unromantic way. We married on a Thursday: July 27th, 1967. (I didn't clock it at the time, but it turned out to be the very date on which the Sexual Offences Bill was passed into law. When I did realise, it was with a vertiginous sense of irony.) Neither Carolyn nor I wanted a fussy performance. So a simple registry office followed by a pub lunch sufficed; I remember I even dropped by the office that afternoon to type up a manuscript. Mother would have liked much more of a 'do', as we say, but managed to bite her tongue. (I've no doubt that she was tremendously relieved that her fears about my proclivities could finally be put to bed ...)

Neither of us was sure we wanted kids, and as Carolyn was enjoying her work well enough, we decided to put off that decision for a while. Others (no guesses) considered us terribly 'modern' (see also: suspect) for doing so. That may have been our undoing; mine, at least. For perhaps with parenthood as a spur, I might have been less likely to return to desultory flings.

It was towards the end of 1972 that I made one bad decision too many, and found myself in the lockup in a central London police station overnight. Gross indecency. The only reason I got released without charge the following morning was that, unbeknownst to me, one of the other chaps in the public lavatory turned out to be a peer of the realm, no less, and he had managed—

I am not Raymond Wallace

god knows how, given us journalists' appetite for scandal—to keep everything under wraps and get us all off the hook. Presumably there was some sort of deal; there usually is.

The following morning Carolyn was waiting for me when I emerged, bleary-eyed and unshaven. I confessed everything. I even confessed <u>us</u>, with the almost certain knowledge that she would leave me. I underestimated her. The stoicism and compassion she showed me that day touched the—though I usually shrink from the word—divine. It is undeniable that the love I came to bear for her grew from this. She insisted that we didn't make any decisions then and there; that there was time. And so it was during these curious days of tolerated uncertainty that we began to take refuge in each other's bodies—and, I would argue, truly and honestly consummated our marriage.

It's hard to write the word, 'honestly'. But it was honest, what we had. Perhaps not 'normal'—whatever that is.

In the summer of 1973, our son was born. We discussed various names, as people do, but when Carolyn proffered her paternal grandfather's name—Joseph—I didn't hesitate for a moment: I could not imagine a purer way of immortalising our love. She must have known; she knew your name, after all. Even so, I know that it was selfish. I named him after your absence in order to make you a present part of this new life. Yet all I actually achieved was to make your absence ever present and ever painful. I also see that with that single decision I erected a permanent, invisible barrier between me and my son. However, since everything in my life has a wound in it, why should fatherhood be the exception?

I'm going to take a break, now, get myself a glass of water, stretch my legs a little. It's draining, this raking over the past; draining but essential, and I still have a lot more to say before I'm done.

Hello again, Raymond. Joey is out rehearsing—a recital tour for the spring—so I can write more. When I finish, I will send this to your publishers. I so hope it gets to you.

Now back to our story. We arrived in New York after ten days at sea, and when our son was born that June there was no argument over his name. By a beautiful coincidence, Giuseppe was the name of my father as well as Sara's, and so in giving our new baby an old name we made sure that his life in the New World was tied to the Old.

Bit by bit we learned the language, and also learned to live among the other immigrants, watching our son—known as Joey, of course—grow into a happy young man who—as Gianna told you that day—often sang his way out of trouble. (He still does, as it happens, but I will tell you all about that later on.)

The summer Joey turned twenty-one, Sara started to complain of pains in her back, a swollen belly and some heavier bleeding than normal. When these symptoms continued, I took her to the doctor. He did some tests, then sent her to a gynaecologist who did some more tests, then sent her to a radiologist…By the time they had anything to tell us, it just confirmed our fears: a cancer which had already spread to her lungs.

She lived another seven months, dying on Sunday 29th January, 1961. Every night when he returned from his shift at the restaurant, Joey sang to her, lullabies that she had sung to him as a child. It was the only pain relief that seemed to work: she closed her eyes and—though it sounds funny to write this—she *bathed* in the sound of his voice.

At her funeral he sang her favourite song one last time: *Bella ciao. Goodbye, beautiful.* (It's an old workers' song, but in the war it became an anthem against fascism. Sara, of course, first sang it to Joey when he was in the cradle...) It was almost unbearable. And then, he stopped singing. He just stopped. And what was funny about this was that no one asked him to sing anymore. It was as though everyone knew and everyone understood. So that night you describe so beautifully in your book—that night I met you—when he sang to us: that was the first time I had heard my boy sing since Sara. And then on Christmas day, when you said that thing about the world being a poorer place without his voice...my god, I knew that you were right, because I had lived in that world already for two and half long years, and it was a desert!

Of course, I blush to read of your passion (as any father would!), but also, reading it described so tenderly in your book confirmed what I always hoped was true: that, whatever pain came after, in the *heart and the heat of it* (as you wrote), was a manifestation of your profound love for one another.

And so to your disappearance, Raymond. When we returned to an empty apartment that night, we were confused, but then after an hour went by, Joey became truly concerned. He went back to Gianna's, then stopped by *Little Navy*. While he was out, I noticed that the photo was missing. He got back, checked and found your clothes also gone, and your bag...So we began to imagine a different scenario...A note would have been kinder, it is true, but there were clues. I remembered, for example, that you had wanted to leave after us that morning. Was that part of your plan: to leave without witnesses?

Because it was a weekend, I had to wait until Monday to visit the offices of the Times. They said you no longer worked there; that you had returned to England. They went to find Dolores for me, but she was off sick that day. Now, of course, I realise that you were just a dozen blocks away with your mother in that hotel, and that if only I could have contacted Dolores, she could have told me your location there and then. But she didn't come back into the office until the end of that week, by which point you'd already left the country. The only forwarding address she had was your old professor's, though she insisted on giving me her number, to pass on to Joey. I don't think he ever called.

For him, those first days and weeks were like another period of mourning. For me, it was like watching someone's heart break in slow motion. Just thinking of it now still brings back the anger I felt towards the person who had done this. Gianna was an angel during this time: she has a sixth sense when it comes to emotions, and gives the best (and best-timed) hugs; she also knows when you just need to laugh. Or sing. She knew about you two, of course; you were wrong about that, Raymond, as was Joey. She can talk for Italy and America combined, but is no fool, and when it comes to family, her lips are sealed.

I don't remember exactly how the next bit happened, but I'm pretty sure it was someone at *Little Navy* who either worked at The Juilliard School of Music or who knew someone who did. Either way, Joey ended up singing for one of the teachers—a French guy called Laurent Berjot. You might have heard of him—a big name in opera in France in the 40s, who moved to New York for a season at the Met in the early 50s, and never left. He had just retired and decided to devote his life to other people's voices. He loved so much about Joey's voice: how it felt as though he was singing directly into the hearts of his audience; how he sang the words as though he had written them himself. However, Berjot also made it clear how much work there was still to be done. He was incredibly hard on Joey—so hard, in fact, that he almost gave up—but Joey persevered, and Berjot would be proved right. Joey flew through auditions for both the program and scholarships, and began his vocal studies in earnest that Fall.

At some point there were coded conversations about his name. The strong implication was that the associations between Gypsy and Maniscalco were unavoidable and undesirable, and that the international career they wanted for him would be impossible without a change. Joey was furious, but I persuaded him that— since Sara had taught him songs from when he was in the cradle— in some way he owed his singing to her, so perhaps he might consider taking her maiden name of Lombardia as a compromise? Eventually, he capitulated like a tamed stallion, and then, of course, he went on to win *every single prize* for voice in his final year!!! Giuseppe Lombardia: look him up, if you haven't already heard of him...

It is agony to see your child suffer. It is invigorating to watch him recover. And it is an absolute privilege to then watch him thrive.

When I listen to that album you gave us that special Christmas, it sounds to me as though Garland knows that—however painful the rest of her life might be—the world is grateful for her voice. And there was something that blossomed in Joey in those years that made me feel the same way about him. When it comes to heartbreak, he sure knows what he is singing about, but the world is, most definitely, a richer place for it. So I hope it doesn't sound odd if I take this opportunity to express my thanks to you, Raymond, for reminding him to share his gift.

Thank you.

His key is in the lock; I will write more tomorrow ...

When I was in the kitchen just now, Joey, I flicked on the radio and there was a singer with a song so intensely evocative that I just stood there, glass in hand, and let tears run down my face. It was in French, and my French has never been all that, but still I was spellbound. He sang with such simple, impassioned sorrow…and though his voice was operatic, classical, and though I am no musician, still there was something about his guileless honesty that made me think of you. Lombardia, his name was. A song by Reynaldo Hahn. And the title?

Infidelité!

Ha, ha.

(In the moonlit snow that falls outside my window I can read the passing of time, of love affairs: history. My son's first footprints, as a child, tentatively making his marks on the whitened lawn, brief traces of evidence, presence, impressions; I was there, he was there: this was important. And the first winter after I'd left, the cold rebuke of February and its inclement weather. And Mother—after some entirely forgettable matinee—shivering crossly on Shaftesbury Avenue whilst I tried desperately to hail us a cab, when all I really wanted was a cab directly to you.)

I did try to call you, once, though admittedly it was shortly after Joe's birth—more than a decade after I had left. A stranger answered. I asked for you but they had no idea who I was talking about. I hung up. Sometime later—it might even have been years—I rang the restaurant, but by then it was a record store. I gave up. Imagined you covering your traces, hiding yourself away—and couldn't blame you. I imagined you and your father, refugees of love, constantly moving on; and in some awfully perverse way, this arrogance—this feeling that I may have broken your heart: this has kept me sane, to some degree. For I hope to god that I did break your heart as I broke mine, if only so that these nineteen years wouldn't be utter vanity.

It's funny, but whenever I try to imagine you now, I draw a blank; it is as though I can't seriously picture you except as a kind of museum piece, a young man who must, by now, be either older, or even—god forbid—dead. That photo of us, the photo I stole? I am afraid that—as Dorian Gray did with that portrait of his youth—I keep it out of sight nowadays. Still, it taunts and haunts me, not because of what the portrait has become, of course—just a little yellowed around the edges—but because all I see when I look at it is the man I failed to honour: the fleeting promise, unrealised. And this failure eats into me like a putrid accusation. So now, I arraign myself, I accuse myself, and await the trial. This will be a long night. This is the repudiation of repudiation; the judgement of the internalised judgement. I can see that I ingested our society's homophobia with such an appetite that I consequently regulated myself far more efficiently than any law ever could. I believe it is no exaggeration to say that I have spent my life making mistakes on behalf of this paradoxical psyche. And the pain of that is nothing compared to the pain of seeing others implicated in this cycle. I think, ultimately, you got the best deal, Joey. I'm sure Carolyn would agree.

In the spring of 1976, Mother died of a series of strokes. Given the strength of her personality it was, I must say, merciful that it all happened so very quickly. Abrupt and brutal for Joan and myself, but kind to Mother, at least. I realised then that I had expected everything to change, afterwards; that I would lose the shackles, somehow. I had not understood that we carry our parents within ourselves, in our blood, bones and minds...however, this new wisdom has made me all the more determined to maintain the distance between

Joe and myself: it is because I love him that I must protect him from becoming anything like me. I stay in the shadows in the obscure hope that I will thereby allow better influences to step into the light, even though I am not confident of success. The absent father is, after all, the magnetic, prevailing trope of our culture, isn't it? Those of us who pray, do so to an absent-presence: Our Father, Who Art Elsewhere.

Grief does funny things, doesn't it? If one isn't careful, it can make one justify all manner of behaviours. And I'm afraid I wasn't careful. I will spare you the details; you can imagine the sort of thing. Carolyn's patience ran out—which I have to say came as a sort of relief; to me, at least—and just shy of eleven years of marriage we divorced in the summer of 1978, shortly after Joe's 5th birthday.

I rented a flat not far from Carolyn and Joe. And I experienced a sudden surge of energy that manifested itself as a kind of neurotic creativity: I wrote a book called Manhattan, 1963, & Other Regrets *in a matter of weeks: it just poured out of me. It was a selective memoir of episodes in my life that I had cause to regret…of course you were front of the line, but by no means alone in that mournful retrospective. It was published the following year and was a modest sensation, largely because of the combination of what people considered to be rather erudite prose alongside what those same people considered to be rather scandalously explicit scenes of a (homo)sexual nature…it is perhaps a sign of my acquired sense of liberation at that time that it never crossed my mind to edit or subdue our passion.*

When Joan read it, she said to me: 'It's a difficult path you have chosen for yourself, Raymond, but you are my brother and I will always love you,' and I was abjectly grateful—because she'd finally put into words the way she had evidently always felt towards me. And would always feel towards me.

A series of other books followed this, each garnering rather flattering praise as well as a perfectly respectable clutch of the quieter prizes. So I am now Raymond Wallace, *celebrated author. Because of the confessional nature of my writing, however, each success is based on yet further self-exposure, so that I feel I have laid myself bare like carrion, and I fear predators.*

Though of course there is no predator as insatiable as my own mind.

I read through the reviews of each book with an increasing impatience and realised—though only relatively recently—that the sole reader's response I care for is yours. Each and every one of these books was a message to you, a torch flashing out code into the darkness; a hand that knocks— two short, one long, two short—on a door that never opens.

I did get a letter from Dolores—Bukowski's secretary, you may remember—once the U.S. edition was published, saying that she had recently retired; that she and Mary had moved out to Long Island; and that Joshua—the salesman in the shop in the Village from whom I bought those clothes—was delighted with his cameo, and apparently remembered me with fond delight. As for Bukowski, well, Dolores' cousin Charles was in town one New Year's Eve, Dolores introduced them, and guess what? They ended up moving to Illinois together...

I exhaust myself with my capacity for envy.

The other week I got a call out of the blue from Stephen Bennett, of all people. You must have heard of him; you may not know that we go way back and that he feels like a sort of terrible salutary lesson in being true to oneself. Having disgraced himself at an early age he fled to Paris, only to return from thence in a blaze of glory a decade ago as the new enfant térrible of the art scene. Anyway, he had read my books and was in town for the launch of a new exhibition. A fancy Mayfair gallery. Would I go? I swallowed my misgivings and accepted. When I got there the room was filled with these happy young men, flamboyant and free, admiring the masterworks through the bottoms of their champagne flutes. Stephen barked when he saw me and embraced me with a suggestion of intimacy that we had never actually shared. He introduced me as his 'long lost pal', purveying—like a street hawker—a list of my published works (chronological order, no less) to all who listened. After a while he released me and I stood in a corner for a quarter of an hour or so, watching the choreography and signature moves of this emancipated group of beings like a decrepit anthropologist who has finally discovered the lost tribe but isn't at all sure that he will live to tell the tale. A rather bookish young man who wasn't dressed at all like the others came tentatively up to me and asked me kindly whether I wasn't the *Raymond Wallace. 'I- I'm afraid I no longer know,' I said, absurdly, before making my excuses in a rather rude and brusque manner and dashing outside into the gasping winter night.*

(I sometimes feel as though I'm under some Greek curse: like Sisyphus, pushing the rock only to have it roll down again; or Tantalus, fruit and water forever out of his grasp. Mine is to feel as though I'm constantly falling from a tremendous height, the threat of mortal impact forever imminent, and forever deferred. Well: almost forever.)

It's nearly over.

I'm going to take another break, now, go to the bathroom.

Hello Raymond. Joey is out rehearsing again, so I am alone in the apartment. I am still keeping this letter a secret, not because I am ashamed, but because, now that I have the opportunity to tell you all these things, I don't want to stop. And I'm worried that Joey might not understand. (I am not sure I understand, myself...)

So here we are in Paris. My third country. My third language. Isn't it funny how my grandparents did everything they could to bury their gypsy roots and, not even a century later, Joey and I have returned to the nomadic life? Perhaps not with the same frequency as our ancestors, but still. Slow-motion gypsies: that's us.

We moved in 1972 for Joey to rehearse Pelléas in a new production of Debussy's *Pelléas & Mélisande* at the Paris Opéra. At first—just like when Berjot went to New York—we were just here for the season, but that job led to another, and something about the timbre of Joey's voice seemed to go down so well over here...plus there is the food...and the wine...and it is also true, looking back, that we both seized the opportunity for a new adventure.

By the way, I did discover the secret as to how Sara's blanket always smelled of her: we had just arrived in Paris, Joey was at rehearsals, and I was unpacking. I found a half-empty bottle of Mitsouko in with his socks...I put two and two together, and just left it out on the kitchen table for him to see when he got back that night. He confessed he used to dab a little on it every few days, just to keep her presence felt. He thought I would be angry, but I just laughed at my own faith in the power of that perfume. And then cried, of course. So now there are no more secrets. (Well…apart from this letter…)

I got a job in a café. Place called *Le Loir dans la Théière*—the dormouse in the teapot! Washing up to begin with, because of my limited French, but we could live on Joey's earnings, and I was gradually promoted to waiter as I gained vocabulary, even adding a suggestion here, a recipe there—Analetta's cake is now on the menu. There is a young woman there called Bernadette who knows the Judy Garland album by heart, and sometimes, when we're clearing up after a late shift, we put it on and sing and dance with Judy! The café is very conveniently located on the same street as our apartment: rue des Rosiers. Perhaps one day you might come and have tea?

Joey's performances are very, very well-received, and last year he recorded his first solo album: *Mélodies* by Reynaldo Hahn. Can you tell I am a proud father? I make Joey blush when I go on about it.

I hesitate to write this, because as you will see it is not uncomplicated, and I must stress that I don't mention this with any desire to cause you pain. But Joey did, after some years of the odd lover here or there, meet someone. Jacques Zaki, a costumier at the Opéra. They have been together a couple of years, now. He is a wonderful man. Just wonderful. And this horrendous disease does frighten me terribly, so for all sorts of reasons I am glad they have found …

I realise, Joey, that there's something terribly historical about my personal perspective—rather like travelling through life in a car, but facing backwards: I only see what is already past and never what might be approaching. I've always been concerned with what I've just missed. I catch the sunset just as the night draws its curtains; the night, in turn, as the dawn draws them back. So, what can be my legacy? What might I make of this rear-view? That it is never too early to wish, and important to make your wishes as flexible as time and the shifting of perspective. Name them if you must, but allow their names to change, to alter according to the present certains and the future possibles. And above all: make your dreams your ambitions, your wishes your intentions. Performativise your hopes and lure them out of the inertia of the fantastical and into the realm of the probable.

(It gets darker as the morning approaches, as though my eyes are becoming less and less able to process the information they receive. I'm losing track of where I'm writing. Even of why I write, given that I have no idea where you are, now. But still, in these final moments I try to home in on what really matters, what is significant, and feel as though I am—at last—running out of things to say. Outside my window the snow now sits mute and expressionless as a tomb. It holds memories, but they are frozen, hidden jealously within its crystals. I feel it begin to crystallise me; to draw me into its cold clarity as I approach my very own freezing point.)

All I ever wanted was either to have something remarkable happen to me, or to be remarkable, myself. My tragedy is that I achieved both, without managing to appreciate either. My remarkable thing—my angel; you, Joey—appeared before I'd had time to make a wish, so I fled in fear. Perhaps the truth is that I never really learned how to wish; only how to long for. After all, people like us don't get to practise with fairy-tales, do we? Who might I be if I'd heard how Cinderello and his prince had lived happily ever after?

(It seems to me now that the very words I am writing are untethered—as though, if I nudged the page, they'd all dislodge themselves and cause havoc, following their own erratic trajectories of meaning. It's all so fragile, so very tenuous.)

That dream; the one where you lie turned away from me: I realise, now, with a sort of detached, disenchanted clarity, that I got it wrong. It is me turning my back on myself, and it is I who disintegrates at the slightest touch. I withdraw from myself; I always have: I am the unreachable, the untouchable, the uncanny. I am the echo of Von Aschenbach: I have paid the deckchair attendant and now sit, casting a waning gaze over the lithe follies of my lifelong obliquity.

I feel lighter, now. I have followed my instructions to the letter, so I won't feel a thing. Perhaps just my head beginning to droop as though presaging a languorous nap. Perhaps just a whistling sound from my mouth: a little sigh, an ee…and might my lips fall forward morphing this vowel into an oo, and might my tongue, obedient to gravity, finish off my final word by dropping onto my teeth? And might I hear this voiceless th, my larynx at last at rest, like the sound of a solipsistic old gas-bag finally deflating: is that how it will be, Joey?

I must go, now.

Always yours—always yours—always yours—Raymond.

Part Three: 2003

Dear Joe,

I hope you won't mind my writing to you out of the blue like this. I got your name from an article I read earlier this year, about your father. I am Joey Maniscalco, now somewhat better known by the name Giuseppe Lombardia. And yes: I am *that* Joey. I enclose a letter from Papà (unfinished; I interrupted him)—a letter which I like to believe I would have gotten my head around sending a few days after its completion, had other things not overwhelmed me, at that time.

I was deeply moved by the anniversary recognition of Raymond's work, and—if it doesn't sound too presumptuous to admit it—not a little proud. When I think of him—as we do of lovers who have departed—I do so with fondness and humour alongside a sadness I can't deny. This morning I was going through some old papers when I came across this letter once more. I had assumed I had thrown it out; I am very glad I hadn't.

Papà's health is deteriorating, and so I've decided it is time his letter finally earns its status as a letter, and gets sent. So here it is. Addressed to a new recipient, and twenty years late—but better late than never, huh? I know nothing about you and your life, and I really don't intend or desire to intrude, so please forgive—or ignore—me if this seems overly forward, but I send you warm wishes, and should you ever find yourself in Paris, please: look us up. I'm sending it via the publisher, so I do hope it makes its way to you, eventually.

Sincerely,

Joey

§

I feel a sudden chill, wish I hadn't worn shorts, reach between my legs into my holdall for a jumper, and pull it on. I fold Joey's letter up and slip it into my pocket. The two letters from Dad and Papà sit side by side on the table before me. I feel as though I know far too much and far too little. Outside, Kent whizzes past as we pick up speed towards the tunnel. I find myself lifting a sheet of one letter, then of the other, then another and another, glancing backwards and forwards between the two like a proof-reader as though, somewhere in between them there lies an answer, a truth, or at least a clarity of some sort. Sudden rain on the window makes me look out, then my ears pop as we enter the tunnel and I turn away from my reflection in the darkened window. I feel a sudden chill, reach between my legs into my holdall for a jumper and pull it on. Despite the undeniable forward thrust of the train I feel as though I am being pulled at an equally impressive velocity backwards into events before my time. Because I am. But then, when I allow myself to own up to the adventure I am now undertaking, I have to admit that I am also thinking most definitely of the future.

When I first read *Manhattan, 1963, and Other Regrets* I must have been fifteen or sixteen. I thought it was clever, believable—and tantalising, in its abrupt ending. But somehow—even though my father is on record describing it as a confessional memoir, the truth (albeit entirely from his viewpoint) about that period in his life—I persuaded myself it was fiction. That Joey—whose detailed image I had constructed in my adolescent mind and about whom, I now blush to admit, I had elaborated numerous intense masturbatory fantasies—was real; that their passion was real: these things simply never entered my mind back then. When, some years later, Mum finally decided it was time for me to read Dad's letter to Joey, I felt comprehensively betrayed. By Dad, of course—I mean, what child wouldn't want their father to be thinking of them immediately before he overdosed? By the book—hoodwinking me, seducing me into shooting my nut over my father's lover like some queer Oedipal spin-off. By Mum—for the timing and manner of this disclosure. And perhaps most devastatingly by my own naïveté: thinking that I was, might have been, or even ought to have been the single most important person in my parents' lives.

I hid it all away. Literally, in cupboards. Metaphorically, in cupboards. And then these two letters arrived and of course, until I opened the envelope, I had no idea what it was that I was opening, and once I'd opened it I couldn't un-read what I had read. At one point it seemed as though, with each new paragraph and each subsequent piece of information from Papà, my world was being re-calibrated, re-jigsawed, and I felt almost jubilantly weightless for a time. Shortly after I'd finished his letter, I went back to those cup-boards and opened them, like a detective—or a pirate—returning to overlooked clues. In these past few days Dad's book has been transformed into a rich seam of memory that has filled my waking and sleeping hours with deadlines and headlines, green-baize doors and unmet lovers in smoke-filled bars, and a longing to assuage a guilt that I have done nothing to deserve.

Now, with Papà and Joey's letters in my hands—and my hands only—I can be certain that, for once in my life, I am the only person in possession of all the available information, and it feels fucking great; now that we have, according to the tannoy, entered France; now as I am, like some determined meteor, hurtling towards a reunion of sorts with Joey and Papà, I feel vivid for the first time in so long, unfettered in a way that is giddily unfamiliar, and full of a faith that I will, shortly, be in possession of my inher-itance.

It is only when I have marched through the Gare du Nord, hopped into a cab and directed the driver to Rue des Rosiers that the reality of my adventure strikes home and I begin to feel a rising, existential nausea.

How *terribly* French.

§

'The diagnosis is conclusive, Monsieur Lombardia—Maniscalco, I mean: dementia. Vascular. Progressive. I also suspect, from the scans, that your father has had a series of minor strokes, which will—may—adversely affect the prognosis, to a greater or lesser extent. Does he smoke?'

I look at Papà, who is examining his fingernails. There is a clock on the wall behind him. Its tick is overly loud, an incessant, unsubtle metronome. I look back to the doctor.

'No,' I say. 'Never has.'

'That's good. Very good. Blood pressure?'

'High, from time to time.' I take Papà's hand in mine. He beams at me as though he is immensely proud of this, and I want to laugh.

'I'll refer you to a specialist. We should keep that under scrutiny and under control.'

I nod. 'I don't imagine,' I say, suddenly needing to clear my throat, 'that you can give me—us—a sense of time?'

'You are correct. There are, however, signs to watch out for. Here are some leaflets which give broad details, but each individual is…individual. Stability, routine, no major changes: these are as good as any medicine yet developed. And the carer needs caring for as well. This is paramount.'

This last comment finally allows my eyes to well. 'Thank you,' I say, hoarse with sorrow.

The doctor stands up and reaches across the desk to shake my hand. 'It is always an honour to meet a great artist,' he says with tremendous sincerity.

I smile. 'Papà?'

'Uh-huh?'

'Let's go get ourselves some cake.'

'Poppyseed?'

'Of course,' I say, nodding my farewell to the consultant.

As we leave the clinic I don't check as we step onto the street and suddenly there's a car horn, a window wound down, a head leaning out, a voice shouting and fingers that flip at us. The gears slam and the tyres screech off. I want to punch someone.

'What was that guy talking about?'

'That was a doctor we needed to talk to.'

'Are you okay?' He looks concerned.

'You know, Papà? Let's talk about this later. I'm in dire need of some cake.'

'Analetta's?'

'Of course.' I raise my arm to hail a taxi and it's only when the driver winds down her window and looks at me with a slight smile that I realise I have done so with my fist still clenched, as though in solidarity of something undisclosed. 'Rue des Rosiers,' I say, and we climb in.

She sets off, looks at me intermittently via her rear-view mirror. I can sense that she's working me out. 'You are ...?'

I smile. 'Yes. But tonight,' I say, taking Papà's hand once more, 'I'm a son taking his father out for a slice of cake.'

She nods as though out of respectful obedience, and drives on.

§

As we pass the Place de la République, my phone vibrates. I reach into the back pocket of my shorts. It's Josie. 'Thanks for calling me back.'

'A foreign ringtone: tell me absolutely everything.'

'I'm in Paris.'

There is a cackle of delight. '*Enfin!* What swung you?'

'Family business. Last minute decision. I'm tying up some loose ends.' I laugh at the ambition of this. 'But I swear to god I'm heading into the Marais now, so I'll make sure I get a table over the weekend and will write up the copy on my way back. The review will be in your inbox by Monday evening at the latest. I promise.'

I hear the click of a lighter and the smack of Josie's lips around a cigarette. 'You're a marvel, darling,' she says, smokily. 'Just make sure you hold onto receipts. You know what Alan's like. Including for this call. Put it all through.'

'Wonderful. Will do.'

'And should you happen upon an impossibly louche, single Parisienne, do feel free to give her my number, won't you?'

'Consider it done.'

There is a pause.

'Are you on an adventure, Joe?'

I hesitate.

'I see,' she says. 'And what would Dolores say to that, do you think?'

I laugh, and then together, in our very best cod-Manhattan accents, we chorus:

'*Do something memorable, this weekend!*'

The taxi drops me off at the corner of rue des Rosiers and rue Malher. I walk past Papà's café which looks as though someone has set up a coffee shop at a house clearance: comforting, familiar, and entirely lacking in vanity. The walls are lined with posters—some framed; others pasted straight onto the rough plaster—art exhibitions, opera productions, films. I look at the menu, pasted onto the door, and am delighted to see 'Analetta's poppyseed cake' listed. I step backwards to take in the full façade but as I do so hear the parp of a car horn. I jump out of the way of a cab drawing up to the kerb—its driver gesticulating furiously with her hands—and head on towards their address. Number 8; flat 6. The main door is a deep red, and each pane of glass is protected by a beautiful panel of wrought iron. I take a deep breath and ring their bell. No answer. I steel myself and press again. Again: no answer. I suddenly feel sullenly stupid: they may not even be in town this weekend. I exhale carefully, then look at my—Dad's—watch, and notice that I've left it on the British side. I flip it so that I am now looking at French time. It's a quarter to six: nearly time for an aperitif; I'll make this work out. I turn left onto rue Vielle du Temple and walk towards my hotel. A few minutes later the pavement widens slightly and there, on the left, is a bar so distinctly, almost parodically Parisian— wicker chairs all facing onto the street, flanking tiny tables—that I consider it rude to resist.

§

'Giuseppe Lombardia and his more famous Papà: *bienvenu!*' says Bernadette as we enter the café.

'Bernadette: how are you today?' I say, as she takes Papà by both hands and kisses him fondly on each cheek.

'Never better,' she says. 'How did it go?'

I shake my head, pursing my lips, but manage a wink.

'In that case, come to your usual table so that I can keep an eye on you two handsome devils.' She leads the way.

'Are we too late for a cup of tea and a piece of cake?'

'Bof,' she says. 'Six o'clock in the evening is the new tea-time. The usual?'

'Papà?'

He looks at me as though out of sudden fear.

'Cake? Poppyseed?'

His face softens, and he nods sagely, then turns to Bernadette and pats her shoulder. 'Has anyone ever told you how beautiful you are?'

She rocks her head back, laughing so widely that her fillings show, then shakes her head ruefully. 'Not today. I'll bring you a pot of tea.'

We sit, and Papà looks around with a benevolent kind of gaze, as though surveying his domain. 'It's nice in here,' he says.

'Isn't it?'

Then he leans forward and whispers. 'Who is that woman? The one who kissed me?'

I smile. 'Bernadette.'

'Does she know I'm married?'

'Yes, Papà.'

'Oh, Ok. Well. Don't tell your Mamma.'

I hesitate. Then, thinking the better of it, say 'I won't. I promise.'

I'm half-way through the piece of cake when he starts tapping my hand, nervously.

'I want to go home, Joey.'

'Absolutely, Papà. Can I finish my slice of cake? Have some tea,' I add, pushing his cup and saucer towards him.

He slams his hand down on the table. 'Don't patronise me!' His voice rises in volume.

I drop my head to my chest and breathe out, hard. I try to take his hand, but he snatches it away and glares at me. He stands up abruptly, and the crockery clatters on the table.

'I'm sorry, Papà; come on. We can go. Let me get the bill and I'll take you home.'

Papà looks at me accusingly, then turns as though to walk up the steps towards the kitchen.

'I'm going home by myself,' he says.

We hear her before we see her. '*You made me love you…(I didn't wanna do it)…da da da da da da da…*' croons Bernadette, swaying side to side and smiling as she wanders nonchalantly towards Papà.

He freezes, turns to me as though to check that I'm listening, too, then turns to Bernadette and begins singing along. It always knocks me sideways, how a song can reconnect the different parts of his damaged brain. After she sings a few more lines, another couple of voices join, until soon it is as though we're in some ridiculous movie. Bernadette indicates for me to sing, too, and though I can fully see the irony of the one professional singer in the place failing to step up to the task, I'm just exhausted, and I know that, if I sing, I'll cry, and I can't do that right now. Besides, it's so, so nice not to be the one singing to him, and I'm delighted to watch Papà calming down and coming back to some semblance of his senses.

§

'And if you will just sign here ... and here ... merci, Monsieur Wallace.'

The concierge smiles broadly at me as though sharing a joke, then hands me my key. I head straight to my room. It's all immaculately white ... Once checked in, I head to my room. It's all immaculately white except for the wallpaper behind the headboard, which is a sensual symphony of oversized flowers—fuchsias, lilies, peonies—punctuated with acid-green foliage. I sit down at the little desk they've provided, take out Joey's letter and place it on the desk in front of me. On hotel stationery I write a short response that takes me a long time.

July 25th

Dear Joey,

Thanks for your letter, and for sending your Papà's letter, too. It did, indeed, take the publishers some time to get it to me, but it finally arrived a few weeks ago.

Better late than never? I couldn't agree, more. And it is in that spirit that I also enclose a letter to you, from my *father. I'm putting it in a separate enve-*

lope so that you can decide when to read it. It was the last thing he wrote. And writing it was the last thing that he did. It makes for difficult reading at times, I'm afraid, but it is most definitely addressed to you, and however complex this might be, I feel strongly that you deserve to read it and to know what you meant to him.

You will notice that this is delivered by hand. I took you at your word: I am in Paris until Sunday evening. I would love to meet. I'm reviewing a restaurant, but that is all I have planned. I realise that this is terribly short notice, but if you are free and would like to meet too, just call.

Love to you and Papà in the meantime,

Joe Wallace

I print my mobile number neatly beneath my signature, seal the copy of Dad's letter in one envelope, then wrap my note around it and slip those into another before sealing that, too, and addressing it.

Halfway across the bridge a guy catches my eye and we share a smile, then pass each other, but I don't look back. At 8 rue des Rosiers once more, I notice with frustration that there is no external letterbox. I step back and look up, trying to guess which windows might be theirs—futile, of course. I go to press their bell, then hesitate—not feeling quite as cocksure as earlier. Besides, I figure, I might leave at least something up to Joey, so I press another bell. In broken French I manage to persuade the woman that I have a letter to deliver, and a few seconds later I hear a buzzer and push the door. In the cool shadows of the vestibule there is a series of wall-mounted boxes. I locate number 6 and slip the letter inside before returning once more to the warmth of the summer evening.

I feel lighter, now, as my father once wrote, though our lightnesses are very different. His was about finality, endings, the anticipated relief of no longer being. Mine, it seems to me, is the very opposite: making connections, reuniting; living.

I pass the bar from earlier and continue down the street until I am at the restaurant Josie has been nagging me to review: *Les Philosophes*. They seat me outside, just around the corner from the main drag. The back of my chair is tight against another customer's. I'm not terribly hungry, so I order a few things—chicken liver salad; crème caramel; a couple of glasses of a chilled red—and figure I'll return tomorrow night for a proper meal. I make a few notes in my notebook, pay the bill and head back towards the river. I look at my phone—notice it's almost nine o'clock—then realise I've not stopped checking it all evening. I shove it into my jacket pocket and implore myself to wait with at least a modicum of patience.

§

It's nine o'clock by the time I put Papà to bed. I sit down and open a bottle of wine. I pour myself a large glass, corking the bottle after I do so and putting it back in the refrigerator: I feel the need to ration myself.

I spread out the literature the doctor gave me but as soon as I try to read it, it all becomes a blur. I've picked up the phone and dialled Jacques's number before I remember. Hanging up, I smack the side of my head with the heel of my palm. It's been nearly ten years, yet—at times of stress, such as this—some stubborn hinterland in my brain bypasses that to dial a dead man's number. I finish the wine, then pour myself another. This time, I leave the bottle out.

There's a knock at the door. I open it to find Sonia standing there in her fluffy pink slippers and one of Jacques's trademark kimonos. This eccentric, intimate vision never ceases to surprise me; it is as though, once we're inside the main door, we are all part of the same family sharing the same home.

'I heard you,' she says, smiling almost flirtatiously, 'on the radio. Such beautiful singing, Giuseppe. Reynaldo Hahn: my favourite!'

I bite my lip. 'Papà's just gone to sleep,' I whisper.

'I won't keep you, then. It's just that my bell went earlier, and someone delivered something. I wanted to make sure that you had received it—whatever it is—safely.'

There is a meow as her cat, Violetta, appears and curls itself around her ankles before approaching me with curiosity. I reach my hand down but Sonia bats it away. 'She'll bite you.' Her eyes glint with a proud delight. 'Violetta is *very* picky when it comes to men.'

I have stroked Violetta many times over the years, but I never tell Sonia. As I wink at the cat, it is as though I replay Sonia's previous statement once more in my head, like an echo. 'Who was it?'

'Well,' she says, her heavily-pencilled eyebrows arched in intrigue, 'it was a young man's voice. Sounded extremely *English*.'

I think of the letter I wrote all those months ago; I can actually feel myself blushing, for god's sake. 'Sonia, would you mind just waiting here while I go and collect it?'

She looks utterly thrilled. 'Of course not,' she says, pulling the lapels of her gown tighter across her chest and pushing past me into the apartment.

I go downstairs to our letterbox and find a thick envelope inside. I tear it open. It is, indeed, from Ray's son. *Wow.* There's another envelope in there. I scan his note.

Shit.

I have to admit that, when I sent Papà's letter to Joe, the most I was expecting was a polite response. But he's here. And then there's this letter from Raymond.

I lean my back against the wall. My excitement is now tempered by a weird sort of irritation, like I'm suddenly under pressure. I read his note once more: he leaves Sunday evening; I've got time. I put everything back into the original envelope and climb the stairs once more. Sonia's at the kitchen window, admiring the sunset; I wonder how long I now have to spend with her before I can politely ask her to leave.

§

I am still negotiating with myself as to how often I can reasonably check my phone, when I reach the river and am distracted by the view. The sky has turned a majestic lilac; the few clouds there are, are tinged by the yolk of the setting sun. I stand and watch for a minute, then turn right and walk along the inner pavement. I realise that whilst I know what I'm waiting for, I'm not sure what I want whilst waiting. I notice a door on the right-hand side with a small light above it. A man appears from my left, presses the bell and is buzzed in. I approach the door. Above the bell is a tiny rainbow sticker. I smile to myself: we always find our places.

Inside is a coat check with a glass cabinet beneath, selling rainbow-coloured gear and condoms, and on the left is a bar with the wall lined with backlit bottles. Up to the right is a television showing porn. The colours are faded, and lines flicker across the screen as though the reception is bad, or the tapes are worn out. There's a close up of a guy's wide-open expression as he takes two cocks at once; this pans out to the other two giving each other a high five. I find this hilarious. I check my coat and, slipping my phone into my jeans, head through a doorway. A guy brushes past me, his eyes hungry. I keep walking. I feel him turn. I keep walking. There is another doorway. I step in and hear sounds of sucking. I can just about make out some flesh in the shadows—a cock here; a buttock there, hands reaching—and there is the sharp, acrid smell of poppers that floats over the ubiquitous scent of disinfectant. I withdraw back into the previous room. The guy is now standing in the centre. When he sees me, he unzips his flies. It turns out I do know that I don't want this—at least, not here. I smile politely, feeling wildly British, then walk swiftly past him, collect my coat, and am outside once more. The sky is now dark, darker than a bruise, and yet I can still feel the residual heat of the day's sun radiating from the building behind me. As I cross the road there is a gentle breeze that comes from downriver. From halfway across the bridge, I see shadows flitting beneath me on the opposite quayside. The flick of a lighter, the glow of a cigarette. I pause and watch various men pass each other—some on benches, others just wandering—and feel them calling me, like sirens. Then my phone rings. I nearly drop it as I take it out of my pocket. It's John. The irony: for months I'd wanted nothing so much as a call from him on a Friday night; now that I've drawn a line under it, of course he gets in touch. I consider hurling my phone into the river but just hold it until it stops ringing before slipping it safely back into my pocket. As I reach the opposite side, I think of Dad and his *Night Climbers,* and descend the staircase to join the Night Descenders, my fellow delinquent philanderers. I step determinedly down into the shadows.

At the bottom of the steps is a group of men standing or sitting against the foot of a tree, smoking and passing a bottle between them. As I reach them, one turns abruptly and holds out his hand to me.

'*Portable.*'

I feel a sudden terror, reach reflexively for my phone in my pocket, I try to retreat, but the steps are larger than I'd thought, and I stumble backwards, gripping the rail for support. He moves towards me. '*Donne-moi ton portable.*'

I manage to right myself, turn and start swiftly back up the stairs but bump into someone coming down. A thick belt, handcuffs attached to one side; some sort of hinged contraption on the other. I look up to see the face of a gendarme, and wonder whether he has come for me.

'*'soir*,' he says, the street lamps glinting in his eye. '*Tout va bien?*'

'I'm sorry, I don't speak French.'

The buttons on his uniform shine like eyes. 'Good evening.' His accent is thick and effortful, his moustache bristling with what looks like amused concern. 'Everything ok?'

I look back down the steps to find that the men have disappeared. I turn back to the policeman and nod.

'Leaving so soon?'

'I made a mistake,' I say, pathetically.

'*Dommage*,' he says, then, 'shame,' and I can't decipher whether this is a slur or an expression of regret.

He steps to one side, bowing in a pronounced, gentleman-like manner. I stammer a *merci*, and our shoulders brush as we pass. At the top, relief rains down on me like a shower and then, as I cross the road towards my hotel, I think of the thick serge of the gendarme's uniform, the bright buttons and the slouching belt, and am suddenly convinced that I saw his hand adjust his crotch as he spoke to me. If I hadn't been so spooked, I realise with a twinge of erotic regret, then I almost certainly wouldn't have been able to believe my luck.

I now make my way unhesitatingly back to my hotel and, as I enter the lobby, remember John's call with a queer, edifying sort of satisfaction. Not only will I not respond, but he'll hear that I am abroad.

I feel like an international man of mystery.

§

'Joey, *chéri*, did I ever tell you about the time I danced with Joséphine Baker?'

I smile, and sigh, and nod.

'It was in '49. The Folies Bergère. Her triumphant return!'

It is nearly half past ten. Sonia has kicked off her slippers and is curled up on our sofa like a coquettish kitten, the lapels of her kimono framing her face as though she is posing for a painting or a photograph. Perhaps it was a mistake to offer her a glass of wine— we are now well into our second bottle and my French is getting fuzzy round the edges—but then again, I didn't want to be alone. I lean my head back against the armchair and close my eyes as she talks. The encounter with the consultant swims before me, as does my schedule for the coming months—the Wagner; the Britten; the recordings for the *Lullabies* album—and I wonder whether I am up to any of this. I open my eyes. Joe's letter sits before me on the coffee table, a ring of wine now staining its envelope like a rogue watermark.

'…and it was at that precise moment that the strap broke—or did she break it on purpose?' she laughs.

I put down my glass. 'I'm terribly sorry, Sonia,' I say, standing up with some effort, 'but I really should be getting some sleep, now. It's been a long, long day.'

She looks at me with a combination of pity and resentment. '*I* will be seventy-five, in April,' she says with immense pride, then stands, only just preventing the folds of her kimono from revealing all with a swift, practised move of her hands. 'The trouble with you youngsters nowadays,' she adds, wagging her finger, 'is that you have no stamina.'

'Guilty, as charged.'

She tilts her chin down, looks up at me from under her heavily mascaraed lashes and purses her lips in a thoughtful twitch. 'You know where I am.'

'We do.' I smile; I would express my gratitude if I could be certain I wouldn't break down.

'No. *You* know where I am,' she says, using the individual, familiar *tu*, and tapping my breastbone with an insistent finger. Then she smiles, and in that flash I get a glimpse of the beam that once lit up the *Folies*. She kisses me lightly on each cheek, looks appraisingly at me—as though verifying whether it is safe to leave me on my own—then nods, evidently sufficiently confident. Her feet slip into her slippers; her hands draw her gown tightly around her and she leaves the apartment like a departing queen, with Violetta, her cat-in-waiting, hot on her heels.

Alone once more, the regular rhythm of Papà's snores emanating from his bedroom, I lift the envelope, open it, and read Joe's letter again. I turn Raymond's sealed letter over in my hands.

'Difficult reading, huh?' I say to myself, then slide my finger beneath the seal. I wonder whether Raymond himself sealed this, his tongue on the paper, but once it's opened, I can see that it is a copy. Of course: the original is presumably in an archive, somewhere.

Joey, I read, *I should have written this letter nineteen years ago, when you and Papà had left for the restaurant and I was alone in the apartment. But I feared then, that if I tried to articulate my reasons for leaving, I might find myself incapable of doing so.*

It's curious, knowing that writing this was, indeed, the last thing that he did; it gives the letter a terrible, haunting weight. I remember the article I read in February, marking the twentieth anniversary of this moment, and of reading that the ten-year-old son—Joe, of course; the Joe who's now somewhere in Paris, awaiting my reply—found his father unresponsive—already, to all intents and purposes, dead—at his writing desk, and my hands begin to shake.

I put the letter down on the surface of the table and smooth out its folds. I glance at the bookshelf which holds his books, then continue reading. I take my time. I turn back to find the date of Raymond's letter and realise with a ghostly shudder that he and Papà were writing at almost exactly the same time: Raymond to me, Papà to Raymond, at that moment when Jacques's ex first got sick and it was all so terrifyingly bleak. The idea that Papà would write to Raymond at that very point had felt so like a betrayal that I hadn't been able to begin to comprehend his motivations.

Yet as I read the history of those intervening years, I think of where I was at those times and feel a kind of survivor's guilt: for as Raymond and I each aged in our respective geographical locations, our lives became more and more different from one another's. Where he has this core of disconsolate shame, I have something secure, solid, somehow. Yet since our time together I have known so many other sad young men who carry Raymond's burden: that of a boy whose parents resolutely failed to protect him from themselves.

A sudden, cool breeze enters through the open window, carrying with it the scent of rain. Sure enough, a few seconds later comes the sound of drops on the roof. I stand up to look outside and breathe in the cooled air. When I sit back down I feel this tug within me between a kind of sullen, angry detachment and a terrible yearning for something different to be happening, to have happened and I resent the contagion of Raymond's regret. Every now and then I lie back, close my eyes for a few seconds. At other times I even find myself answering him out loud; then I laugh at the absurdity of trying to reason with a dead man. And when I read that he's imagining me responding, it all feels so ravishingly, despondently romantic that I want to weep.

When he writes that he heard me sing the very night he died— well, that does for me, and I let myself go. *Guileless honesty?* Guilty as charged. Still, this crap about angels has never done it for me. I never wanted that, to be the man of someone's dreams, to be considered incredible; I only ever wanted to be the man of someone's rainy Thursday afternoon: something real, that could be held and understood; the ordinary-extraordinary man of someone's quotidian hopes and disappointments. As for fairy tales…*They lived happily enough together, until one of them died*: isn't that the most precious outcome we can ask of love?

I read on, with the encroaching feeling that everything is running away from me—as though no matter what I do I cannot prevent myself from losing grip. When he writes about the feeling of constantly falling, I actually laugh because I, too, feel caught in such a curse—a kind of nightmare, yet now that I have read them I have no choice but to accept Raymond's words as part of my own history.

In those final passages—when he is evidently already under the influence of his chosen poison—I am chilled by a hideous sense of complicity, as though I'm somehow in the room with him...and as though, in reading his letter written to me I am—once again— being written by him.

Then I realise that it is *that* which I resent. I am not written by him, and never was; I am not determined by him, and am not circumscribed by his foibles, failures and flaws.

And it is out of this—this profound sense of our great differences—that I begin to soften, and I feel for Raymond, in such abject pain on that deliberately lonely night, and for his poor, poor kid who must wear his father's death as indelibly as a tattoo.

I finish the letter, fold it up and put it back in its envelope. I check the time: it's two o'clock. I spritz Mamma's blanket with some perfume, then replace the bottle on its shelf.

I should call Gianna, tell her about the confirmed diagnosis. *Tomorrow.*

§

I dream that I'm back at my father's flat in Quernmore Road— though it isn't anything like his actual flat was—and that I've used my key to let myself in. I call upstairs but there's no answer. Mum's car is still running: I've forgotten my watch, and am just popping in to collect it. I go upstairs, and grab my watch from my bedroom. I'm about to leave when I hear a dripping coming from Dad's office. I make my way along the corridor. His door is ajar and I push it gently open to find the most astonishing sight, at once neither entirely a memory nor resolutely a dream.

The walls are covered in writing—indecipherable, to me at least—and sprouting from the walls, ceiling and floor is a spider's web of wool that fills the entire room: a web which holds my father at its centre, slumped over his desk. There's a sticky black liquid dripping from the wool which I know is his blood, and which explains the noise I heard. Outside it is snowing—I know that it's been snowing all night—and the room is absolutely freezing. There's a crack in the windowpane above his desk through which one end of the wool has been pushed. A label hangs from it, and although I am only on the threshold, I know that the label reads:

TO:
Joey Maniscalco
Somewhere Else

I hear sirens, and I know that they are coming here, but they are at a distance: I still have time. I walk towards Dad, at first navigating the web quite deftly, though strokes of blood still mark my hair and face. As I get closer, the wool catches and I have to push. He starts to move, and my heart leaps: *he's alive*. So I move faster, and he sits right up, but then I get stuck, and I'm suspended in the web's tension. I steel myself and make one gargantuan push, but as I do so something snaps, he is flung backwards into his chair like a marionette whose strings have been cut, and I realise that he is—was—already dead. Still, his eyes look into mine with loving kindness. His chest is bare, and there is an incision where the nib of his now defunct quill has entered—perhaps as he slumped forward at the moment of death—between his ribs to the right of his breastbone, puncturing the skin and entering his heart. The other end of the wool is in this wound.

Then the sirens get louder and I begin to panic, knowing they are coming to take him away. I look at his watch on his wrist—it has numerals, but no hands. I take it off and turn it over; the reverse is identical. I slip his watch onto my own wrist, and mine onto his. As I do so a team of scientists and curators in protective clothing enter and begin photographing, cataloguing, analysing. I see Dad being taken away from me into posterity. Then I feel my mother's arms shaking me, her hands trying to turn my face away and I want to scream *let me look* but the more I try to make a noise, the tighter she holds me, and I realise that the only way to escape is to open my eyes.

My throat is dry. I breathe. I feel bereft. I close my eyes again and find that whilst his room is still there in my mind, I am no longer in it. I open my eyes and think of Dad alone in that room that night, writing to Joey but not to me; not to *this* Joe. I lie awake, hand resting on my breastbone. These feelings make me itch, and I want to escape them. I hear a foreign siren, remember the gendarme, try to conjure the image of his hand at his crotch, the brush of his moustache, and stroke myself as though to insist that I come. Then the image of that ten-year-old boy walking into his father's office comes into my head and I begin, instead, quietly and peacefully, to cry, cry, cry myself back to sleep.

I am awoken by my telephone, buzzing on the bedside table. I grab it, drop it, pick it up again. It's not Joey. 'Hi Mum.'

'Where are you?'

'Paris.'

'You didn't say. Did I wake you?'

I yawn. She laughs. I look at my watch. It's eleven thirty. 'Don't judge me.'

'Never.'

'Josie sent me. Last minute.'

'Fancy.'

'I guess so.'

'Everything ok?'

I sit up, suddenly alert. 'Yes. Why?'

'You sound sad.'

'Oh.' I laugh—sadly, I suppose. 'Maybe a little. Still sleepy. Nothing to worry about.'

'Paris helping?'

'So far, so good. You okay?'

'Yes. Roger's out playing golf. We're seeing Joan and Gerald tonight.'

'Give them my love. I'm back tomorrow night. Can I call you then?'

'Do. Love you.'

'Yep. Me too.'

When I hang up I see that there's been another missed call from John. I put my phone back on the bedside table, next to the small radio. I turn it on, tune it in to a music station and—after a few minutes—feel a rush of delight at hearing the twinkling, plangent piano introduction before the smoke-tinged voice of Sarah-Jane Morris begins the Communards' '*Loverman*'. Jimmy Somerville takes over with his aching, piercing vocals, singing of a man making love to him, and I'm back in our living room watching Top of the Pops. I must have been about thirteen, and had gazed at their performance from my position on the sofa without daring so much as a glance at Mum, reading in her chair in the opposite corner of the room. Still, as the performance had drawn to a close and the audience had applauded and cheered, she'd looked at me over her glasses as though placing under scrutiny something in me that I'd only just discovered myself.

I realise with a shudder that this is almost certainly the song—albeit a different version, of course—that was playing in *Little Navy* when Dad met Joey—and that the world is full of ghosts and echoes.

I shower, slip on a T-shirt and shorts, wonder whether Joey will call. I laugh at myself: have I simply substituted waiting for my own lover's call with waiting for my father's? Then I see the simple gift of Joey: it really doesn't matter whether or not he calls. What matters is that I am no longer in thrall to the vicissitudes of John's bleeding heart: that alone is worth the trip.

I bounce out of the hotel into the midday heat.

§

By the time I get up, Papà is sitting at the table by the window, looking down at the street. I follow his gaze to see a young woman with a red jacket getting out of a car, shouting at the driver before slamming the door. Another young couple, a man and a woman, have stopped to watch, but the car screeches off and the woman in the red jacket walks quickly away in the opposite direction, her heels ticking noisily on the cobblestones.

Papà turns to me, raising his eyebrows at the commotion, and smiles. 'How did you sleep?'

'You know? Once I got to bed, not bad at all. You?'

He smiles again, then nods and says, 'I was tired,' as though in explanation of something.

'Me, too. Now listen. I have a piano rehearsal with Céline this afternoon: you want to come?'

'Sure.'

'Great. So shall we go for a walk, grab a bite to eat with Berna-dette, maybe, then head over to the studio?'

'Sounds good to me.'

At times like this I doubt everything any doctor has ever told me, and then have to remind myself of episodes such as yesterday's. I pick up his jacket from the chair and hold it out to him. He puts his arms through the jacket sleeves and pulls it on, automatically adjusting the collar.

'Great work, Papà. Let's go.'

On the stairwell he becomes momentarily fascinated by the banister, pressing his thumb into it as though trying to mark it. 'Ouch,' he says.

I laugh gently. 'Yeah, go easy, Papà.'

He slips his thumb into his mouth. We leave the apartment building and look up, as we always do when we leave together, to our windows on the third floor.

'Nice place you got there,' I say.

'Ditto,' he says, and replaces his thumb in his mouth.

We walk down onto the Rue de Rivoli where there's such a big crowd that Papà begins to look a little agitated, so I steer him deftly towards the river where we sit on a bench and watch people wander past.

We must be there for about half an hour, just watching and listening, before Papà speaks. 'Am I losing my wits?'

It's like a punch in the stomach. I take his hand and look at him. 'Not if I can help it.'

'I sometimes get this fog in my brain and I can't clear it, and I can't think straight or remember.'

I nod, and squeeze his hand. I turn to him. 'I know.'

He looks straight ahead. 'Do you get that, too?'

'Not exactly, Papà.'

'Is there anything they can do?'

I ruminate for a minute or so, remind myself that Papà and I have always been honest with each other. And that more recently, from time to time—as he began to talk of Mamma as though she were still alive—I've reneged on that. He turns to me and in his eyes is a look of such simple, yearning need that I have to give him some hope, or some comfort.

'Routine is our friend,' I say. 'As is song, fortuitously.'

He nods as though this makes sense to him and we sit there in the shade a while longer, he humming lightly; me feeling as though I've let go some ballast.

After another ten minutes or so I suggest we get something to eat. The sun's almost at its peak and we move as swiftly as I can persuade Papà to do so—from tree to canopy to tree—until we reach the café.

Bernadette seats us at our *usual* table, and I want to kiss her.

Papà looks around him, taking it all in. He looks contented. We order, and then just sit, smiling every now and then, each of us in our own little world. I think of Joe, whom I still haven't called, and I find myself enjoying, in a funny sort of way, this little bit of power. I know it's neither fair nor rational—after all, it's not Raymond who's awaiting my call—but there's something about it being *me* who gets to decide when to call that I'm not yet ready to let go of.

We sit and eat in silence, watching the bustling of the waiting staff and the customers, enjoying the repartée of Bernadette as she charms the crowd, and I can almost believe it's the old days: me joining Papà on a break between shifts. It's only the quality of the silence that has changed.

Bernadette brings us a tray of madeleines still warm from the oven and Papà and I bask in the scent. Papà takes the fork and stabs a cake, then lifts it into the air like an aeroplane.

'Chagall,' he says, flying the cake around the table.

'Chagall?' I ask, and he looks behind me, and nods. I follow his eyeline to find a poster of two lovers, flying above a church. 'Ok, Papà: now eat it,' I say, turning back and laughing.

Papà puts the fork in his mouth and squeezes his lips down onto the fork, before pulling it out and savouring the flavour.

'Good, huh?' I say, taking a bite, myself.

He looks at me, picks up another cake and breaks it into pieces, each of which he then holds up to the light like a precious stone before popping them, one by one, into his mouth.

Then Papà points over my shoulder at another poster, this one of a necklace of pearls.

'Perfume,' he says, knowledgeably, and I remember that sequence in Ray's book and know exactly what Papà's referring to, and I feel glad that I do and at the same time sad at the sheer number of moments which I don't, won't and can't understand. It feels like a code, or a club.

'Spoils the lustre, right?'

He winks. 'What are we doing next?'

'Studio. Rehearsal. With Céline.'

He nods as though at a distant memory.

I go to the counter to pay, and as I do so I hear the most almighty fart behind me. I turn back to find the entire restaurant—or so it seems—looking at Papà who, in turn, is glaring accusingly at a demure old lady to his left who is sipping her tea in blissful ignorance, her miniature dog on her lap. I bite my lip. Papà puts his thumb back in his mouth.

'I'm going to the John, Papà; see you in a few minutes.'

I look to Bernadette who is already making her way over to him: I can pee in relief.

When I return they are at the front door, looking out onto the street. I kiss Bernadette goodbye, she glides back into the café, and I take Papà's arm to lead him along the street. As I do so he turns to me—a wry smile wrinkling his eyes—and whispers conspiratorially: 'Made 'em think it was the old lady, didn't I?'

A laugh escapes my mouth like a bark.

Then he says, deadpan: 'I saw Raymond.'

I stop abruptly. 'What?'

'Raymond Wallace.' He looks at me as though daring me to cross him. 'There isn't any fog today,' he says, tapping the side of his head. 'I know what I saw: Raymond's eyes.'

'Ok, Papà, I believe you,' I say, and I mean it. I think of Joe, somewhere in Paris at this very moment. 'It's possible,' I say, accidentally out loud.

'Anything's possible,' says Papà, reflexively.

I have a brief urge to tell him about Joe's letter, but think better of it. In the taxi en route to the studio I decide to call Joe later, once Papà's in bed: get it over with.

§

I wander, now trying to keep out of the sun, crossing the rue de Rivoli, back towards the Marais, before realising—with a fierce embarrassment—that I'm back on their street. I walk swiftly past Papà's café, where there's an old man in the doorway, a waitress by his side. The heat is gaining on me. Just past their apartment building is a falafel counter from which I buy a pitta filled to bursting and a bottle of water. I eat languorously in the shadows, between sips.

On the wall opposite are a number of posters. One is for a production at the Opéra Bastille of an opera called *Les Maîtres Chanteurs de Nuremberg* by Wagner, and I note with a thrill that Joey's stage name is prominently displayed: Giuseppe Lombardia. Maybe I'll come over to see it. Him. Another poster advertises the Louvre, its pyramids sparkling in the image. I realise that I'm only twenty minutes away and as I finish my food decide that my time would be better spent in the edifying auspices of a museum than in stalking my late father's erstwhile lover.

I pass the afternoon wandering the cool, air-conditioned spaces, my body relieved that the burden of heat has been lifted. Periodically I sit on benches and wonder at the execution of such tremendous works of art. Then I enter a gallery and see the most extraordinary image: a young man, seated, entirely nude, in profile, the creamy curve of his back like a gorgeous bow; the creased shadows of his stomach; the full muscularity of his thigh and the languid, pensive resting of his head on his knees. Seated on a faded topaz gown laid on a flat rock, his heels rest on the edge; beyond him is the sea. I am filled not with erotic desire, but with admiration both of the model's peaceful solitude and the painter's artistry. A phrase from one of my father's lesser-known works comes into my head: *As with all the best art, at its centre I find myself.*

Though I subsequently leave this gallery to see other works, again and again I return to the intimacies of this painting and its simple, evocative elegance. Each time I do so, I also return to the wisdom of Dad's phrase, which strikes me as something of an anomaly—the hallmark of my father's writing, the letter included, after all, is a compelling, plangent powerlessness, as though his trajectory can be summed up in a single word: inexorable. I think of Stephen Bennett, and of how there are always people—braver or more robust?—who don't succumb to the homicidal fantasies of the prevailing phobes, but blaze a different trail. Then I wonder whether it is truly possible to redirect one's own trajectory. I think of last night on the bridge; John's call; my phone in my hand about to be hurled into the Seine, and know that I, too, have a dark compression within me that absorbs all light and guards furtively against reflection, and that I allow it to retain its determined unexaminability at my own peril.

Then—and I couldn't say why—I remember the moment when Mum found my stash of *Gay Times* magazines under my bed. I had just got back from school—I must have been sixteen or seventeen—and had opened the door to find her sitting on the floor beside my bed, the magazines before her. Into my taut, embarrassed silence, she had said: 'Are you sure?' and I had swallowed and nodded. She had smiled in a concerned kind of way, then said, 'You will be careful, won't you?' and I had nodded once more, just longing for the moment to be over.

And I don't know what the timing was for this, but either then or at most within the next couple of weeks, she had sat me down and given me a copy of Dad's last letter. And even at the time I hadn't been able to escape the feeling that the two events were somehow linked, that she had felt that it was now time for me to know. She had said almost nothing as I read the letter, but had watched me as though monitoring my reactions, and I feared then that she had chosen this timing in order that the letter would function as a kind of cautionary tale; as though my being queer could all too easily end in premature death, whether from suicide or disease.

Then I remember last night's dream, the blood and the wool, the moment when I pushed through the web and the kind look I received from Dad having done so, and think of how surprises take place, how people surprise us—and of how, too often, we freeze in our tracks when more of us really ought to push through the web at the point of greatest tension, because when we do, something new always comes out of it. I'm considering what my own web might be when my phone pings with a text. It's John: *Where are you?* Three little words. A museum guard wags his finger at me. I nod conscientiously and switch my phone off with obedient satisfaction.

Now as I sit and gaze at the tender isolation of this nude I realise that I'd always worked on the principle that all John needed was persuasion and love, whereas now I see that all he truly recognises is the silence of neglect. As I identify this, I see that—in actual fact—while that may or may not be true of him, it is most definitely true of me: I'm always in the market for a sad young man, after all. Could that be my own web? If so, what might happen if I let someone push through to me, rather than the other way round? I laugh and think that I really ought to travel more often, as it seems that simple geographical distance dips the clutch on entrenched patterns of behaviour; I am delighted by this realisation.

§

'I know you're not convinced by '*When Angels Cry*'—' Céline says, shuffling her scores on top of the piano and looking at me over the top of her glasses.

'I love it when Janis Ian sings it,' I say, interrupting, trying not to appear a snob. 'And I appreciate that Deutsche Grammophon want something contemporary on the album.'

'—but I have done an arrangement of it, to take it out of the folk world and into that of its bedfellows on this album—the Brahms, for example.' She looks at me as though throwing down a gauntlet.

I glance over at Papà leafing through a magazine on the other side of the studio, then back to Céline.

'Can I at least play it to you?' She sits down, fingers twitching above the keys.

'I'm all ears,' I say, not entirely truthfully, but nonetheless I lean over the body of the piano, rest my head on my folded arms and close my eyes.

As soon as she begins, I know I'm done for. The chords are the same, of course, but instead of a delicate, picked guitar, they're rich and dense, as though she's taken the Schumann Ave Maria and superimposed it on this song. She starts low down on the keyboard, creating an almost sombre texture. The first quaver of each bar is missing, which means that you're always feeling as though you're catching up with something: a fall before a swell.

After just a few bars, I wave my hands. 'Take it from the beginning,' I say with almost embarrassed impatience.

She smiles and droops her head, eyes closed, then starts again. As I sing the very first phrase, the hairs on the back of my neck rise. I can barely look at Céline; it is as though she has cast a spell on me. Out of the corner of my eye I see the magazine drop from my father's hands as he leans his head back against the wall to listen. I realise at once the genius of Janis Ian and of Céline: a song to a friend, relative or lover dying of AIDS—what could be a more intriguing addition to this album of Lullabies? About halfway through I feel a release deep, deep inside me, and begin singing it as though directly to Jacques in his final days, and it is then that the song fulfils something I hadn't known I'd been looking for, something intrinsically about me and my life and my loss and my people, and I feel its potency and its politics as a balm. And then I am released from a much more immediate struggle: by admitting Raymond—in the forms of his letter and his son—back into my life, I had feared I was cheating on Jacques, somehow, but now I see that they aren't in competition with each other but are just sweet evidence of my capacity to love.

When Céline places the final chord, I look at her with tears streaming down my face, then begin to laugh. And she laughs, too. And then Papà starts laughing, and then we're a trio of laughers, and I lift her up from the piano stool and hug her. 'Céline, it's like you've wrapped the song around my voice.'

'Like a blanket?'

'Like a cradle.'

§

When I leave the Louvre and re-enter the contemporary world my eyes are dazzled by the light, even though at six thirty the sun is on its way down. I walk back towards the Marais where, rounding a corner, I see the bookshop Papà had mentioned in his letter—only it must have moved, as I'm sure I'm nowhere near where he said he was.

The shop window is full of books and videos and I can see an assistant's back just behind the display. I climb the few steps and enter. Inside, the air is refreshingly cool. To the left is a spiral stair-case that leads down to a basement.

'Bonjour, Monsieur.' His skin is as pale as that of the model in the painting, his thick, dark hair gelled in a taut quiff.

'Bonjour.'

'If you need anything, don't hesitate to ask.'

'Thank you,' I say, smiling embarrassedly at how easily people just switch into English when they hear my terrible accent.

On the left are shelves of magazines—Beyoncé and oiled torsos. One bears the tagline, *Raymond Wallace: martyr ou lâche? 20 ans depuis sa mort.* I pick it up, flick to the article. Heading it is a portrait of Dad at his desk, very much alive. I close it reflexively, return it to the shelf and hide my flushed cheeks in a corridor of books.

In bookshops as in libraries I usually feel a curious pride in my father, perhaps heightened by the reassuring knowledge that—

however absent he might be from the rest of my life—in these places his presence is undisputable. At the back of the shop I find the section Papà mentioned—*Littérature de L'étranger*: foreign authors in their original language—and look for *W*. I draw a book from the shelves. *Feathername/Warname*—published posthumously, it's his final musings on identity and personal history. The cover is a blurred-out photo of Dad's handwriting: indecipherable, like that on the walls of my dream. I open the book at random, let his words flow over me.

I employ an interpreter to write to a friend in Welsh, he writes. *A reply comes—also in Welsh—and my interpreter tells me that my friend's use of the language is good: 'He's mutating,' she tells me. I have never heard this expression outside of science, or science fiction. That mutation could be linguistic, and positive, was news to me.*

It makes me think: if we have no way of conceiving of our own existence except through language, then just as language mutates, so might identity. When we die we are ghostwritten, ventriloquised by those who outlive us. Posthumous identities are colloquial: an accumulation of received memories, events, utterances. Shame and glory; exaltation and disappointment; bold interpretations and downright lies. What might happen if we, the living, pronounced ourselves in a different way? Could we mutate ourselves?

I turn to the last page. I've read it before, of course, but it feels different today, and a novel peace envelops me as I read the final passage.

So what's in a name, exactly? We introduce ourselves with names given to us by others in a system that—by default—accords us our father's surname. Thus, I am my mother's late uncle, and a patriarchal tradition. But since—rather like an inherited suit—such a name may well be made to fit but can never be made to measure, who, exactly, am I?

('Can I call you Ray?'

'You can call me anything you like.')

Hello. I am not Raymond Wallace; who aren't you?

I feel a hand on my shoulder, turn my head to find the shop assistant behind me, his rich, blue eyes revealing a level of bemused concern.

'*Tu sais que tu parles à haute voix, mon ami?* You know you're speaking out loud?' He pats my shoulder, then withdraws his hand.

'What? Oh, I'm so sorry.'

'It's no problem, it's just that, well—' And he gestures around the shop. He's pulled the blind on the door; the lights are now dimmed and the place is completely empty: closing time.

'Oh, god, I'm sorry, I was completely lost in thought. I should leave.'

'I have a few things to do, anyway, so please don't feel that there's any pressure. I just wanted to let you know.'

'Did you move?'

'Sorry?' he says with a frown.

'This shop. Has it moved?'

'No.' He hesitates. 'I mean, twenty years ago, yes. It was up in the 18th.'

'Ah,' I nod.

'He's good, isn't he? Wallace.' He gestures to my father's book, in my hands. 'I mean, I love reading him in the original, but I usually need a dictionary.'

'Your English is astonishing,' I say.

He smiles a sudden, broad smile, looking at once pleased and shy. He drops his arms, his left hand holding his right wrist just like the figure in the painting. 'Thank you,' he says. 'Have you read any? I mean, apart from the words you were just reading out loud.'

I feel as though I'm playing some silly game by withholding, but it's always the same: once I've said, I can't unsay. 'Yes.'

'I recommend him all the time.'

'Thanks.'

He frowns like a child at my gratitude, and I decide to confess. We speak at the same time:

'You want a drink?'

'It's my father.'

Then again:

'What?'

'Sure. Raymond Wallace,' I say, to clarify, 'is—was—my father. And I'd love a drink.'

'Wow,' he says as a shadow crosses his face. 'So you're the son who—?'

'Yes,' I say, gently and firmly, as though to take control of it. 'I'm the son, who.' I know everyone knows, but it is always a complex surprise that the most traumatic moment of my life is public knowledge. I hold out my wrist. 'And this is the watch. I am a walking museum.' I try to ascertain whether he pities me or not.

'I am Marc. With a C.' He says this as though it is an entirely logical response to my comment.

My shoulders drop. 'Nice to meet you, Marc with a C. I'm Joe.'

'Nice to meet you, Joe.'

It's funny, but the simple act of introducing myself is almost aphrodisiac. 'That drink,' I say, raising an eyebrow.

'Yes. I have something we can share here.' He goes over to the shop window and ducks behind the cash register before reappearing with two small shot glasses and a label-less green wine bottle. He walks back towards me, pulls the cork out and fills each glass with a syrupy, amber liquid. 'Calvados. From my parents' apple trees.' And then, as though in explanation of the bottle's presence in the shop, 'You never know when a toast may be called for.'

I remember reading in some gastronomic magazine about a certain mouth cancer specific to a region in Normandy which doctors had put down to the favoured local combination of calvados, strong black coffee and thick cigars; I decide not to mention this as I accept the proffered glass.

'*To new friends and old countries*,' he says, grinning.

I raise my glass and take a large draught. It bites the inside of my mouth, whistles at the back of my tongue then suffuses my throat with appley warmth.

Marc takes another volume of Dad's—*Interlogue*—from the shelf, turns to a certain page and begins to read it out loud. '*We all have our legacies, our histories.*' His accent is thick and his reading almost glamorously ponderous. I can't help but smile at the passage he's selected. '*We live through them, repeat them, and periodically try to unravel them. We suffer them, indulge them and profit from them. We forget them, but they never forget us, and sometimes we may find ourselves, randomly and wonderfully, being offered a choice: repeat or change. And if Liberty is less the freedom to do* what we want *than the responsibility to do* what we ought, *then a crucial moment in our lives is when we take the possibility of simple repetition and become innovators in our own lives. We assume responsibility for our presents as we cannot take responsibility for choices others made for us in the past.* The past is not to be thought away. *It is to be studied and plundered, researched and interpreted, warts above all.'*

When he stops there is a delicious, embarrassing silence. It is as though he wanted to reveal something of himself by both his selection and his delivery, but now that it has been revealed, neither of us knows quite what to do with it. I look at him and see a man dedicated to the pleasures of the text, a pedlar of uncensored reading and interpretation, a collector and collator of stories and analyses and I realise that simply by being here I am adding myself to the biographies of Marc and his shop: I am contributing to history. And while at so many points in my life I have felt circumscribed by my father—part of the *wound* of his fatherhood, as he put it—I can see now that I am not yet written. And with this resilience comes another, crucial acknowledgment: that wounds, by definition, can heal.

'I fear I may have broken a spell,' says Marc, evidently unaware that he has, in fact, cast a rather brilliant one.

I shake my head and take a final sip. Marc immediately lifts the bottle to refill, but because his hand is now shaking rather charmingly, he spills some onto my hand. As the fluid begins to roll down my bare arm he looks to me as though asking for consent, then leans and licks the errant liquid from my elbow to my wrist. I catch my breath. He is removing traces and at one and the same time creating new tracks, new marks, new residues. He pauses, swallows. I smile and nod, sip slowly and deliberately, let my head fall back against the bookshelves. I feel unfamiliarly, invigoratingly present.

'You're handsome.' He takes the glass out of my hand, puts it on the floor beside me, then takes my hand in his and rubs it between his palms. 'And cold.'

'A little.'

'You should eat something.'

I laugh, remembering my professional task for the weekend. 'Undoubtedly.'

Marc drops my hand, replaces the cork in the bottle and takes it, along with our empty glasses, back to the desk.

'I need to eat at *Les Philosophes*, actually' I say, slightly louder than I'd intended. 'I have to write a review.'

'Marvellous.'

'Will you join me?'

He steps out from behind his counter and makes a small bow. 'It would be an honour.'

I swat playfully at him. 'Stop it, immediately.'

We step out onto the street. While Marc locks up I watch in delight as a child kisses a balloon, releases it into the pale sky, then—as it disappears out of sight—jumps in unexpected glee.

§

I tuck Papà in—just as he used to tuck me in—then pick up the phone and dial Joe's number; it goes straight to answerphone.

His voice is the very print of Ray's. I leave a clumsy, embarrassing message before hanging up. It's the weirdest feeling—as if I'm anticipating a first date, yet of course the truth is wildly divergent from that. Still, I feel similar anticipatory nerves. I've now handed the power back to Joe, after all, and then—as if to mitigate this power shift—I do something I'd sworn I wouldn't do: I Google him.

His articles appear on numerous websites and I am impressed— proud, even. I realise that that's exactly the word I'd used in my letter to him about his father's literary success, and feel curiously close to this person I've never even met. I can only find a single online image, in which he appears both like and unlike his father: the same eyes with their compelling sadness; but the look Joe is giving the photographer conveys a resilience that is his alone. I have to admit finding him terribly handsome, and even wonder whether he's gay. That, however, feels almost incestuous, so I distract myself with a few more of his articles. He writes beautifully— with wit and style—but then again, with Raymond Wallace as his father, Joe would be hard-pressed not to be at least a half-decent writer. I return to his photo, this time as though seeking evidence of the effect of Ray's death. The shock; the loss; the publicity; the shadows those things must have cast. Once again, it is resilience that I perceive. I take out his note once more and feel a different sort of pride at his bravery and determination in contacting me, then realise that I am really skirting around my own loss and impending loss, and feel deep sorrow, but also—like sunshine and rain at once—a vibrantly unexpected sense of inspiration at this unequivocal proof of life after death.

I take a shower to wash off the day's heat and exertions. I dry myself but don't dress; it's too hot for clothes. I listen for Papà's snores: his breathing is even and peaceful. On a whim I take the necklace Ray gave me that Christmas out of its box and slip it over my head. Then I do another thing I swore I would never do: I take the copy of *Manhattan, 1963 & Other Regrets* into my bedroom. I lie down on my bed, relishing the breeze that creeps tauntingly in from the open windows and across my skin. I flick to our first meeting in *Little Navy*, but soon turn to the morning after our first night together. Then, drawing the sheet up just to my waist, I allow myself—urge myself, even—to remember.

§

I slip into the bathroom while Marc is still sleeping and splash my face with water. I pee, then come back into the bedroom. I can already feel the heat of the morning beating on the closed blinds beyond the bed. In muted shadow, the supersized blooms behind the headboard now appear almost pornographically sensual. Outstretched like a living statue, Marc is on his back—one arm covering his eyes; his cock snaked across his thigh. I think of the pleasure we took in each other's bodies during the night. Then he shifts, his dick slips into shadow, and I suddenly recall the demure figure in the painting yesterday, the cool solitude—loneliness, I guess—of the gallery, and how quietly alive I now feel. Then I remember the museum guard, John's text, and realise I still haven't heard from Joey, so pull my phone from my pocket only to find I never switched it back on. *Shit.* My heart beating fast, I stab my PIN into the keypad and wait. Seconds pass, then there's a double beep to indicate a voicemail and a text that tells me I have three messages. The first two are from John. I just delete those; I'll deal with him when I get back. Then I hear the deep baritone of Joey's voice, the residual American twang in his accent, speaking to me as though hesitant yet determined:

'Gosh. Joe. It's Joey,' he says. *'It's Saturday night. Thank you for your letter—letters, actually—and I, er, well, sorry it took me a day. Look: I'd love to see you. We're here all day tomorrow, just me and Papà, so come by when you're free. I, um…yep.'* He leaves his number.

I grin as though I've won something.

Marc opens his eyes. *'De bonnes nouvelles?* Good news?' he says, yawning, then 'Good morning.'

'Good morning,' I say, dropping my phone and climbing onto the bed. 'Yes. Very good news.'

He turns to lie on his back once more and slips his hands behind his head. He smiles at me. I lean down and we kiss a delicious, lingering kiss.

He pulls away abruptly. 'What time is it?'

'Quarter to nine.'

'Shit. Shit. Shit! The shop!' Leaping out of bed, his cock flailing comically, he dashes into the bathroom. I hear the stream of his piss and poke my head round the door. He looks over his shoulder at me.

'What time do you need to be there?' I ask.

He shakes his cock then turns and looks at me like a school-teacher. 'By ten o'clock,' he says, sternly. 'And we are a quarter of an hour from there, at a fast walk.'

'And it is eight forty-five.'

'Eight forty-five!' He throws up his arms with sudden, relieved understanding. 'Quarter *to*; not quarter *past*. *Fantastique. En ce cas*,' he adds, sidling up to me and placing his hands on my hips as though measuring me up, 'might I suggest we take a shower together?'

By the time we check out it is half past nine. As we cross the river he takes my free hand with a simple affection John could never show.

'What time is your train?' he asks, looking straight ahead.

I smile. 'Oh, nine o'clock or thereabouts.'

He nods, looks once again like a child. 'Can I come and say goodbye?'

'Yes,' I say, with a laughing smile.

'I might even finish a little early.'

'Great. Call me,' I say.

When we reach the bookshop I check my watch: ten to ten.

'I should get on,' he says, unlocking the door and stepping inside. 'I will call you. What are you doing today, by the way?' he adds, leaning out of the doorway.

'Have you heard of Giuseppe Lombardia?'

'Of course. He's wonderful. Why?'

'He knew my father.' I take a few steps away from the shop and swing my holdall over the other shoulder.

'Wait,' he says. 'Is that where you're going? To meet *him*?'

'I'll tell you all about it when I see you later,' I say, and his intrigued laughter follows me down the road.

§

When I wake up, I hear Papà in the kitchen. I slip on a pair of pyjama trousers and pad through to join him. He's standing at the window, looking down onto the street.

'Papà?' I say.

He turns to face me and I see tears in his eyes. 'I want to send it,' he says. 'Now.'

'Send what, Papà?'

'Don't treat me like a fool. I want to send my letter to Raymond. Let me,' he adds, and his eyes are so imploring that I capitulate.

'Sit down, Papà. I've something to tell you.' He looks at me with suspicion, but sits. I join him at the table and take his hands in mine. 'Raymond died, Papà. Some time ago.'

'Did I know this, once?' he asks, quietly. I nod tentatively, uncertain as to whether I've made the right decision. He looks down at our hands, his face a mask of concentration, then back at me. 'Did he take life away from himself?'

His phrase is so distinctly, idiomatically Italian that it is almost comical. I squeeze his hands and nod again. 'But I get the impression it was exactly what he wanted.'

'Did he reply?'

'What?'

'When you sent my letter. Did you get a reply?'

I don't know whether we're making sense, anymore. Then I think of Joe's letter, and—with a jolt—of my open invitation to him last night. 'Yes…kind of. Not from Raymond. But I did get a letter from his son. Joe.'

Papà looks at me in astonishment. I take a deep breath. I figure I'm in so deep, I may as well continue. I go into my room and collect the letters. I give Joe's to Papà and watch him carefully as he reads it. His eyes light up like a child's.

'He's in Paris!' he says, delightedly—then, cautiously: 'Will he come, do you think?'

'I've invited him, so I hope so.'

Papà nods, and bites his lower lip. Then he looks covetously at the other letter, the one from Raymond.

'It's really long,' I say, keeping a tight hold on it, 'but it's also—perhaps unsurprisingly—pretty disturbing. And that's not me thinking you're losing it, or anything like that, but I don't want you to get upset, Papà, and I think that his letter could—would, in fact—upset you.'

Papà reaches his hand up to my face and brushes his thumb against my cheek, wiping away a tear of which I was unaware until then, before pressing his damp digit onto the paper of Raymond's letter.

'Watermark,' he says, with a wink.

'Watermark,' I echo. 'You look exhausted.' I stroke his face. 'Did you sleep?'

'Not really,' he says with a yawn.

'Well, why don't you go lie down for a while, then you'll be ready when—if—Joe comes to visit. Okay?'

Papà nods and I lead him to his room where I tuck him in just as he used to tuck me in. I sing a few lines of *Bella ciao*—just until he closes his eyes—then shut the door behind me. *Second childhood*, indeed.

I make myself some coffee, then stand looking out of the kitchen window, just like Papà. Way down on the opposite side of the cobbles a solitary figure looks up from the shadows.

§

I stand across the street from the door to Joey and Papà's apartment building knowing that everything I have always known is about to be qualified by something at which I can only guess. I look up to where I imagine their apartment might be but only see framed reflections of the sky. I'm nervous of making a fool of myself, but then I remember his halting voicemail. I cross the road and press the doorbell. After a few seconds there's a click.

'Joe.' He says my name as though establishing something incontrovertible.

'Joey? How—?'

'I saw you looking up. Come in!'

The door buzzes and clicks as I push it open and step into the shadows of the stairwell. It feels so different from how it had felt on Friday: realer now; portentous, even. I walk up the flights of stairs, look at the worn curves of the steps and think of how they have been scratched and splintered: moulded by the passing of time, shoes, wardrobes, coffins. On the final flight I hear a door opening above and Joey calling my name gently. As I reach the top he's buttoning up his shirt and I am touched to see the pearl on its gold chain glinting amid his chest hair. The only image I've seen is the photo of him and Dad—and of course he's now greyer, a little heavier—but it seems as though I've known him my entire life. I stand stock still, suddenly hesitant, feeling as though I'm about to cry, but then he steps forward and draws me into a fulsome embrace.

'Jesus,' he says after a moment, gripping my shoulders and leaning back slightly as though to take a proper look. 'Yes,' he adds, as though either confirming or overcoming something.

We stand there for a few seconds just looking at one another. We are both blushing fiercely.

'I'm so sorry,' he smiles. 'How rude of me. Come in,' and as he steps over the threshold he glances down the corridor, then turns and whispers, 'Papà's taking a nap in his room; he'll join us later.'

He closes the door behind us and I slip off my trainers as though following instructions he hasn't issued. He ushers me into the kitchen, pulls out a seat for me at the table. I sit, put my bag on the floor beside me. On the table is my letter, next to which is Dad's. We both look at them, then at each other, and laugh.

I purse my lips. 'Quite the read, huh?'

'No shit.'

In the pause that follows I look around. Between the windows hangs an astonishing image: dressed in psychedelic, punked-up kimonos, Grace Jones and Naomi Campbell lean in towards one another. Where Jones's profile is all stern, pouting attitude, Campbell is roaring with infectious laughter. The name *Jacques Zaki* is emblazoned across the top, with *Costume-Couture: L'Exposition* beneath it. At the bottom it reads: *Octobre-Décembre, 1992.*

'He'd just made her laugh,' says Joey, his eyes following mine. 'His last exhibition; he died the following Autumn.' We turn and look at each other as though in solidarity. 'Actually, they want to do a 50th birthday retrospective, next year.'

'"They"?'

'The Pompidou Centre.'

'Right,' I laugh, impressed. 'How wonderful.'

He taps my letter. 'Your hotel licensed some of his prints, so you might have seen them around the place. Cushions, throws: that sort of thing.'

'Joey?' His name still feels both familiar and strange in my mouth, like a word of which I haven't quite established the true meaning. 'Can I ask you a question?'

'Anything.' His sincerity seems almost compulsive.

'What does "*lâche*" mean?'

He blanches, frowns. 'French for "coward"—why?'

'I saw it on the cover of a magazine yesterday—an article about Dad.' I bite my lip. '*Raymond Wallace: martyr, or coward?*'

He pulls out a chair and sits down, looking intently at the surface of the table—as though reading a map, you might say. 'It's possible they were just trying to sell a magazine. They make a habit of doing that sort of thing to people who can't answer back.' He glances momentarily at Jacques' poster, then frowns as though he's working something out. 'Then again, *coward* was a word Raymond sometimes used to describe himself, wasn't it? In which case, *martyr* could be seen as a kind of upgrade? Saint Raymond, anyone?'

I laugh, then suddenly remember what I've brought. I unzip my bag, withdraw the parcel and slide it across the table. 'A present. Well, more a form of restitution.'

He looks puzzled as he pulls off the paper, but smiles broadly when he sees the photo of the two of them. 'Thank you. Papà will be especially delighted.'

'You're wearing the pearl.'

'Oh. Yes,' he says, blushing once more, his hand touching the necklace through his shirt. He smooths his hair, then takes my wrist with an ease so intimate it feels familial. 'And you're wearing the watch.'

'I am a walking museum,' I say, like it's my new catchphrase.

'Aren't we all? Now then,' he says, pushing back his chair and standing up, 'Can I make you a coffee?'

Before I can answer, however, our attention is drawn to the doorway, where a figure—the man I'd seen at the café, yesterday—is rubbing his eyes. He looks at me, nods, walks forwards. I stand clumsily, uncertain as to whether we should shake hands or hug; I look to Joey for guidance, but his eyes are on his father.

'I thought I heard voices,' says Papà, batting my hand away and taking me in his arms. His body feels fragile, though his hug is powerful. Then—just as his son had done only moments earlier—he holds my shoulders, leaning back to get a good look. I laugh, a little self-conscious; he drops his arms and takes my hands in his.

'Joe,' says Joey, 'This is my Papà, of course. Papà this is…'

'We've already met,' he says, confidently.

'It's good to meet you, properly, Mr—'

He silences me with a squeeze of the hand and says:

'I think you'd better call me Papà, too.'

Author Note

The inspiration for this book came in part from a New York Times article written in 1963 by journalist Robert C. Doty. Whilst a character bearing this name and professional role appears in this book, it is an entirely fictionalised character and is in no way intended to represent the man himself. All other characters are also fictional, and any resemblance to actual persons, living or dead or events (other than historical events) is entirely coincidental.

Acknowledgments

Nathan and Justin, two new heroes in my life: you have given me the greatest gift and fulfilled a lifelong dream. Immeasurable and eternal thanks to you both for your passion, determination and patience.

Early drafts and sketches of this book were aired at the Gay London Writers Group, spearheaded by the late Jeremy Trafford and run by Peter Slater. Thanks to them, as well as all those who heard and responded all those years ago—amongst others, Roy Woolley, Peter Daniels, Warwick Stanley, Philip Donovan, Ernesto Sarezale. Peter McGraith for his enduring enthusiasm and encouragement. To Jonathan Kemp from that same group who, in early 2019, retweeted a request for submissions from Inkandescent…I am indebted to him and to that tweet.

Thanks to readers of early drafts—Erica Whyman and John Grantham—and to Pippa Hill for her candid reflections on a recent one. To Laura Barber and Laura MacDougall for much-appreciated advice, and to Caroline Wood. To Mike Whyman for his memories of JFK's assassination. To Eliza Lumley for walking Raymond's walk to Brooklyn with me way back in 2004. Huge gratitude to Gabriella Le Grazie for her linguistic and idiomatic advice, as well as culinary recommendations: Gianna and Sara are particular beneficiaries of this knowledge.

Now to the songs: thanks to Paul Higgins for introducing me to 'The Ballad of the Sad Young Men'; to Jeremy Sams for so very many things, but most recently for 'Infidélité' and Reynaldo Hahn; to Paul Farrington for opera expertise; and to my parents for introducing me to Janis Ian from a young age. Thanks to the songwriters: Jay Landesman and Theodore J. Flicker (The Ballad of the Sad Young Men); Jimmy Davis, Roger Ramirez, and James Sherman (Loverman (Where Can You Be?)); Reynaldo Hahn & Théophile Gauthier (Infidélité); Janis Ian (When Angels Cry)—And their interpreters: Rod McKuen, Jimmy "Loverman" Davis, Billie Holiday, The Communards, and Janis Ian herself.

Thanks to all my students, particularly those who came 2002-4 and 2021-22. To Jean Gottlieb for nudging me towards Le Loir Dans La Théière, and to the staff of that cafe as well as those at Les Philosophes. To Les Mots à la Bouche for providing a beautiful and visible shop for all these years: you are a sanctuary. To Bryan for relieving my pain, and especial thanks to Gun for helping me unpack over all these years. Thanks to the late (or, rather, later) Steve Sondheim for reminding me that news comes on the radio, too. To Murray Melvin and Lexi Taylor for their memories of New York in the 60s. To James Conway and David Braniff-Herbert for specialised help. And to Charles Kaiser and John Loughery for their utterly inspiring work as well as their quick and enthusiastic responses.

Above all, thanks to Catherine Hall: you have cheered and championed me beyond my own energies. You always said this would happen, and you were right. "Rarely wrong," as you'd say ... To Mitch for, quite simply, everything. And final unspeakable gratitude to G and J, the original Raymond and Joey, for surviving your pain, and for meeting again…you give me hope.

I wanted to include the email I received from Justin David of Inkandescent, as it shows so beautifully the clarity and passion these guys feel about their work.

Sam Kenyon
2022

Date: 20th August 2020
Subject: I Am not Raymond Wallace

Dear Sam,

I write to you with wet eyes and a rather blotchy red face after just finishing *I am not Raymond Wallace*.

I feel privileged to have read such a deeply moving portrait of thwarted love, set in a time when men of a certain persuasion, tormented by guilt and shame, remained oppressed and closeted. Your evocations of New York City and Paris, tinged with emotional deprivation and solitude, render a rather magnetic backdrop, not unlike the work of one of my favourite painters, Edward Hopper. I couldn't put the book down until I'd got to the devastating conclusion.

This is such an important work that will offer younger readers a glimpse into what life was like for gay men really not so long ago in the Western World, and of course older readers will feel understood by it. Moreover, the prose is so beautiful and the story so engaging, I'm sure it will be cherished, too, by a wider audience.

I rather feel that it needs a little bit of work to make it as good as it possibly can be, and with that caveat, we would love to be your publishers if you would still like us to be. I have a few notes on the manuscript but Nathan is more the structural editor than me, so maybe that discussion should wait?

We should either fix a time to meet in person, or perhaps set up a Zoom meeting. We're crazy busy with the new book, so it may be a week or two before we can make that happen but do give me your reaction as soon as you wish.

Thank you again for giving me the opportunity to read such a beautiful, albeit heart-breaking piece of work.

Drying my tears,

Justin

Inkandescent would like to thank—

Joe Mateo for his marvellous design,

Alex Hopkins for his meticulous proofreading,

Rebecca Carter for her magnanimous advice.

And in loving memory of our cat, Genet.
Thank you for brightening the Inkandescent offices—
we know you are now shining somewhere else in the universe.

Supporters

At Inkandescent, we believe books can save the world, particularly books of diversity. Stories make us feel less alone. They can educate. They can challenge us to reflect on different points of view. They can bring us great pleasure. Most importantly, stories help us to develop empathy. They make us better people—more socially, culturally and emotionally aware human beings, able to understand and feel compassion for voices different to our own.

It is widely known that mainstream publishing has consistently failed to raise up voices from a number of diverse groups; these are namely writers from LGBTQ+ and BAME backgrounds, those who are financially disadvantaged or who identify as working class. We started Inkandescent Publishing to provide a platform for underrepresented writers and artists.

We are small. Very small. But with the help of a growing readership, we have been able to publish eleven books since 2016. Enough to fill a small bookshelf! The following list of names are people who supported the production of this book by pledging or pre-ordering a copy from our publishing partner, Unbound, long before the release date and to whom we are eternally grateful. For small indies like us, a bit of extra cash upfront means creative freedom. It means we can stop worrying about cashflow and balance sheets and instead focus upon bringing brilliant books to you. We have a lot more in the pipeline.

Whether the book you're holding in your hand was pre-ordered from Unbound or purchased more recently from a bookseller, we think you're inkredible! Because by buying one of our books you're helping to keep independent publishing alive.

THANK YOU!

Acting Out
Alan Wright
Alda and Juris Steprans
Ali Jay
Alice Strang
Andrew Buckingham
Andrew Jones
Ben Hladilek
Benjamin Napper
Beth M Allen
Bob Hughes
Caspar Aremi
Catherine Bellsham-
Revell
Catherine Hall
Chloe Campbell
Chris Arnephie
Cocker Family
Conor McFarlane
Danny Scheinmann
David & Natalie
David Bailey
David Scotland
Dee Jones
Eamon Somers
Edwards Family
Eliza Lumley
Emma-Jane Bould
Esther Shanson
Faye Moore
Gabriella Le Grazie
Gemma Parker
Greg Barnes

Guy Foord-Kelcey
Harry Waller
Helen Mumby
Helen Watkiss
Ian & Jennifer Hall
James Conway
Jane S Brown
Jennifer Hall
Jeremy Sams
Jesika Steprans
Jess'n'Ceri
Jo Riley
John Abbott
John Atterbury
Jon Trenchard
Joshua Davis
Judith von Orelli
Julie Hazel Young
Justine Cottle
Kate Calico
Katie Baxendale
Laura Riseborough
Laura Thomas
Lexi Taylor
Lucy Rix
Marie & Steph
Mark Vent
Martin Roderick
Matthew and the
Family Sharp
Natalie Schenk
Natasha Bernard
Nicola Goodchild

Noa Bodner
Oliver Rix
Paul Farrington
Paul Higgins
Penny
Philip Battley
Pippa Hill
Rachel Dufton
Rachel V Crompton
Red Lion Books
Sally Fielding
Sarah
Sharanjit Paddam
Simon Smith
Sophie, Rob,
James and Beatrice
Stephen Minay
Stuart Dixon
Susan and Sean Truman
Susanne Stohr
Tarek Merchant
Tim Baker
Tim Jackson
TR Guest
Trevor Norris
Vicky Horner
Vita Plūme
Vivienne Aspin
Zinta, Ēriks, Imants
and Zigis

And an extra special thanks to Alan & Rose Brookes

Also from Inkandescent

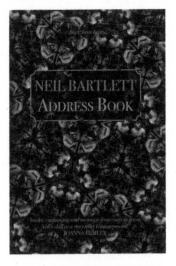

ADDRESS BOOK
NEIL BARTLETT

'Neil Bartlett is a national treasure. I read everything he
writes and am always lifted by his skill, humour,
political purpose and elegance.'
DEBORAH LEVY

Address Book is the new work of fiction by the Costa-shortlisted
author of Skin Lane. Neil Bartlett's cycle of stories takes us to
seven very different times and situations: from a new millennium
civil partnership celebration to erotic obsession in a Victorian
tenement, from a council-flat bedroom at the height of the AIDS
crisis to a doctor's living-room in the midst of the Coronavirus
pandemic, they lead us through decades of change to discover
hope in the strangest of places.

"Address Book is completely absorbing; tender, enchanting
and a mesmeric read from cover to cover. Neil's skill as a
story-teller is unsurpassed. This book is something else.
I adored it.'
JOANNA LUMLEY

Also from Inkandescent

MAINSTREAM
edited by Justin David & Nathan Evans

'A wonderful collection of fascinating stories by unique voices'.
KATHY BURKE

This collection brings thirty authors in from the mar-gins to occupy centre-page. Queer storytellers. Working class wordsmiths. Chroniclers of colour. Writers whose life experiences give unique perspectives on universal challenges, whose voices must be heard. And read. Emerging writers are being placed alongside these established authors—

Bidisha, Elizabeth Baines, Gaylene Gould, Golnoosh Nour,
Jonathan Kemp, Julia Bell, Keith Jarrett, Kerry Hudson,
Kit de Waal, Juliet Jacques, Neil Bartlett, Neil McKenna,
Padrika Tarrant, Paul McVeigh and Philip Ridley

'A riveting collection of stories, deftly articulated.
Every voice entirely captivating: page to page, tale to tale.
These are stories told with real heart from writers
emerging from the margins in style.'
ASHLEY HICKSON-LOVENCE,
author of *The 392* and *Your Show*

Also from Inkandescent

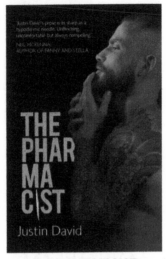

THE PHARMACIST
by Justin David

Twenty-four-year-old Billy is beautiful and sexy. Albert – The Pharmacist – is a compelling but damaged older man, and a veteran of London's late '90s club scene. After a chance meeting in the heart of the London's East End, Billy is seduced into the sphere of Albert. An unconventional friendship develops, fuelled by Albert's queer narratives and an endless supply of narcotics. Alive with the twilight times between day and night, consciousness and unconsciousness, the foundations of Billy's life begin to irrevocably shift and crack, as he fast-tracks toward manhood. This story of lust, love and loss is homoerotic bildungsroman at its finest.

'As lubricious as early Alan Hollinghurst, The Pharmacist is a welcome reissue from Inkandescent, and the perfect introduction to a singular voice in gay literature.'
THE TIMES LITERARY SUPPLEMENT

'At the heart of David's The Pharmacist is an oddly touching and bizarre love story, a modern day Harold and Maude set in the drugged-up world of pre-gentrification Shoreditch. The dialogue, especially, bristles with glorious life.'
JONATHAN KEMP

Also from Inkandescent

Kissing the Lizard

by Justin David

Justin David's newly-released novella is part creepy coming-of-age story, part black-comedy, set partly in buzzing 1990s London and partly in barren New Mexico wildlands.

When Jamie meets Matthew in Soho, he's drawn to his new-age charms. But when he follows his new friend across the planet to a remote earth-ship in Taos, bizarre incidents begin unfolding and Matthew's real nature reveals itself: he's a manipulative monster at the centre of a strange cult. Jamie finds himself at the centre a disturbing psychological nightmare as they seize the opportunity to recruit a new member. Pushed to his limits, lost in a shifting sagebrush landscape, can Jamie trust anyone to help him? And will he ever see home again?

This evocatively set desert gothic expertly walks the line between macabre humour and terrifying tension.

'There's not much rarer than a working class voice in fiction, except maybe a gay working class voice. We need writers like Justin David.'
PAUL McVEIGH, author of *The Good Son*

Also from Inkandescent

THREADS
by Nathan Evans & Justin David

If Alice landed in London not Wonderland this book might be the result. Threads is the first collection from Nathan Evans, each poem complemented by a bespoke photograph from Justin David and, like Tenniel's illustrations for Carroll, picture and word weft and warp to create an alchemic (rabbit) whole.

On one page, the image of an alien costume, hanging surreally beside a school uniform on a washing line, accompanies a poem about fleeing suburbia. On another, a poem about seeking asylum accompanies the image of another displaced alien on an urban train. Spun from heartfelt emotion and embroidered with humour, Threads will leave you aching with longing and laughter.

'In this bright and beautiful collaboration, poetry and photography join hands, creating sharp new ways to picture our lives and loves.'
NEIL BARTLETT

'Two boldly transgressive poetic voices'
MARISA CARNESKY

Also from Inkandescent

CNUT

by Nathan Evans

'Poignant, humane and uncompromising'
STEPHEN MORRISON-BURKE

As King Cnut proved, tide and time wait for no man:
An AnthropoScene, the first part of this collection, dives into the
rising tides of geo-political change, the second, Our Future Is Now
Downloading, explores sea-changes of more personal natures.

Nathan's debut, Threads, was longlisted for the Polari First Book Prize.
His follow-up bears all the watermarks of someone who's swum life's
emotional spectrum. Short and (bitter)sweet, this is poetry for a mobile
generation, poetry for sharing – often humorous, always honest about
contemporary human experience, saying more in a few lines than
politicians say in volumes, it offers an antidote to modern living.

*'a kaleidoscopic journey brimming with vivid imagery,
playfulness and warmth—a truly powerful work'*
KEITH JARRETT

Also from Inkandescent

THE PALE ONES
by Bartholomew Bennett

Few books ever become loved. Most linger on undead, their sallow pages labyrinths of old, brittle stories and screeds of forgotten knowledge... And other things, besides: Paper-pale forms that rustle softly through their leaves. Ink-dark shapes swarming in shadow beneath faded type. And an invitation...

Harris delights in collecting the unloved. He wonders if you'd care to donate. A small something for the odd, pale children no-one has seen. An old book, perchance? Neat is sweet; battered is better. Broken spine or torn binding, stained or scarred - ugly doesn't matter. Not a jot. And if you've left a little of yourself between the pages – a receipt or ticket, a mislaid letter, a scrawled note or number – that's just perfect. He might call on you again.

Hangover Square meets Naked Lunch through the lens of a classic M. R. James ghost story. To hell and back again (and again) through Whitby, Scarborough and the Yorkshire Moors. Enjoy your Mobius-trip.

'A real addition to the literature of the uncanny and an impressive debut for its uncompromising author.'
RAMSEY CAMPBELL

Also from Inkandescent

AutoFellatio
by James Maker

According to Wikipedia, only a few men can actually perform the act of auto-fellatio. We never discover whether James Maker—from rock bands Raymonde and RPLA—is one of them. But certainly, as a story-teller and raconteur, he is one in a million.

From Bermondsey enfant terrible to Valencian grande dame—a journey that variously stops off at Morrissey Confidant, Glam Rock Star, Dominatrix, Actor and Restoration Man—his long and winding tale is a compendium of memorable bons mots woven into a patchwork quilt of heart-warming anecdotes that make you feel like you've hit the wedding-reception jackpot by being unexpectedly seated next the groom's witty homosexual uncle.

More about the music industry than about coming out, this remix is a refreshing reminder that much of what we now think of as post-punk British rock and pop, owes much to the generation of musicians like James. The only criticism here is that – as in life – fellatio ultimately cums to an end.

'a glam-rock Naked Civil Servant in court shoes.
But funnier. And tougher' MARK SIMPSON

by outsiders for outsiders

Inkandescent Publishing was created in 2016
by Justin David and Nathan Evans to shine a light on
diverse and distinctive voices.

Sign up to our mailing list to stay informed
about future releases:

www.inkandescent.co.uk/sign-up

follow us on Facebook:

@InkandescentPublishing

on Twitter:

@InkandescentUK

and on Instagram:

@inkandescentuk